YOURS FOR THE TAKING

NAI

URBAN AINT DEAD

URBAN AINT DEAD
P.O Box 448
Maybrook, NY 12543

No part of this book may be reproduced or transmitted in any form by any means, electronic or mechanical, including photocopying, recording, or by any information storage system, without written permission from the publisher.

Copyright © 2024 By Nai

All rights reserved. Published by URBAN AINT DEAD Publications.

Edited By: Shawna Brim / Ladies Of Lit

URBAN AINT DEAD and coinciding logo(s) are registered properties.

No patent liability is assumed with respect to the use of information contained herein. Although every precaution has been taken in the preparation of this book, the publisher and the author assume no responsibility for errors or omissions. Neither is any liability assumed for damages resulting from the use of the information contained herein. This is a work of fiction. Names, characters, places, and incidents are either the product of the author's imagination or are used fictitiously. Any resemblance to actual events, locales, or persons living or dead is entirely coincidental.

Contact Author on FB: Authoressnai / IG: @authoressnai / TikTok: @authoressnai / Website: hoodloverssociety.com / Email: hoodloverssociety@gmail.com

Contact Publisher at www.urbanaintdead.com

Email: urbanaintdead@gmail.com

Print ISBN: 979-8-9906748-3-7

STAY UP TO DATE

To stay up to date on new releases, plus get information on contests,
sneak peeks and more,
Click the link below...
https://mailchi.mp/6d21003686d1/subscribe

Scan the QR Code below to listen to the Soundtracks/Singles of some of your favorite U.A.D titles:

Don't have Spotify or Apple Music?
No Sweat!
Visit your choice streaming platform and search URBAN AINT DEAD.

Currently on lock serving a bid?
JPay, iHeartRadio, WHATEVER!
We got you covered.
Simply log into your facility's kiosk or tablet, go to music and search URBAN AINT DEAD.

URBAN AINT DEAD

Like & Follow us on social media:

FB - URBAN AINT DEAD

IG: @urbanaintdead

Tik Tok - @urbanaintdead

Submission Guidelines

Submit the first three chapters of your completed manuscript to
urbanaintdead@gmail.com, subject line: Your book's title. The
manuscript must be in a .doc file and sent as an attachment. The
document should be in Times New Roman, double-spaced, and in
size 12 font. Also, provide your synopsis and full contact information.
If sending multiple submissions, they must each be in a separate
email. Have a story but no way to submit it electronically? You can
still submit to URBAN AINT DEAD. Send in the first three chapters,
written or typed, of your completed manuscript to:

URBAN AINT DEAD
P.O Box 448
Maybrook, NY 12543

DO NOT send original manuscript. Must be a duplicate.
Provide your synopsis and a cover letter containing your full contact
information.
Thanks for considering URBAN AINT DEAD.

1

———

AMIKO

Electric bill, cable bill, credit card bill, rent. If I saw another damn bill, I was gonna lose it. This whole adulting bullshit was for the birds, and I was beyond over it. Sometimes, I wished I could've stayed in a child's place like my mother used to tell me. Shit didn't seem near as bad as being in an adult's place. And here I was again, rambling in my own thoughts. I found myself doing that more often these days.

At twenty-six, I was trying to hold everything down while still holding onto what sanity I had left. I'd become all too familiar with living paycheck to paycheck and robbing Peter to pay Paul. I knew struggle, but it seemed as if it was easier to maintain when my mom was around to help. And not financially but mainly her guidance. There was nothing like hearing her words of wisdom or just telling me that we'd be alright. Unfortunately, she died four years ago from breast cancer, leaving me and my twin sister, Ming, semi lost with my now four-year-old nephew.

My mother had to be the strongest woman I knew. She worked two jobs to raise me and Ming with no help. Not once did I hear her complain about being tired or needing a break. Mieko was my super woman, and she held it down, refusing to let her daughters see her fall. We didn't even know she was sick until I stumbled across paperwork she had from one of her visits to the doctor.

I told Ming about it first before we both approached her. Downplaying it, she told us God had the last word. I wished God hadn't spoken so soon because within two months, my beloved mother was gone. Still to this day, burying her was the hardest thing I'd ever had to do. Ming took it harder than me, while I more so internalized my pain to be there for her.

She was in her third trimester at the time, and the dude she'd laid down with to procreate wasn't on shit. I was determined for my nephew to be delivered in a safe and stable environment. Having long ago deemed myself the more responsible of the two of us since we were kids, it was natural for me to step into the role of "caretaker" when my mom passed. As far as I was concerned, Ming and I only had each other. Our dad, whoever that bastard was, said *fuck us* from the time we were in the womb.

I was older than Ming by a full twenty-five minutes. According to my mom, I came out with no problem. Ming had to be forced out butt first. So, although we were the same age, I was still the big sister. I took my role very serious too. That could have contributed to where we were today, even though I hated to admit it.

I was an enabler. I never made it a priority for Ming to help financially. I just figured she would on a consistent basis. I mean, she did chip in here and there, and at times, she even came through in a clutch. That every now and then help had nothing on consistent assistance though.

My mother struggled alone our whole life. I was determined not to see the same result for Ming, Case, and myself. That was why whenever she needed me to hold my nephew down, I would, even though that was on rare occasions. Ming was usually home while I worked because every job she had, she'd quit within three months. Her excuse was always that she'd found a better opportunity. I loved my sister to life, but I needed her to do better —_not only to help me but more importantly for her son.

"Hey, Miko. What you doing out here on the couch?" Ming came out from her room, still in her pajamas with a bonnet on her head, protecting the sew-in she'd slayed the night before.

"Girl, I came in late from working overtime and couldn't even make it to my bed. Where's Case?"

"Still sleeping." I peeked over at the time on the cable box, and it read seven fifteen. I figured he must've gone to bed late because he was usually up by seven looking for me. "Are those the bills for this month?" she inquired, taking a seat next to me.

I wanted to say, *Why yes, yes they are. Would you like to draw one and pay it?* It was too early to put on my petty hat though. "Yeah. And one, maybe two of them, may not be paid on time. I already know Uncle Sam gon' tax the shit out of my check because of this overtime."

"Damn. Well, I have an interview at a dental office downtown tomorrow. It's a receptionist position. Oh, and I got the approval letter for food stamps."

I nodded, relieved that the stamps would free up the money I had set aside for groceries. "That's good. Hopefully, everything goes well with the interview, and the stamps are gonna come in handy for sure. We have a good amount of food already, so that will add to it. Did you get a chance to drop the check off to the daycare?" Gathering the bills, I stacked them in a neat pile on the coffee table.

"I did, but the check bounced."

I hung my head, so she wouldn't see the tears threatening to fall from my eyes. It was like no matter how many hours I worked, it never matched the amount of bills we had. My check bouncing was the last thing I needed right now. Just that fast, I calculated the fees that I would incur, not only with the bank but possibly with the daycare as well. The only good thing was I knew Case wouldn't be kicked out since the owner was my friend, Jasmine's, mom, who knew our situation.

"Alright, I'll take care of it." I went to stand up, still fighting back tears. Ming stood with me and threw her arms around my neck to hug me. That gesture alone made me cry. "I'm tired, Ming. I'm just so tired." I always tried to hide my breakdowns from her because I didn't want her to feel bad. I didn't regret making sure my nephew was straight or that we had a roof over our heads, but that didn't mean I wasn't overwhelmed.

"I'ma do better, Miko. I promise. Case is not your responsibility; he's mine. And I'ma get my shit together, forreal."

Something in her declaration was different than the other times she'd said that same statement to me. I couldn't stress enough how much I needed her help, more now than ever. Pulling away from her, I wiped my eyes and forced a smile.

"I know, sis. I know. Let me go get in this shower and lay down in my bed. I'll call the daycare later and get everything cleared up with the check."

Entering my room, I stripped out of my clothes and put on my robe before walking out into the hallway where the bathroom was. Our three-bedroom apartment may not have been huge, but it was cozy enough for the three of us. A one-shot deal from housing afforded us the ability to get into an apartment in a new building on the Eastside of Harlem.

I was so against the idea of having to ask the government for help in the beginning but had to swallow my pride and do it anyway. I hated the way the workers treated you, as if it was their money that aided in you getting on your feet, when, in fact, it was your paycheck that got taxed before your check even hit your account. I wasn't a slouch ass bitch by far, and I hated to be treated as such.

In the shower, I let the sounds of the water soothe my aching muscles and take my mind to a peaceful place. Here, I was able to get away from my stressful job at a telecommunications company and the mountains of bills I had. Here, I was able to let my tears fall freely and lay down my burdens. I often thought that maybe if I had a man, he'd be able to help me out in more ways than one. Not just financially but sexually. Ughh, I missed sex so bad. I was ashamed to admit how long it'd been since I'd been fucked.

The last guy I dealt with was a scrub. Dre knew his way around the bedroom and kept this pussy more than satisfied, but he lacked commitment, common sense, and most importantly, a home. In his mind, he thought he was slick, running from my bed to his baby mama's, but the joke was on his dumb ass because I knew all along. He didn't know how to lie, and I never cared to listen when he did. He was simply good for dick and dick only.

I hated that I had to cut him off on account of him not having his baby mama in check. She'd come up to my job one day, and we had a verbal exchange that turned physical. The bitch word had passed through her lips one too many times, resulting in her being picked up and escorted off the property. I got my first write up that day, but I took it on the chin because I knew I had no business fighting outside my job. Best believe I let Dre have it as soon as I got home and cut him off immediately. There wasn't a dick that good to risk my employment over.

At this point, I was through with men —_well, boys in Dre's case. My focus was making money. That's it, that's all. Stepping out of the shower, I slipped my robe back on and returned to my room. My bed was screaming my name.

Wanting to ease my mind, I turned on the humidifier, and the German chamomile oil permeated the air. With heavy lids, I skipped my moisturizing routine and pulled the sheets back, ready to get a solid few hours of sleep. Before my head could hit the pillow, my phone rang. I let out a frustrated sigh as I stood to fish it out of my purse.

Seeing my supervisor's name dance across the screen of my iPhone 14 Pro Max, I sucked my teeth and plopped down on the bed. My finger hovered over the red phone button, ready to decline the call, but I foolishly hit the green button to answer.

"Hey, Sheila." I answered sweetly but mouthed, *What you want, bitch?* I couldn't stand her, and that was crazy seeing as I got along with everyone I came in contact with at my job. This ho just rubbed me the wrong way and didn't know how to talk to people.

"Amiko, I need you to come in to cover the afternoon shift," she said without so much as a hello in response.

Rude bitch, I said to myself while throwing my head back and squeezing the bridge of my nose. **"I just got in not too long ago from working a double."** This bitch knew that. She was the one who did the damn schedule. **"Is there anyone else you can call? I really need to get some rest, and this is my only day off this week."**

"If I had someone else to call, I wouldn't be calling you, now would I? You wanted this position as team lead. Be a leader and be

here at eleven to lead your team." She disconnected the call, leaving me hot.

This bitch really let her position go to her head. If I didn't need this job and the benefits, I would've tapped Sheila in her mouth months ago. Sucking my teeth, I threw my phone across the bed after checking the time. It was already eight thirty. My job was thirty minutes from my house on the train and maybe fifteen minutes in an Uber.

I desperately needed at least a good eight hours, but sadly, I'd learned to function on four. Covering myself with a sheet, I knocked out. This was my life.

2

MING

"MOMMY, IS AUNTIE MIKO HERE?" MY SON, CASE, ASKED AS HE OFTEN did when he awoke in the morning. He adored my sister.

In the beginning, it bothered me how attached he was to her. As I battled with navigating being a new mom, little things such as putting him down for a nap or getting him to latch onto my breasts for feeding was a challenge. As much as he cried, I just knew my newborn didn't like me. He never gave Miko a problem though. She was always able to put him to sleep and even helped with my breastfeeding, making sure I was set up right and that he was positioned correctly to latch on with ease. I quickly came to understand that their bond was one that I couldn't compete with. In fact, it was something I never wanted to come in between.

"Auntie Miko is sleeping, handsome. She got in late from work. You can give her a big kiss after you finish getting dressed for school. Up and at 'em, big man."

He smiled wide, tore his Spiderman covers off him, and stood. My son meant the world to me, and I was grateful every day that God saw fit for me to be his mother. Case saved me from sinking into a deep depression after the loss of my mom. He'd made his debut a month after we laid her to rest. A few days after his birth, his father got swept up in a drug raid. It was one loss after another, and I didn't know how to handle it. I was close to a breakdown, but my son was my saving grace.

Being able to wake up to his smiling face every day made the days a little easier as they passed. Miko played a big part in helping me as well. She took on so much as the big sister. Oftentimes, I didn't know where she mustered up the strength.

Seeing her breakdown this morning broke my heart. She was the emotional one of the two of us, while I was the spitfire. I rarely cried and tried not to wear my emotions on my sleeve after my mother died. My demeanor often made people think that I didn't give a fuck when, in fact, I did. I just showed it in my own way. I knew my sister was struggling to balance everything, and that was why whenever I got a couple dollars from doing hair, I would put it into the house.

I wasn't a job kind of girl. Whenever I was hired somewhere, I'd still be out looking for something better. Terrible, I know, but it had been my method... up until today. I planned to give my all in the interview I had lined up for tomorrow. I was determined now more than ever to keep our heads above water. Right now, we were drowning, and I could no longer act oblivious to that fact.

"Okay, big man, last one to the bathroom is a rotten..." He raced into the hall before I could even finish my sentence. "Yo' little cheating butt."

I laughed, catching up to him, playfully tackling him to the floor, and tickling him. Moments like this I cherished because my little man was growing right before my eyes. As I stood back, watching him brush his teeth and wash his face without asking for help, I teared up like a lame. I'd become one of those moms who cried and cheered at every little milestone.

"Mommy, I'm finished," he said, pulling me from my thoughts.

I turned for him to climb on my back, and he was full of giggles.

"Did you brush twice?" I questioned like I hadn't watched him do it.

"Yep. My tongue too cause that's the stinky part, right, Ma?"

I laughed because he got that from Miko. She was a stickler about oral hygiene. "Yes, son. Come on. You wanna eat breakfast at school? Or you want Mommy to make you something?"

"At school, Mommy. It's waffle day!" He threw his hands in the air in excitement. I'd be too. Ms. Pat made her waffles from scratch, and they were bomb. "Mommy, can you put my hair in a ponytail?" Case had hair similar to mine and Miko's. It was full and had a wavy curl pattern. It reached a little past his shoulder blade, and I usually kept it braided.

"Sure, baby." I brushed his hair into a low ponytail and braided the end of it. I didn't want anyone mistaking my baby for a little girl. "Alright, all done. Here, put this on then we out."

Case was independent, so I didn't need to stand over him while he dressed himself. I would give him a few minutes to put himself together and step in when I needed to. While he dressed, I went to peek in on Miko. Her door was slightly ajar, giving me a chance to check in on her without having to wake her up. My sister was exhausted. I could tell by the way she was sprawled on her bed with her mouth hanging open. Closing the door quietly, I let her get the rest she needed.

"I'm ready. Can I go give Auntie Miko a kiss now?"

Case stood before me in a pair of cargo shorts and a black Gap shirt. He even had his sneakers on. Well, the back of his heel was hanging out, but my baby tried. I bent down to fix it then, grabbing his hand, I led him into the room where he crept over to Miko. Giving her a soft peck, he tiptoed back over to me.

"I love you, Case," Miko said in a groggy voice.

I smiled and so did he. As we went to walk out, he stopped mid stroll.

"Mommy, your head." He pointed out.

I laughed, looking in the mirror that hung in the hallway near the door. Pulling my silk bonnet off my head, I let my twenty-six-inch lace front fall to the middle of my back. Finger combing the hair in place so that I was presentable, I was ready to step outside.

"Better?"

He gave me a thumbs up and a smile. I didn't really need a weave, but I swore I was addicted to them. They made me feel like a different person.

The daycare was a twenty-minute bus ride uptown from where we lived on One Fourteenth between Seventh and Lenox. I used our daily bus rides as a time to teach Case new things. He was gonna be both book smart and street smart. At four, he was a sponge, so I made sure that he soaked up as much education as he did YouTube, if not more.

We made it to the daycare in time for the first round of breakfast. Ms. Pat was the perfect caretaker. She loved all the kids she had like they were her own and always made sure they had one-on-one time with her. What made it even better was that the daycare set up was in the bottom half of her brownstone, so I felt my son was safe. Picking Case up to ring the buzzer, Ms. Pat came to the door seconds later.

"Ms. Pat!" he yelled excitedly.

"Hey, Mr. Handsome." She greeted him with a kiss on the forehead before allowing him to run in and join the other kids at the breakfast table. Inside the daycare had such a warm and homey feel to it. The walls were decorated with educational posters and different projects the kids had done.

"How you doing, sugar?"

"I'm hanging in there, Ms. Pat. About that bounced check, we…" She cut me off with a wave of her hand.

"Ming, you don't have to explain anything to me. This building is already bought and paid for by my nephews. The money y'all give goes to lights, food, and anything else I may need for the kids. I know times are hard, baby. Just know that Case will not lack because of no bounced check."

I wanted to cry so bad, but I held it down because I didn't want Case to worry. I didn't want our struggle to be known; shit was embarrassing.

Thanking her, I went to give Case a kiss goodbye. He wasn't trying to be mushy with me because he was around his friends, so he held his fist up for me to pound. Laughing inwardly and respecting that my boy had somewhat of a rep, I pressed my fist against his. I left feeling a little better since Ms. Pat wasn't tripping over the check. I was now even more determined than before to get my money up.

Case was my child, and while I appreciated my sister, I needed to be able to be his sole provider. Walking out onto the street, I pulled out my phone to check the DMs on my hair page on Instagram. I constantly received messages about different hairstyles and what I charged. I usually did hair for fun, but right now, I needed that quick money like yesterday.

"Damn, whatever nigga you texting gotta be important for you to be risking your life by not looking up while crossing the street."

Lifting my head, I swallowed hard, looking into the grey irises of a fair-skinned man. The tattoos on his neck were on display in the V-neck polo shirt he had on. I took in his biceps and broad shoulders, surveying him all the way down to his feet, before focusing back on his face.

"Excuse me?" I snapped, making sure my voice didn't match the way he had my body feeling. The smirk that lined his face let me know he was about to either crack a joke or say something smart.

"I'm saying though. It's not good to have your eyes on your phone all the time, especially while you're walking." He stared back at me, awaiting a response, but I was stuck. His eyes were so captivating. "Damn, so you a mute now?"

And there it was, my reason to snap on his ass.

"First off, no, I'm not a mute. Second, don't worry about what I do with my phone." I flipped with a mug on my face. He had some damn nerve.

"I'm just trying to prevent you from bumping that pretty little head of yours but do you, shorty. I hope that iPhone got wings in the event a car tosses yo' lil' ass in the air." Sidestepping me, he kept walking and entered the daycare. I didn't know who he was, but I didn't like how he gave me goosebumps when he spoke. *Lord, keep that man away from me. He don't mean me nor my lady parts any good.*

Just as I went to put my phone in my pocket, it rang. The incoming call was from an unknown number, and I knew it was a jail call from Case's dad, Karter. I sucked my teeth, prepared to not answer. Our last conversation ended with me hanging up on his ass, and knowing Karter, this call had the potential of ending the same way. He called himself trying to check me and make rules from his five-by-nine-inch jail cell. It was no way he missed the memo of us no longer being together, so he couldn't check shit over here.

Sighing, I connected the call and listened to the automated

message system. I knew one thing. I wasn't about to argue with Karter Stone today, so for his sake, he had better keep it cute. Once he said his name, the call connected.

"**Wassup, baby?**" His gruff voice came through in a rather pleasant tone.

"**Hey, Karter.**" We were no longer on a pet name basis. At least on my end we weren't. We hadn't been together in three and a half years, but the only person who seemed to acknowledge that was me.

"**What you doing?**"

"**Just dropped Case off to daycare and about to go handle my business. Wassup?**"

"**Oh, what business?**"

"**The business that pays me, Karter. Why you all up in mine?**"

"**I hear you,**" he replied, not taking the hint that I didn't want to talk. "**My mans ain't hit you up about dropping off no bread?**"

I chuckled to myself because the question was comical to me. "**No, Karter. No drop offs have been made.**" The fact that he even thought that somebody was bringing me anything from him was crazy. The people that claimed they were gonna make sure Case was good while he was away had up and disappeared. It was how shit went when you played in the streets. You got knocked, and life went on.

"**Don't worry. I'ma make sure somebody comes through and hit you off.**"

"**I would appreciate it if you didn't send anyone where I rest my head. If you wanna send something for me, Cash App, Zelle, and Apple Pay work just fine.**"

"**Aight, man. Yo, I need to ask you something.**"

The line got quiet for a few seconds, and I was glad the bus had pulled up because by the pause, I knew whatever he was about to say wasn't gonna go over well with me.

"**They're having family day up here, and I want you to bring Case to meet his little sister.**"

I laughed out loud, and when he didn't join in, I stopped immediately. "**Case don't have no sister, Karter.**"

"**Look, I didn't know how to tell you...**"

You have one minute remaining, the automated system announced, cutting him off.

"I can tell you more in person. Can you please just bring him for me?"

The phone clicked off before I could tell him hell no. It was just like his trifling ass to tell me he had another child on me while he was in prison. Karter was a fucking joke, and the best thing I could've done was drop his ass before he dragged me into doing a bid with him. He'd thrown my whole mood off, but I knew I had to shake it. There was money to be made.

3

———

CHANCE

The foreign looking chick I bumped into on my way into my aunt's daycare was fucking breathtaking. She had a lot of attitude, and her small stature held some fire. She reminded me a lot of the singer, Jhene Aiko, only there seemed to be nothing peaceful and serene about her. Shorty looked like she wanted to bite my head off when I mentioned her getting hurt by not paying attention. I towered over her at six-foot-three, but she was bucking up at me like I was five-foot-one. I was drawn to that nutty shit. And if I had it my way, if I ever saw her again, she would have to give me her number.

"Aunt Pat, I'm here." I announced myself as I entered the daycare with my key. As soon as the kids heard my voice, they all came running toward the door.

"Chanceeee!" they shouted in unison, making me chuckle.

Whenever I came by, they would show me mad love. It was weird at first because I was the first one to admit that I didn't like kids. However, being around these little ones made me realize that I was a kid magnet, just not beat for the bad fuckers.

"Wassup. Wassup, fellas?" I dapped up the boys. "And ladies." I bent down to give the girls half hugs. I always made sure to treat them different without them noticing. I didn't play rough with the girls, and I didn't do soft shit with the boys.

"Alright now, go 'head and finish up your breakfast before it gets cold, little people," Aunt Pat said, interrupting our bonding moment. "These kids sho' love you, boy. I don't know why." She smiled and hugged me.

"C'mon, Auntie, you know I'm the sugar honey iced tea." We laughed, and I followed her to the laundry room. She didn't play that cussin' around her kids shit.

"So, it's the dryer that messed up. It won't start for nothing, and I don't know what happened. Me and Jas are the only ones that use it. Take a look at it for your auntie and see what you can do."

"Auntie, if it's broke, why didn't you order a new one on the card?" My brother, Truth, and I had given her a credit card months ago that was linked to our business account. The card was to be used for anything she needed at the daycare. It seemed like we had to fight her to use the free money.

She put her hand on her hip and cocked her head to the side. "Now why would I go and waste money when I have you to come and fix it good as new?"

"Aight, Auntie. Let me see what I can do."

There was no sense in going back-and-forth because she could go all day. I was already hip to what she was doing anyway. I'd gone to Job Corp as a teenager because I couldn't seem to get it right in school. While there, I was able to learn a little bit of everything. Fixing appliances was one skill that really stuck with me. Aunt Pat would give me odd jobs around the daycare every now and then, hoping it would sway me from my current occupation, supply and demand.

Aunt Pat was my mother's older sister who had taken me and Truth in after our parents were gunned down at the gambling spot they owned. Growing up, I heard different stories about why it happened and who was responsible. Truth called bullshit on all the theories. He promised that when it was time for us to find out who did it, we wouldn't have to look for the perpetrator; they'd bring themselves to us. He was older than me and more aware, so I didn't know what to think. All I knew was that my mom and dad were gone, and that shit fucked my head up.

Without the nurturing and love from Aunt Pat, I don't know

where I'd be. I couldn't speak for Truth because he was a thinker above all. Me, on the other hand, I was a loose cannon. Every now and then, I would go off, but as I got older, I'd been able to maintain a certain level of calmness before I blacked on motherfuckas. She had taken us in with no questions asked and raised us as her own. Truth, Jasmine, and I were like the three amigos. For that, we were forever indebted to Aunt Pat, and there was nothing that we wouldn't do to make her happy — including fixing a dryer that she could've replaced.

It was a good thing that I came in sweats. I had a feeling this wasn't going to be no three-step job. Two and a half hours later, I had fixed the problem, saving her a cool four hundred dollars had she replaced it. Maybe she was right about wasting money.

"How you do that?" a small voice asked.

I looked up from behind the dryer after snapping the back piece on. One of Aunt Pat's most popular kids, Case, stood in the doorway of the laundry room with his arms folded across his little chest.

"I got skills, lil' man."

"How you get skills?"

I had to laugh because his facial expression followed by his question made it seem like he was tryna get put on. "Gotta be taught, lil' man. The next time I come by, you can watch me fix something, aight?"

He gave me a head nod before running off. He was a cool lil' kid, probably one of my favorites.

"Aunt Pat, you're good to go!" I yelled out while checking my text messages. There were two unread. One was from this chick I met uptown while running errands and the other was from Truth. I opened bro's text first.

Truth: Board meeting today at one.

Me: Say less.

Checking my AP, the time read eleven forty-five. I had enough time to run by the crib, shower, and change clothes. With my messages still opened, I scrolled to Tiara's text while heading up front.

"Goddamn!" I let out and zoomed in on the pussy pic she'd sent. She had the lips spread open, showing her inner folds, making my dick brick up. Along with the picture was a text that read, *whenever you're free, so am I.*

I texted back immediately, requesting her address. A few seconds later, the phone chimed with the info. Scrolling back to the picture, I analyzed it while licking my lips. Yeah, I had to go see what that wet box was hittin' on.

"Watch your mouth in front of these kids, Chance," Aunt Pat scolded me.

"Oh, my bad. I'm done. I'll take my payment in the form of chicken and dumplings and buttered biscuits. Thank you." Kissing her cheek, I waved bye to the kids.

BACK IN MY CAR, I drove down Amsterdam Avenue and cut over onto Broadway to get to 135th Street where Tiara lived in 3333. I texted for her to have the box ready when I got to the door. I was on stick and move type of time. I couldn't be late for the meeting. Always aware of my surroundings, I made sure to scope the scenery as I maneuvered through the buildings before reaching the C side. Taking the elevator up to the nineteenth floor, I got off and headed straight for her door.

Once I confirmed I was at the right place through text, she responded that the door was unlocked. That was odd. Although her building wasn't located in the hood, leaving the door unlocked for a stranger was weird. It let me know that she was a careless broad. Knowing that I was only here for pussy and not commitment, I pressed forward. Shit, if she didn't care about her safety, why should I?

I said a silent prayer that her house was clean because if it wasn't, she could keep the pussy. It didn't matter how wet she was or how good she looked, if her house was dirty, I was straight. Letting myself in, the smell of vanilla and almond hit my nose, causing a nod of approval.

"I'm in the back. In the bedroom on your right," she called out.

Still cautious, I looked around while walking to the back where I'd heard the voice. Turning to my right, I found an open bedroom door, and there she was, sprawled out on the bed with her head back and a pocket rocket up against her clit.

"Damn, shorty, you started without me?" Licking my lips, we locked eyes.

She stared up at me through her heavy lids and bit her lip. That shit was sexy as fuck. "Mmm, you can join in whenever you want. Sssss, I'm so wet," she let out in a lust filled tone.

I watched as she replaced the toy with her fingers, skillfully twisting them in and out of her wet box. My dick threatened to burst through my sweats. Knowing I was pressed for time, I pulled them down, leaving my boxers on. As I made my way over to her, she sat up and crawled over to the edge of the bed. With a sexy smirk, she put her hand up and went to place her fingers on my lips.

I didn't know shorty that well to taste her just yet, so I grabbed her hand and placed it on my dick. She didn't seem offended. Instead, she went with the flow, pulling my dick from my boxers. Her eyes widened when she saw the length and the curve on this motherfucka.

"Oh, he's beautiful," she marveled.

I chuckled. "Thank you. Let me see how he look in your mouth."

Licking her pouty lips, she opened her mouth wide and wrapped her lips around my shaft. My dick was fat, so just watching her do her best to take all of me in was a sight to see. Watching the spit pool in the corners of her mouth as she bobbed up and down on my shit made me harder. I gripped the back of her head, fucking her face slowly. The gawking sounds she made was like music to my ears.

"Yeah, shorty. Just like that. Eat that dick up. It's good for you."

"Mmmm," she moaned, really getting into it.

I reached over and slapped her ass, watching it jiggle before slipping my fingers in her pussy. She wasn't snug, but not crazy loose either. I could work with it. Feeling my nut build up, I stroked her face faster. She got the hint and did the jack and suck combo. Not wanting to be disrespectful, I pulled out and let off in my hand. Her eyes lit up like I had just asked her to marry me.

"Where's your bathroom, Ma?"

"Down the hall to your right."

I followed her directions and washed my hands quickly. Returning back to the room with my dick sticking out of the hole in my boxers, I smiled at her waiting for me with her ass in the air. She was down with the program. Reaching down to grab a condom from my sweats, she stopped me.

"I got you covered, boo." She held up a gold Magnum wrapper and stretched her hand out to me.

"Nah, I got me," I assured her while continuing to fish for my own protection. I flashed a fresh golden wrapper of my own and proceeded to step out of my boxers to put it on.

You could never be too safe. Trapping niggas had become somewhat of a sport, and no chick was about to score with me. I caught the slight look of disappointment on her face but brushed it off. This grade A beef would put her in the right state of mind.

"Turn around for me and toot that ass in the air."

She didn't respond verbally but turned to do as I said. Gently pulling her closer to the edge of the bed, I slid my fingers down her slit. She looked back just as I put my fingers up to my nose. I gave her a wink, acknowledging her cleanliness. I wasn't hard up for pussy to where I'd let anyone skate past the smell test. Placing my dick at her opening, I slid in with ease.

"Sssssss," she hissed as I stroked her at a medium pace.

I needed her to feel every inch of this dick. Gripping her waist, I moved my hips in a circular motion, making sure to massage that g-spot.

"Oouu, yes. Gimmie that dick, nigga." She threw her fat ass back like she was tryna show me something.

I commended her in my head cause she was doing her shit. *WHAP!* I smacked her ass hard, pulling a soft whimper from her lips. Taking a handful of her braids, I gently tugged at them, pulling her toward me. "I'm bout to bust," I whispered in her ear. "Wet this dick up, Ma."

"Ooh, fuckk, ohh, damn, I'm cummin'," she announced. Reaching around, I got ahold of her clit and slapped it before rubbing it in a fast motion. "Yesssss!" she cried out and started to shake as she came.

Pulling out, I stroked my dick a few times before letting off in the condom. Carefully taking it off, I tied it in a knot and left to flush it down the toilet. It was a practiced routine that I never failed to do.

"You don't have to leave," she said once I returned to redress. "We can chill for a little while."

"Can't today, sweetheart, gotta get to a meeting. I'ma hit you though. That thang got my approval." I leaned over where she now sat up against her headboard and kissed her cheek. "Come lock up."

I didn't bother checking the time again because I knew I was cuttin' it close. Heading home, I changed clothes and walked right back out the door. I hated to be late, but Truth took it to another level. In his eyes, if you were on time, then you were late. I managed to pull into the parking lot of the warehouse/gambling spot at exactly one o'clock.

Parking my whip, I made my way inside and downstairs to the boardroom. From the outside, the building appeared to be a normal warehouse in Gramercy Park. Inside was anything but that. Inside, me and my brother ran one of the largest gambling spots in the five boroughs, along with the most exclusive escort service in the north region. The Porter House was our family legacy, and those who knew of it knew that here, you had to pay to play.

4

───────

TRUTH

"Nice of you to join us, brother," I said to Chance as he bopped into the boardroom and gave me a brotherly hug.

"That's my fault, bruh. I'll tell you about it once the meeting is over. Ladies, gentlemen." He gave a head nod to the staff assembled for the meeting.

There was Robin, Nyema, Brock, and Troy, along with me and Chance that made up the team. Chance and I had inherited the Porter House by birthright when my parents passed. Being that I was only fifteen when it happened and Chance twelve, I didn't take over immediately. My uncle, Boss, stepped in and held it down. Little did he know, I was watching his every move. My pops had groomed Chance and I to take over. And I soaked up the knowledge like a sponge. I knew the ins and outs of the gambling spot and the Elite house by the time I was fourteen.

When I found out my parents had been killed in their place of business, everybody was a suspect, including Uncle Boss. I didn't seek out the persons responsible. I kept my ear to the streets, knowing that no matter how many years went by, someone would talk. I also stayed close to the warehouse as well as the home that the Elites shared. My Aunt Pat didn't agree with our line of work, but she never steered us away from it either.

She knew my mother played a big part in the success of the business. My mom was everything, including a rider, but not to be confused with a ride or die chick. Some ride or die chicks claimed the phrase until shit got real. Not Tammy Porter. She was the queen that stood tall alongside her king and took whatever came with it. Unfortunately, she rode with my pops all the way to those pearly gates.

"Truth, you okay?" Robin asked.

"Yeah, my bad. I zoned out real quick. I called this meeting because I need to make a few changes. I want you all to hear it here first before I get the ball rolling." Everyone gave their undivided attention, listening for the changes I was referring to. "For one, management for the Elites is changing. Nyema, I no longer want you in the house. I need you to take your talents down to Tantra and manage the girls there."

Tantra was one of my newest ventures, an all-female staffed tapas bar and lounge that I opened two years ago. It exuded sex appeal and had a euphoric feel to it. I wanted Nyema there because it was the one place I didn't frequent often, and she wouldn't be into it with the women. Nyema was my off again, on again girlfriend. We had been doing this song and dance for the past two years. For a minute, I had her over the day-to-day operations at the Elite house, but lately, I had been getting too many complaints about her from the ladies.

The Elites consisted of a group of five women who provided companionship for what I liked to call the big dawgs. The big dawgs were prominent lawyers, politicians, musicians, doctors, etc. My ladies took care of them and were paid very well to do so.

"Let me guess, somebody had something to say about the way I run things?" Nyema inquired with a roll of her eyes.

"It doesn't matter. What does matter is that's the decision." I wouldn't engage in a back-and-forth conversation with her. My word was law.

"Next, Chance, I need you to be here holding down the Porter House for a little bit while I get some sense of normalcy back down at the Elite house. Brock and Troy, y'all are good where you are. Robin, you always straight. We'll meet later and talk numbers."

Brock and Troy worked security, and Robin was the business

accountant. Everyone seemed to be okay with the slight changes. The only person who had an obvious problem was Nyema. It was written all over her face. Adjourning the meeting, I sent everyone on their way while Chance hung back.

"Bruh, that's a pretty big change you're making here. Wassup with Boss? Why he ain't here?"

"Unc is getting old. It's time for him to start living for himself. It's not really a big change. We just have to be more hands-on than before."

"I hear you. Nyema out there ready to lose her shit right about now. The Elites can't stand her ass."

We both shared a laugh because he was telling the truth. They complained all the time about how difficult Nyema was to be around.

"I know it, man. Hopefully, she does better at Tantra. Shit, the only female she seems to get along with is Robin."

"That's because she don't have a choice in the matter. Robin will shoot her ass and count twenty stacks right after, not skipping a fucking beat."

I nodded, agreeing. Robin didn't play about me or the business, which was why I'd always keep her close. She had been working for the Porter House since before I'd taken over.

"Aight, I'm outta here. Ya aunt had me up early this morning working on a damn dryer she could've replaced."

"You a regular ol' Mr. Fix It." I snickered.

"You told her to call me, didn't you?"

I held my hands up, still laughing.

"You ain't shit, man. I'll hit you later. And I'm telling you now, don't be calling me tryna hang out after Nyema cuss yo' ass out."

"You know me well enough to know that Nyema treads a thin line with me, bruh. She can jump crazy if she wants and get her feelings hurt. Hit me later so you can tell me why yo' ass was late."

"Aight."

Locking up the boardroom, we walked out together, and he made his way to the exit. As I went to turn the corner and head over to Robin's office, Nyema switched over to me with a scowl on her face.

"We need to talk, Truth."

"Meet me in the car. I gotta go holla at Robin one-on-one real quick." I walked away before she could respond. Porter House didn't open until seven in the evening, and I needed to make sure everything was in place, especially the money.

"Wassup, Robin? How we looking for tonight?"

"Good, boss. Last night, we brought in eighty thousand dollars. Bringing in those penny machines was a brilliant idea."

"That's wassup, and how are the Elites?"

"Let's just say if you wanted to shut this spot down for a month, everybody could eat off of what the Elites bring in."

I smiled and rubbed my hands together. That was the kind of news I liked to hear. Anything attached to the hustle and getting some money made me feel good.

"Thank you for all you do. Go home and get some rest. Chance will handle money tonight."

"Okay. Oh, and can you try not to blindside me when you plan to shake up my world next time?"

"What you mean?"

"Nyema."

"Oh."

"Yeah, oh. This is y'all business at the end of the day, so I know who run things. You know how I feel about bs though. I'll short fuse and be on the news. And you know my husband and children would miss me dearly."

I laughed a little. "I can ensure you that won't happen. And though we make the rules, you're family. What affects you affects us, subsequently affecting the business. I got you, sis."

"That's all I need to hear. Be safe and I'll talk to you later."

"Aight."

Robin was a valuable asset to our team, and before I let Nyema come in and shake up the atmosphere, I'd drop her ass.

Making my way outside, I hopped inside my all-black custom Maybach S-Class where Nyema sat waiting for me. I knew she wanted to argue, and I would hear her out for a moment, but if the conversation went too left, I was dropping her ass off at home —_her home.

"So, which one of the Elites has an issue with me?"

"None."

"Bullshit. Someone definitely has a problem. And it's news to me because I do a damn good job at managing that house and keeping them in line. Make me understand why I now have to change lanes."

"The fact that your understanding of the position is to keep them in line is why you're changing lanes. We don't keep the Elites in line, Nyema. For one, they're grown ass women. And secondly, they govern themselves, and we manage their client list. You're not losing your managerial position; you'll be doing the same thing at Tantra."

"Yeah, sure, tell me anything. As your woman, I don't want you in that house all times of the night either. I already know they wanna fuck you, Truth, and you know I have no problem going toe-to-toe for what's mine."

I stayed silent, not engaging in crazy talk with her. The Elites were like family to me, and even if there was an attraction, I never gave off the vibe that I was interested. She was so wrapped up in thinking she was checking me that she didn't notice the direction I was driving in until the car stopped. Knowing that this conversation was going to be never ending, her destination was home.

"I'll call you later," I said, popping the locks on the door.

"Really? Wow, okay. You don't have to put me out. I'll gladly go." With an attitude, she got out and slammed the door behind her.

Things between Nyema and I hadn't been the same since I brought her onboard to work down at the Elite house. She had become difficult to deal with and had a sense of entitlement that I just couldn't rock with. The slamming of my door didn't faze me none. She wasn't a kid, so me yelling out the window to chastise her would do nothing. Denying her access to my presence would really fuck her up. When she had her melodramatic melt downs, I'd go ghost on her ass for a few days, and she'd come back with a new attitude. I'd learned from my father a long time ago that your presence had to mean something.

Before heading home, I made a detour to the Elite house. I made sure the ladies lived a life of luxury, and the beauty of it was that they were able to take care of themselves should they want to go off on their own. You could tell they were kept women by the way they lived. I purchased a townhouse for them on the Upper Westside. The 3,422 square feet townhome had been redesigned with a woman's touch and all up-to-date amenities. It was equipped with everything they needed, and if there was anything they wanted, they had the means to get it.

Ringing the buzzer, I waited for one of them to buzz me in. I made sure to have my tech guy, Brock, install the latest security system to ensure the ladies' safety. They even knew their way around a few guns, which I had strategically placed throughout the home. I flashed my pearly whites into the camera, and the door buzzed, giving me clearance. Entering the house, the scent of maple syrup filled the foyer. I'd come at the right time.

"Why do you insist on being buzzed in when you have your own key, Truth?" Nicole asked as she descended the steps in her silk kimono and fuzzy heels.

Along with Nicole, there were four other girls that lived in the Elite house. There was Joi, Olivia, Kane, and Jomary. Nicole had been in the Elite house the longest. At thirty-seven, she was like the mom of the house and had her loyal clients that stuck to her like glue. She started out at twenty-one as the youngest on my mom's team and had gradually matured under her wing.

"It's a respect thing, Nic. You know that. Who in the kitchen working the pots?" I asked, walking in that direction.

"You know that's Joi in there trying out a new recipe. You staying for brunch?"

"Yeah, I gotta talk to y'all anyway. Gather the ladies for me and meet me in the dining room."

She walked off to do as I asked while I kept forward toward the kitchen. Joi was currently in her last year of culinary school and had deemed herself the house chef. At twenty-four, she had a good head on her shoulders, and no matter how much I tried to push her into her destiny as a chef, she always pushed back. I made sure all of the ladies had something going for themselves because the life we lived wasn't forever.

"My Joi. What you in here cheffing up?" I leaned over to kiss her cheek, and she blushed.

"Hey, Truth. I'm making stuffed French toast, egg whites, and turkey bacon. You want some, greedy?"

"Hell yeah. I'll be in the dining room. We're having a quick meeting too."

Once the ladies were assembled at the table and the food was placed in front of us, we bowed our heads to say grace. I silently thanked God for all my triumphs and trials and asked him to forgive me for my transgressions. Looking up, I noticed there were only five people at the table including myself.

"Where's Liv?" I inquired.

Olivia was the wild card. She marched to the beat of her own drum and made her own rules. I always gave her enough room to hang herself, and lucky for her, she never went too far.

"She had a date last night and stayed out. She checked in though," Kane reassured me while placing an egg white in her mouth.

"So, what's this meeting about, Truth?" Jomary asked, taking a sip of her mimosa.

Both Jomary and Kane were fairly new to the house, almost a year to be exact. They were brought in by Joi, and so far, they seemed to fit in well.

"I'll start as soon as we get Liv on the phone. Nic, call her for me, love."

She dialed Liv on her phone and put it on speaker. The call connected, and her voice came through in a chipper tone.

"Hey, Nic. Wassup?"

I cut in. **"Olivia, we're having a meeting. How soon can I expect you here?"**

"Oh, hey, Truth. I didn't know you were there. Give me about twenty minutes. I'm close by. And save me some of whatever Joi made. I can hear y'all smacking through the phone."

We all laughed, and she hung up. Exactly twenty minutes later, I could hear her heels clicking across the marble floor.

"Alright, now that Liv is here, I can tell y'all what's happening. I will be managing the house hands-on until I find someone more suitable for the job." They all remained quiet, as if what I'd said didn't faze them, but I knew better. "Y'all can go 'head and say how you really feel."

"Ding dong, the witch is dead, the wicked witch is dead," Kane joked, making the girls laugh.

Liv leaned over and kissed my cheek. "I knew you loved us, Truth. I swear, if we didn't value and love you, we would've jumped her ass a long time ago."

Damn, Nyema was that bad? I guess I'd made the right decision. I couldn't let anybody fuck up the money, and fucking with the Elites was a sure way to fuck up the cash flow. Hopefully, I could find someone they liked and soon.

5

———

AMIKO

"**Ms. Johnson, I completely understand how you feel. For a year, your bill has been one set price, and now, you're seeing something different. However, you had a promotion last year for the ultra-upgrade, and that expired.**" I tried to reason with the irate customer who I'd been on the phone with for the last twenty-five minutes. For some reason, in her mind, my answer was going to change.

"**Well, y'all ain't tell me that shit, so y'all need to put it back on because I ain't paying no extra money for this trash ass internet!**"

I took a deep breath in an attempt to compose myself because I was two seconds away from cussing this bitch out. "**Ms. Johnson, I'm unable to extend that discount at this time. I can...**"

"**Don't tell me what you can't do. Get your supervisor because clearly you don't know how to treat yo' customers!**" She cut me off for the third time.

There was no reasoning with her, so I politely put the call on hold to get Sheila on the phone. Using our internal chat, I messaged her what the problem was, and she took the call. Annoyed by the whole interaction, I put my phone in a personal state and went to the bathroom. I swore I couldn't take rude ass people, and then, she had the nerve to tell me I didn't know my job. I knew this shit like the back of my hand. Taking five minutes to get my mind right, I went to return to the floor, only to be stopped by Sheila.

"Can I see you in my office, Amiko?"

"Sure." I put on my fake smile and followed behind her.

"Can you tell me about the conversation you had with the customer you transferred to me?"

I looked at this bitch like she was crazy. Again, taking a deep breath, I explained what happened play by play. Her facial expression remained sour, like she had just finished sucking on lemons.

"So, you couldn't de-escalate the customer like you were taught in training?" Her tone was offensive as she called herself reprimanding me.

"If you play the call, you'll see I did all I could to calm the customer down and explain the reason for the change, but she was not trying to hear me."

"I see. Unfortunately, I have to let you go. This is the second customer complaint we've received about you within the last month regarding your attitude. From the way you're interacting with me right now, there's no need for me to dispute her complaint."

"Let me go? Are you serious right now? What ever happened to a write up?"

"These are the rules, Amiko. I'm sorry, but we can't have our employees treating customers any kind of way. It reflects badly on the company. Please hand your badge in to the security. He'll walk you out."

"Treat them any kind of way? You mean like how you treat us? 'Cause you should be the last person talking about customer service. You know what? Fuck you and these customers." I stormed out of her office on the verge of tears.

Snatching up my purse, I ripped the badge off my waist and handed it to the security, who was waiting at the door. His face showed genuine empathy, but I didn't need anyone feeling sorry for me. I couldn't believe this shit was happening. I could've taken the issue up with human resources but fuck this place. I had given this hellhole five years of my life, and if they didn't appreciate me, they could have it.

The ride home on the train seemed to be the longest it had ever been. The bitch could have at least waited until the end of my shift to let me go. *Ole snagga tooth looking ass bitch*, I thought to myself as I fiddled with my phone. Getting off on One Sixteenth Street, I heard my name called as I walked toward the steps to get to the street.

"Miko, Miko, wait up." I turned slightly to see Dre bopping in my direction. I rolled my eyes hard as he got closer, flashing his gold fronts that lined his bottom teeth.

"You stopping me? I know ain't nothing good to come out of it. What you want, Dre?"

"Damn," he put his hand over his chest, faking like he was hurt, "you ain't gotta carry me like that, Ma. I saw you getting off the train and wanted to see what was up witchu."

"I'm good. Anything else you wanna know?"

"I miss you," he said, grabbing at my hand, only for me to snatch it back.

"Come on, don't act like that. You don't miss a nigga, Miko?"

"I sho' don't." Rolling my eyes again, I turned on my heels to walk away.

As persistent as I'd known him to be, he followed, wrapping his arms around me from behind. Feeling his dick pressed against my ass, I pushed him back.

"Boy, back up off me."

"I got something that can help with that little attitude of yours." He licked the side of my neck, making my body shiver without my permission.

"There's nothing you can help me with, Dre. I'm cool on you. Been cool on you for a minute now."

"You sure about that?" he whispered in my ear.

"Positive."

"Shit, Dre," I cooed out loud as he sucked on my pussy from behind. Don't ask me how I ended up here, sober with my ass in the air. I had no alcohol to blame for the position I was in. "Ooouu, shit, eat this pussy. Ughhh, you gon' make me cummmm!"

Dre was a lot of things —_a liar, a dog, and a pussy eating ass fool. The feeling of his lips pressed against my wet box made me temporarily forget why I left him in the first place. And as my clit swelled in his mouth, I humped his tongue until I released. Caught up in trying to regain my composure, I gasped when I felt him slide inside of me bareback. It had been so long since I'd had some dick that I lost all the good sense God gave me.

"Goddamn, this pussy still good as fuck." Slapping my ass hard, he held onto my shoulder and plunged into my wetness, making my pussy very happy. The feeling of his balls slapping against my clit made it that much better. "You gon' cum on this dick for Daddy?" He was doing such a great job at working my middle that I told him what he wanted to hear.

"Yesss, yes, Daddy."

My pussy got wetter as he slowed down his strokes and put in overtime on my g-spot. I'd reached my peak again, pinching my nipples as I rained down on him for the second time.

"Shittt," Dre crooned, pulling out just in time to nut in his hand.

Satisfied, I climbed out of bed and slid on my robe. "I'll walk you out," I said, letting him know that I didn't wanna kick it and definitely didn't want to rekindle any flames. This one-time double back was just that, a one-time thing.

"It was good seeing you too, Miko," he spoke through a chuckle while putting on his pants. "That thang still grip tight."

"Yeah, nigga, this still that. Thanks for the tune up, Dre." Guiding him to the door, I made sure to lock up right behind him.

"Feel much lighter, don't ya?"

I jumped hearing Ming's voice. Turning around, I caught her smirk. Just as I went to lie about my sexcapade, I burst out laughing.

"Sis, I feel like I need a blunt, and you know I don't even smoke."

She laughed along with me, slapping me five. Laughing with her in the moment felt freeing until reality set in that I was unemployed. My smile instantly fell, and she picked up on it.

"What?"

"Come to my room real quick."

"Ummm, you not gonna let it air out?"

"Don't even try to play me, Ming."

"Alright," she giggled. Following behind me, she stood against the wall while I chose to sit. "Wassup?"

My head dropped, not wanting to face her due to the embarrassment. I was the oldest; I was supposed to hold shit down. I felt like a failure, and for a minute, I wanted to retreat and not tell her anything about me being fired. But as I looked up, the worried expression on her face let me know that I had to tell her what was up.

"I got fired today, Ming. That bitch, Sheila, let me go on some bullshit." I was mad all over again, and the tears that fell down my cheeks pissed me off even more.

All I could do was think the worst. Me, my sister, and my nephew on the streets with nowhere to go scared me. This couldn't be life. At twenty-six, I had more problems than a little bit.

"Miko, don't cry. Come on, sis, we're built Ford tough. Mommy made sure of that." She rubbed my back while encouraging me. "Everything will fall into place. I already put it in the atmosphere." She hugged me tight, and I calmed down a bit. "Alright now, don't mess up my shirt with all this crying you doing."

Chuckling, I pulled back from her embrace, shoving her a little. "Shut up."

"How 'bout I see if Ms. Pat can hold Case down for the night, and we can go grab a drink with Jas or something? My interview was rescheduled for next week, so let's turn up. You need it, sis."

I agreed because I knew she wasn't gonna take no for an answer. With most of my time spent at work, I barely got out anymore. Tonight, I was gonna let my hair down. I'd worry about finding a job tomorrow.

"You do know that Tantra is an all-female staffed lounge, right?" I reminded Ming as she entered my room in a pair of cut-up shorts, a bustier, and thigh-high boots.

It was going on ten o'clock, and we were getting ready to go out with my homegirl, Jas. Ming had crimped her hair, and her face was lightly made up. The fire red matte textured lipstick really set the makeup off.

"Girl, with the luck I've had with the opposite sex, I might as well go and get me a girlfriend." Sticking her tongue out, she walked past me and over to my dresser to get a closer look at herself.

I was nowhere near that fed up with men that I would ever consider carpet munching. I didn't care how good females said bumping kewchies was, I'd take a hard dick for 500, Alex. Keeping it light in an off-the-shoulder jean jumpsuit and a pair of stilettos, I put my long hair in a low ponytail, applied a little mascara and Fenty gloss, and was ready to go. After a few mirror selfies, the doorbell rang. As soon as I opened it, Jas was dancing through the door, already turnt.

"Yess, bitch, put these hoes to shame and give them body, honey!" Spinning me around, she popped me on my booty.

I giggled at her antics. If you were feeling down, one call to Jasmine would have you feeling on top of the world. For some reason, she was always in good spirits, and I loved it. We'd met Jasmine when we enrolled Case into daycare at six months. Ming was so against the idea at first, but we both understood that we needed to be on the grind. And unfortunately, she couldn't drag her six-month-old on interviews with her.

Jas and I instantly clicked the first day we met, and she, along with Ms. Pat, were like family to us. She often kept my spirits up when I would complain about work or bills. She even let me borrow money every now and then. My friend was the shit.

"Thank you, boo. You already know you out here killing shit."

She stepped back and posed in her Balmain jeans with a matching t-shirt and nude red-bottom heels. Them fucking shoes were the devil. I made sure to keep the one pair that I owned at the farthest part of my closet.

"Grab ya bag, we 'bout to turn up. Oh, and everything is on the house."

"On the house?" Ming and I said at the same time.

"Yes, my cousin owns the place. The drinks are gonna taste that much better knowing we don't have to pay for them. Whoop, whooppp!

"You would like him too, Miko, and he got a brother, Ming." She didn't give us a chance to answer before heading back out the door, yelling for us to hurry up.

I looked over at Ming, and she shrugged her shoulders.

"What you looking at me for? I told you I'ma 'bout to find me a girlfriend."

"Girl, bye." I waved her off, and she laughed.

Locking the door, I gave myself a pep talk. Tonight, I was throwing caution to the wind and going with the vibe. We all climbed into Jas' Acura TL with me behind the wheel of course. I was always the designated driver because unlike Lucy and Ethel in the passenger and backseat, I knew how to hold my liquor.

"Ooh, sis, turn that up," Ming requested as Summer Walker's hit, *Stretch You Out,* featuring A Boogie played through the speakers. I turned up the volume and sang along.

Niggas be insecure, claiming that you ain't doing enough, claiming that they need more. What you on your last breath, your last sweat, your last dime? Out of your fucking mind, can't you see I'm fucking trying? You want pussy six times a week, and you never wanna clean up. And you talk to me like shit, and you handle me too rough.

My good sis, Summer, was speaking from experience. These niggas wanted the fucking world and had the nerve to be fucking up. Just stretch me out and get on at this point.

Pulling up to Tantra, the parking lot was packed with cars. I had never been to the lounge before, but Jas had told me about it, and I couldn't wait to see if everything she said was true. Parking, we got out and maneuvered through the people to get inside. Once we entered the place, Jas guided us up to the second floor where a section was roped off for us. I loved the VIP treatment. Looking over the balcony, the blue lighting in the dark club screamed sex.

This wasn't your average lounge. It had character. There were aerial dancers doing all types of tricks on that little ribbon thingy throughout the place. None of the women were fully naked, and I could appreciate them leaving something to the imagination. It was tasteful. Whoever the interior designer was knew a thing or two. The designer had gotten everything right, even down to the two massive bars on the lower level.

"Sis, you gon' daydream? Or you gonna partake in the festivities?" Ming asked, directing my attention to the spread in front of me.

We hadn't been in the place five minutes and already had all kinds of liquor on the table, along with an assortment of finger foods. I'd never eaten at any lounge I'd gone to, but the food looked too good to pass up.

"What's good, cousin?"

My eyes shot up at the voice, and I'd be damned if I didn't see my future ex-husband enter the section. He was so goddamn fine I wanted to lick him.

"Miko, this is my cousin, Truth. Truth, this is my bestie, Amiko." Jas introduced with a smile.

6

TRUTH

"You're beautiful," was the first thing that came out of my mouth when Miko placed her small hand into mine.

"Thank you," she replied in a confident tone while blushing.

That shit was cute as hell. I guess I may have held onto her hand too long because Jasmine picked up on it.

"Well, damn, cousin, you gon' get on one knee and ask for her hand in marriage or what?" We both laughed, but I didn't let her hand go.

"My answer is yes. Yes, I will marry you, handsome," she joked.

"I'ma hold you to that." Giving her hand a few strokes from my thumb, I hesitantly let it go to hug Jas as she introduced me to Amiko's sister, Ming. Her demeanor wasn't so friendly. She sported a mean mug that had me on defense. "I know you from somewhere? You look like you wanna box, shorty."

"Oh, no, this mug is not for you. It's for the asshole headed up here." She rolled her eyes as she spoke, and I turned to see Chance coming up the stairs.

"What my brother do to you?"

"Oh," Jas giggled. "This my other cousin, Chance. What you do to my homegirl?" She chastised Chance once he was closer.

"I ain't do nothing to her little ass but help her cross the street without becoming part of the pavement. Wassup y'all?" He hugged Jas, shook hands with Amiko, and smirked at Ming, who rolled her eyes and turned away from him. "Maann, yo mean, fine ass ain't gotta speak."

I shook my head at the backwards compliment while Amiko snickered. "Well, I didn't come to interrupt y'all party. Enjoy y'all selves and let the waitress know if you need anything." I gave Amiko one final look and a wink and made my exit.

"Wait up, cousin," Jas called out to me as I started to walk down the steps. "I saw you back there eyeing my girl, so what I'm about to ask you should be no biggie." I nodded for her to continue talking. "I know she's gonna kill me for telling you this, but I'll deal with that later. Miko recently lost her job. And when I say recently, I mean earlier today. Normally, I wouldn't speak on her behalf, but right now, she's in a tough spot. Do you have any openings here?"

I rubbed my goatee, considering her question. I wasn't just selective about who I had in my personal circle but my business as well. Jas knew that, so I figured if she was coming to me for the hookup for her homegirl, she was vouching for her being solid. My wanting to hear Amiko talk more may have also sparked my consideration.

"She can come down and check out the Elite house."

Her brow raised, and she shook her head. "Oh, unt unh. You know I love the Elites like family, but I don't think that's quite her speed."

I laughed at her assumption. "Nah, not like that. I made some changes. I relieved Nyema of her duties there. I'm in need of a house manager. Right now, it's just me."

"Ooh, okay. I think she'll be cool with that. I'll tell her about it and get back to you. In the meantime, yo' girl down there waiting and watching. Ol' guard dog ass."

Turning my head slightly, I could see Nyema downstairs with her arms crossed tightly across her chest.

"Let me go see bout this girl."

"Yeah. For she get to cuttin' up and I get to showing my natural Black ass before I can consume this top shelf liquor." Leaning in to kiss my cheek, she patted my back. "Love you. And let me know if you need me."

"Love you too, cuz."

I made my way down the steps and over to Nyema. "Wassup? Why ya face all tight?"

"Who's up there in VIP?"

"My cousin and her homegirls."

"Well, Shika just put in a big order for that section, so I hope you ain't giving no family discount."

I was used to Nyema being extra and fake trying to boss up, but now, she was overstepping her boundaries. What I charged or didn't charge my family when it came to any of my businesses was only mine and Chance's decision.

"Would you consider free a family discount? If so, then that's what it is."

"You need to remember that you're running a business, not a nonprofit organization." She called herself checking me.

"That's where you're wrong, Ma. I'm running an empire. My kids' kids will be straight even if I decided to do a free night once a week. What you need to remember is you work for me, not with me. You've been getting real fly witcha mouth lately, and I've been lettin' shit slide. Don't make me get on bullshit witchu, Nyema. I promise you won't like it." I left her to think about what I said while moving through the crowd and to the bar to help the bartenders with the rush.

My lead bartender, Amina, stopped me as soon as she saw me coming. "No, Truth, we got it." She constantly fussed at me about taking over the jobs that I paid her team to do. "Here you go, Shika." She placed two bottles of Don Julio on the counter for one of the waitresses and turned to me.

"You sure y'all good?"

"Positive. You see all these men standing here? They don't mind waiting. We got it, boss." Smiling, she gave me a thumbs up and went back to serving her customers.

I stood off in the corner and watched the women run my club using the art of seduction. From the aerial dancers in bikinis covered in body art to the waitresses in their thonged leotards, they were all shapes and sizes, handpicked by me. A little bit of everything for every man or woman that came through the door. I created an ambiance that made you want to spend money. It was nothing to bring in twenty to thirty bands a night. This wasn't your ordinary strip club or gentlemen's club. This was Tantra.

"Yo, I need to go see a doctor, bruh."

"What the hell you talking 'bout?" I asked Chance, who stood in front of me with a lost look on his face.

"I think I'm in love. I gotta be sick. I'm sick, right?" He ran his hand down his face, and I cracked up.

"That shit ain't funny, bruh. This chick got me feeling weird as hell, and it's only my second time encountering her mean ass."

"Love at first sight I guess." As the words left my lips, my eyes shifted to Jas' section and met Amiko's. It felt like she was staring into the depths of my soul. Shit was so powerful I had to look away.

"Nigga, only you believe in that fairytale shit. That's why I'm saying I gotta be sick."

"Yeah, aight."

"You staying here 'til closing? I was gon' chill and make sure Jas and her people got home safe."

I listened to him lie his ass off. "If that's the reasoning you're going with, then I'm staying to make sure the club is closed down properly."

"That's what it is then." He smirked and dapped me up before disappearing into the crowd.

Once I was done scanning the room for a final time and checking on VIP again, I retired to my office downstairs. Using my hand imprint to gain access, the door unlocked, and I walked in.

"Truth, baby, hold on."

Hearing Nyema behind me, I held the door open for her. Taking a seat at my desk, I turned on the security cameras to watch the club from different angles. Even with security, you could never be too careful.

"I'm sorry about earlier. I was out of line, and I may have overstepped my boundaries." I stared, unmoved, waiting for her to correct the last part of her statement. "Okay, I did overstep. This is your place of business, and I respect that."

"Apology accepted." I wasn't the type to hold a grudge. That was for kids. Plus, what Nyema did didn't faze me.

As I watched the cameras, I felt her eyes stalking me. Stepping in front of the screen to get my attention, she sauntered over to me and placed herself in my lap. I knew she was about to show me just how sorry she was. I could say a lot about Nyema's fucked up attitude, but one thing for sure and two things for certain, she knew her way around this dick. Leaning in to kiss me, she grinded in my lap, making my dick spring to life. All she owned was thongs, so bare ass was what I felt when I lifted her pleated skirt.

"Lift up a little," I instructed.

She lifted enough for me to free my dick from my Amiri jeans and pulled her thong to the side for me to slide in with ease. Throwing her head back, her mouth fell open. Her pussy was warm and inviting. It was good enough to put up with a headache every now and then.

"Yes, Daddy. I love it when you fuck me like this." She talked her shit while I dug into her pussy something vicious.

Having a need for control, she held onto my neck and bounced up and down to her own rhythm like she was begging for me to nut. I spread her cheeks and thrust into her while she creamed on my dick. Nyema couldn't outfuck me no matter how hard she tried.

WHAP! "Bounce that ass, girl," I encouraged, prompting her to contract her pussy muscles around my shaft.

I felt myself about to bust. She thought she was slick, trying to kiss me so that I couldn't concentrate. I wasn't ready for kids right now, and she knew that. More importantly, I didn't want to have kids with her.

"Oooouu, this dick so good. Nut in me, Truth. Nut in your pussy."

All the moaning in the world couldn't get me to grant her secret wish. Lifting her up by her ass cheeks, I pulled out and stroked my dick, bussin' on her back. Sucking her teeth, she hopped up off of me with disappointment written all over her face.

"Fix your face. Here." I handed her a towel from my desk drawer and used another to clean myself up.

"Why you got a towel in your drawer? You do this all the time?" This girl was bugging.

"Ay, don't go ruining a good moment. Let a nigga enjoy his nut in peace, damn."

Shaking my head, I tucked my dick away and pulled up my pants. Glancing up, I caught the frame that showed the VIP area where Jas sat. I didn't know what song was playing, but the way Amiko was slow dancing and touching all over herself made me rock up again. Hoping Nyema didn't catch on, I focused back on her.

"What?"

"Nothing, Truth. Nothing," she snapped before storming into the bathroom with her skirt still up over her ass.

I heard the water running and got up to walk closer to the screen. My eyes studied Amiko's body intently.

"I'm headed back upstairs. You coming?" Nyema questioned from behind me.

"I'll be back up before closing. You know being amongst a bunch of people ain't my scene."

Circling around so that she was in front of me, she pecked my lips twice and headed for the door to leave.

"Oh, my bad. Am I interrupting?" Amina asked, standing at the door with her hand up to knock.

I went to respond, but Nyema interrupted me. "As a matter of fact, you are. Is there something you need?"

I watched Amina's head cock to the side before she answered. "I was just coming down to let Truth know that Shika has to head out early. Her daughter is sick."

"Oh, well then, you can deliver that information and anything else that goes on with the ladies to me. I'll be managing the place from now on."

I waited to see Amina's reaction as she looked to me for confirmation. I nodded. She never really had to deal with Nyema up close and personal, and I had yet to tell her about the change. I sure didn't want to spring it on her like this.

"Okay, cool. Well, welcome aboard. Hopefully, you'll be planning a meeting soon with all of the ladies, so they're aware of the new change and not as blindsided as me." I knew that was a shot at me. Amina was a godsend to the club, so I knew I had to make up for it later.

"Thank you for letting me know, Amina. Let Shika know she'll be compensated for tonight," I spoke. Nyema's head spun in my direction with a hard look, as if to ask if I was serious. "And yes, we'll be having a meeting tomorrow before we open. I can assure you nothing else will be changing other than Nyema stepping in. Your bar is still your bar," I assured her.

"I'm happy to hear that. Again, welcome to the Tantra family, Nyema." She turned to leave, and Nyema didn't let the door fully close before she went in.

"Compensated? Really? Compensated for what when she's leaving early?"

"There you go again. Ny, I don't have to explain to you how I run my shit. Stay in your lane cause you swerving and ain't shit stopping you from crashing."

"You do know that with me being manager now, there may be some changes I might need to make, right?"

"And that's cool, so long as you run those changes by me first. Tantra is doing well, and Amina has been doing a pretty good job as interim manager. Now that you're coming in, you can lighten her load. I don't expect your presence to cause friction. I put you in position, but shit can change and will if it starts to affect my bottom line." I let her know in not so many words that at the end of the day, I was the HNIC around these parts.

7

MING

"It's good to see you having a good time, sis!" I yelled out over the music to Miko. I enjoyed watching my sister dancing, laughing, drinking, and living her best life. I wanted her to soak up every bit of this night out because she deserved it.

Finding out that she had gotten fired threw me for a loop. Miko was a hard worker, and though it was no secret that she hated her job, she got up every morning to be there. Her getting fired was a sign of better things to come. I'd prayed for it, and I knew that she would bounce back. It was what we did.

"I know. I am too. I would be having an even better time if I could climb on top of Mr. Truth. Girl, that man had me all kinds of hot and bothered."

I cracked up laughing at her drunk ass. "Ooh, that 1942 got you acting different, sister. I'm here for all the antics. Go shoot ya shot, boo."

Her facial expression suddenly became serious. "You think he can help me get a job here?"

"Miko, be so fuckin forreal. How you go from thinking about dick to a job in five seconds? You a trip. Here, let me fix you another drink."

"No, Ming, I'm deadass. I need a damn job like yesterday."

Ignoring her, I got up to look over the balcony and people watch. I didn't want to think about bills or work while I was out trying to escape our problems for a few hours. My eyes scanned the room and landed on Chance at the bar, talking to one of the bartenders. His cute ass was aggravating as hell. He came over in our section all friendly like he hadn't tried to get me together the other day. Gone talk about some, 'so we meet again.'

I wanted to say something smart, but I couldn't think of anything. Something was clearly wrong with me because I always had a witty response on standby. With him, I felt stuck. It was a good thing he didn't stick around long after his brother left the section. As I continued to watch the crowd, the sudden urge to pee came over me.

"Jas, where can I find the bathroom, boo?"

"You wanna use the public one or private? You know, just in case you gotta do a number two."

Miko laughed, knowing damn well Jas was serious.

"Jasmine, what kinda girl you think I am? I ain't about to be shittin' in no club. What I am about to do is pee on myself though." I rocked side to side, waiting for her to point me in the direction of the damn bathroom.

"Okay, that's nasty. Oh, look, Chance is coming up. I'ma have him take you to the one in his office."

"No. Uhn uhn, I'll find it myself," I said, but it was too late.

She had already opened her mouth, and he'd nodded to follow him. Jas thought she was so damn slick. I gave her the finger and mouthed that I was gonna kick her ass when I got back. Following Chance downstairs, we walked down a dark hall and down to a lower level where he used his handprint to open a door. Stopping in front of a smoke-gray door, I watched as he typed in a code, and the door unlocked. Pushing it open, he let me walk inside first.

"Straight ahead to your left. And don't be nosey tryna go through my shit while you're in there either."

"Shut up. Don't nobody care what you got in here," I spat while going into the bathroom.

Even though it was clean, I still squatted before I peed. There could have been some disease-infected ass ho up in here just the other day. Why him having another female in his office crossed my mind was beyond me. Reminding myself that it was none of my business, I emptied my bladder and felt a few pounds lighter. Pulling up my thong and shorts, I washed and dried my hands before walking back out. Chance sat on the edge of his desk with his head in his phone.

"Thank you. I can find my way back upstairs."

"Oh, nice things do come out of your mouth," he said smartly.

"And condescending shit still makes its way out of yours."

"Fly shit too!" he yelled out behind me as I exited the same way I came.

I giggled but didn't stop my stride. Back in the section, I caught Miko starting to nod off. She had partied her ass off, and I had accomplished my goal of getting her fucked up. I'd kept my drinking to a minimum tonight so that she could thoroughly enjoy herself and not have to worry about being the driver.

"I think she's had enough, Jas. We can Uber if you don't wanna leave now, and if you're too drunk to drive, I can hold it down."

"Uhn uhn. When I come here, I come to enjoy myself. I already knew I wasn't gonna be able to drive home. Don't worry. I'ma leave my car here and get Chance to drop me off since I'm closer, and then, he can take y'all."

Here she was, trying to lowkey play matchmaker, but I was onto her ass.

"You do know I can just drive, right? We can drop you off home then Uber from there. No big deal." I was trying to avoid having to be around Chance.

"We're riding with Chance, girl. Stop acting scary."

"Yeah, Ming, don't be scurred," Miko slurred, making me laugh.

"Whatever, drunk heffa. C'mon." I helped Miko stand and guided her down the steps and over to where Chance stood, waiting for us by the exit like this whole thing had been planned.

"Y'all want anything to go?" he asked with his eyes on me.

I shook my head no, but Miko's greedy, drunk ass requested the teriyaki wings that she'd bust down at the table. He handed Jas his keys and told her he'd meet us at the car. Following Jas outside, I almost fell out when she led us to a Mercedes AMG GT 4 Deurs Coupe. It was my dream car. Matching color and everything. The matte black had me in awe, and if I wasn't afraid of being embarrassed, I would've kissed the hood.

We got inside, and I fell further in love with the peanut butter interior. His seats looked custom, further letting me know that he and his brother were some boss ass niggas. I admired the car while Jas and Miko talked amongst themselves until Chance finally walked out with a big bag in his hand. I was almost positive that one order of wings didn't require three containers.

"Here you go. I had them add in a couple of other things I saw y'all eating up there too."

I held in my smile for his consideration.

"Aww, thank you. That was so nice. He's nice, right, Ming?" Miko eyed me.

"She doesn't seem to think so. It's cool though. Don't give her none of the food." He winked at me, and Miko laughed.

During the ride to Jas' house, I was quiet and in my own thoughts. We had fun tonight, but tomorrow, it was back to our regular day-to-day. The fact that the dental office rescheduled my interview had me less than optimistic, but after finding out Miko was let go, I was gonna do my best to snag the job.

By the time we stopped again, I felt someone shaking me awake. I didn't even know I had fallen asleep. Opening my eyes, Chance was staring at me from the front seat. There were those damn grey eyes again. I wiped the side of my mouth, hoping he didn't catch me drooling. I caught his smirk which let me know that he did.

"Y'all have a goodnight," he said as we got out the car and headed for the building.

"Get home safe," I responded out of habit.

"Ohhh, so you care?"

"No, but you know what they say about driving at night."

"Nah, what they say?"

"Don't." We both laughed, and I found myself watching his car as he drove off.

"Hmph, I see you didn't meet your future girlfriend, but you sure met yo' future husband," Miko commented while pushing the front door open.

"I don't know what you're talking about."

Chance couldn't be anything other than my future pain in the ass.

I WOKE up the next morning to my loud ass ringtone. Peeking out from under my covers, the clock on the cable box read nine thirty-two a.m. Given the fact that we hadn't gotten in until a little after three, the only call I was willing to accept was from my son. Reaching up on my nightstand, I unplugged the phone from the charger. Upon seeing unknown caller on the screen, I hit ignore and put the covers back over my head. Karter would just have to count this collect call as a loss. However, he was ever so persistent this morning because the phone rang again.

"Ughhh. This nigga here!" Snatching up the phone, I answered and waited for the automated system to do its thing.

"**Yo,**" he spoke, irritated. I knew there was some bullshit to follow.

"**Yeah, Karter,**" I replied with my eyes closed.

"**You ain't see me calling a second ago?**"

"**I did, and I was sleeping, still trying to do that actually. Case isn't here. You can call back around three. He'll be home by that time.**"

"**What you mean he ain't there? Where he at? Out with your sister?**"

"**No, he's over at a friend's house, Karter.**" I wanted him off my line, and he wasn't getting the hint.

"**What friend? I know this friend? And why he had to spend the night out when you're home?**"

I shot up, annoyed at his line of questioning. "**A friend of mine and why he spent the night is none of your business. Now, like I said, he'll be home around three. Call then.**" I was about to bang up on his ass because it was too early to have an attitude and a migraine. I felt like I was on the verge of both.

"**Yeah, aight. You ain't his only parent, Ming.**"

"Says who? I know you ain't tryna pull rank and you been gone how long?"

"Maannn, whatever. I ain't call to argue." He backed down, knowing he couldn't argue the truth. "You bringing him to the family day? I really want him to meet his sister, you know, so they can develop a bond while I'm in here and shit."

"No, Karter. I'm not bringing him."

"Why not?"

"Well, for one, prior to this, you never asked for him to come for a family day, and now, all of a sudden, it's imperative that he be there. And two, my son doesn't need to bond with nobody."

"Wow, you're foul for that, Ming."

The automated message announced that the call was coming to a close in a minute, and I said one last thing to wrap the conversation up quicker.

"I'm not going back-and-forth with you about it. Enjoy your family day. Talk to you at three if you call back."

I hung up before the system disconnected us. I wasn't entertaining Karter. Now that he'd decided he wanted to come clean about having another child, I was supposed to bring my son into the fold like everything was cool? Hell no. I threw my phone next to me on the bed and closed my eyes, needing at least another couple of hours before I was ready to present myself to the world.

Two and a half hours later, I was up and still sleepy. Getting out of bed, I brushed my teeth and washed my face before going to check on Miko. I knocked on her door lightly, and she didn't answer. Twisting the knob, I peeked in, and she was still asleep —_at least she looked like it. Sis partied hard last night. Knowing she would need to put something in her stomach after drinking all that liquor, I decided to make breakfast. First, I needed to call Ms. Pat to check on my baby.

"Good morning, Ms. Pat," I greeted once the call connected.

"Good morning to you, sugar. You calling to check on that precious baby of yours?"

"You know I am." I smiled just thinking about my son.

"Alright. Well, here he is." I could hear her call out to Case, letting him know I was on the phone.

"Hi, Mommy," he said.

"Hey, handsome face. What you doing?"

"Eating breakfast. I just woke up."

"Okay, baby. Well, I was just checking on you. I'll be there in a few to get you, okay?"

"Okay, Mommy. Love you."

"I love you too, handsome. Give the phone back to Ms. Pat for me."

"Girl, that little linebacker you call a baby is on his second bowl of oatmeal."

"Oh, my gosh. He's so greedy, and he loves oatmeal."

"He sure shocked me because a lot of kids don't. When he woke up requesting it, I was like whatttt?"

"I know, right? Thank you again for watching him for me. We had a good time. I'll be by to pick him up later, and I also have something for you when I get there."

"Now if it's money for watching him, you can keep it because you know I ain't gon' take it," she fussed as always.

"Ms. Pat, you know I don't feel right if I don't pay you. Now you can either take it or I'ma hide it somewhere in your house." I let her know just as I'd done plenty of other times.

"Well, do what you gotta do then. I'll see you when you get here, sugar."

We hung up, and I shook my head. She always refused my money, noting that if she didn't wanna watch Case, she wouldn't, so when she did, it wasn't for the money. Having heard my baby's voice, I continued on to the kitchen. Quickly cheffin' up some French toast, maple bacon, and cheese eggs for me and Miko, I set up our plates on a tray and headed back to her room.

"Miko, I made breakfast. Open up." A few seconds later, she pulled it open with her hand covering her eyes.

"Girl, I can't eat," she said, retreating back to the bed and under the covers.

"C'mon, get up. Once you get something in your stomach, you'll feel much better. Trust me, I does this." Unlike Miko, I'd had my fair share of hangovers and had all the remedies to get her back up and going.

"What time did we get home this morning? My damn head is spinning."

"Around three. Get this in your stomach and I'll grab you something for your head." Setting the food down, I went to the kitchen and grabbed the bottle of 1942 I had in the fridge. The best way to get over a hangover was to drink a shot of the very thing that had you drunk the night before. I poured the shot, grabbed a bottle of water, and took it to her.

Now sitting straight up in her bed, she looked at me with wide eyes. "You got me so fucked up. Who you think drinking that? I just told you my head was spinning."

"Girl, don't question my method, just trust me. Drink this shot and then drink this water. Here." I put the shot in her hand and opened the bottle of water. Hesitantly, she took it and scrunched up her face before chugging the water.

"So, did I have a good night last night?"

Now it was my turn to look at her crazy. "Bitch, you were not that drunk." The look on her face said otherwise. "Damn, Miko, you're a lightweight. You had a good time though. The vibes were good, and you were lusting over Jas' cousin."

"I'm sorry. I was doing what?" Again, her chinky eyes widened. Snickering, I snacked on a piece of bacon. "Stop playing, Ming!" she shrieked and shoved me. "What was I doing?"

"Harmless flirting, girl, nothing crazy. Chill out, Worry Wanda."

"You and Jas were supposed to be watching me."

"We were watching you. Watching you watch Truth."

"Girl, please, okay. What time you going to get my nephew? I miss him, and I feel like I see you more now than I do him. I ain't feeling that."

"I'm going to pick him up after I catch a few more Zs. I know he's gonna be bouncing off the walls when he get here." While eating, we recapped the night, and unaware of how tired I was, I fell asleep in Miko's bed.

Waking up for the third time today, I felt well rested. I rolled out of the bed and made my way to my room to get ready to pick up Case. Throwing on a pair of leggings and a hoodie, I ordered an Uber to cut my travel time in half. My account looked less than desirable, but today, I was making an exception.

The only thing I hated about Uber was those drivers that always wanted to talk. And it was just my luck that I got stuck with Mr. 21 Questions. I practically ran out of the car when we pulled up in front of Ms. Pat's house. It would've been petty of me to give him a one star for talking too much, so I didn't rate him at all. Ringing the bell, I pulled out my phone to check my social media accounts. When the door opened, Chance stood on the other side of it, smiling.

Rolling my eyes, I tucked my phone away. "Whatchu doing here? How you know Ms. Pat?"

"Shorty, me and Jas are cousins, remember? How you know my aunt though?"

Of course she was his aunt. I was beginning to think I wasn't gonna be able to shake this man.

8

———

CHANCE

SEEING THE LIL' CHINKY EYED MING AGAIN FOR THE THIRD TIME THIS week had me feeling a way. And like the other two run ins, her mean ass had an attitude. That shit didn't move me none. If anything, it just made me wanna agitate her more. I liked my women with a little spunk. Ming was only turning me on.

"My son attends the daycare if you must know."

"Case yo' lil' one?"

"Yes. Now, can you move out the way?" She pushed me to the side before I could move. I heard my aunt laugh when she asked how she dealt with me.

"Auntie, don't tell this woman nothing about me. She's mean as hell."

"Don't nobody wanna know nothing about you anyway, sir. Where's my baby, Ms. Pat?"

"I'll go get him for you. He got the headphones on, watching YouTube," I spoke.

"I can get my own child. Thank you very much."

I put my hands in the air, backing up from her little hostile ass. I was gonna write my name on one of the bills I had in my pocket and slide it to Case to give to her, but she fucked that up. I glanced over at my aunt, and she had a smirk on her face.

"She like that all the time?"

"Nope," she responded, giggling.

"Okay, Ms. Pat, we're gonna head out. Thank you again for watching him for me. Case, go give Ms. Pat a hug." Case ran over to Auntie then over to me to dap me up.

"Aight, lil' man, stay up." Returning to Ming's side, I caught her rolling her eyes again before they headed for the door.

"Ming," Aunt Pat called out, making her turn slightly. "I hope you didn't leave no money in here."

"I plead the fifth!" she yelled before closing the door behind herself.

Auntie just shook her head. "That girl is something else. When I find that money, I'ma put it right toward her childcare like I always do."

"What's the deal with her?" I questioned, thoroughly intrigued.

"It's just her, Case, and her sister. She's a great mother, very hands-on with her son. She's very close with her sister as well. They're all each other has. The rest is her story to tell."

"Okay, I'll handle the rest. Care to share why she's giving me such a hard time?"

"You should ask her that if you really wanna know." Auntie was holding out on me. "Pick up your face. Every woman ain't gon' fall for a cute face and good hair all the time." She was a regular ol' comedian.

"Auntie, you tryna say a nigga ain't got no substance?"

"No, I'm saying you like chicken heads who like surface level. That woman that just left is gonna make you work for it."

"Hmm, noted. I'm outta here tho." I kissed her cheek and snuck a piece of bacon she was frying from the pan.

"I'ma whip yo' ass," she threatened as I ran out the door.

With my schedule clear for the next few hours, I decided to pull up on Tiara. I hadn't been by to see her since I hit a couple days ago, but we did a lot of talking via text. She seemed really cool. She didn't bug me if it took an hour or so before I responded back to her messages, and I could fuck with that. I wasn't looking for anything serious at the moment — at least not with her.

As far as Ming, I wasn't letting her attitude deter me. No female was that mean for no reason. Pulling up on Tiara's block, I spotted her posted outside with a couple females, shooting the shit. I stopped the car in front of them and rolled down the window.

"What's good, T?"

The females with her almost broke their necks trying to see who I was. *These the chicken heads Aunt Pat was talkin' bout,* I said to myself. Tiara stood from where she was leaning against the gate with a bright smile on her face. She was dressed in a pair of Nike leggings and a matching hoodie. For a quick minute, my mind drifted to Ming. She had on a similar outfit when I saw her earlier, only hers was black.

"Bitch, who that pulling up talking 'bout what's good?" one of the women asked Tiara, and I waited to hear what her response would be.

"That's my business, boo." She gave a simple answer and switched over to me. I hit the lock for her to hop in.

"Hey, handsome," she sang, leaning over and pecking my cheek. "What you doing over this way?"

"I was in the neighborhood. Wanted to stop by and see what you was on." I made small talk, so it wouldn't seem like the sole purpose of my visit was pussy, even though it was.

"Nothing really. I wanted to go get my hair and nails done, but my money is funny until I get paid next week."

There was a begging undertone in her statement that I picked up on immediately. I was far from the tricking type, but I was giving at heart, so if she was in a tight spot, I'd help her out. I mean, it wasn't like I didn't have it. I went in my pocket and peeled off three hundred-dollar bills from the knot to hand to her. She slid it in her bra, cheesing the whole time.

"C'mon, let's go upstairs so I can properly thank you, boo."

"I think I deserve it."

I RODE up to Porter House feeling good. The tricks Tiara did on this dick for that three hunnit should be studied. I fucked around and gave her an extra two just for the performance alone. Had I been a nigga who let pussy control him, I would've been an easy mark for her. Shorty knew what she was doing in that bedroom.

Parking, I entered through the employee entrance of Porter House. Business had been going smoothly within the past week since I'd been running things. That was to be expected though. I was known to be the jokester, but I didn't play when it came to the money. It had to be right every time, or it was off with ya head. I didn't believe in second chances.

"Afternoon, ladies and gentlemen," I spoke to everyone on my way back to Robin's office.

Robin was the best when it came to holding things down for us. Next to Jas, she was the closest thing to a sister Truth and I had. "You busy?" I asked, peeking into her office.

"Not at the moment, come in. What you doing here so early?" She lifted her head briefly to acknowledge me then went right back to her paperwork. Robin was about her business one hundred percent of the time.

"I ain't have shit else to do. I wanted to run something by you really quick." Placing her pen down, she gave me her undivided attention. Taking a seat in front of her desk, I continued. "How do I approach a mean ass woman who I wanna get to know?"

She gave me a blank stare before responding. "That's really what you wanna talk about?"

"Yeah. I need advice from a woman's point of view."

"Well, first, start off by not referring to her as a mean ass woman."

"She is mean though. Since the day I met her and was trying to prevent her from being hit by a car."

"And how was your approach with that, Chance?" She had me there. Maybe the approach wasn't the best, although I thought it was smooth as hell. "You have to change your approach in order to get to know a, as you've described her, mean ass woman. More than likely, she's been through some things, and she's guarded. If you're interested, start by doing something nice. And I don't mean buying anything because technically you don't know her, but something that shows you're a decent guy."

That advice wasn't so bad.

"Aight, I can do that. Thanks, Robin. I owe you one." I stood to leave.

"You can start by giving me next Friday off, so my husband can take me out to dinner. Thank you. Now get out my office."

I laughed at her request because she knew if she asked, it was as good as done.

On my way out, I doubled back. "Aye, I'm decent and shit, right?" I was curious to know.

She giggled. "One of the most decent men I know."

Nodding, I walked back out to check on the floor to make sure everything was in place for tonight. Making my rounds, I spotted my uncle, Boss, coming out of the money room. Usually, I wouldn't think twice about him doing so, but his shifty eyes as he looked back-and-forth made me question what he had going on. That and Truth had already retired him, so there was no need for him to be in the room at all. I didn't wanna think Unc was on bullshit, but you could never be too cautious. After all, this was the money room that only me, him, and Truth had access to.

"What's good, Unc?" I came up from behind him, making him spin around quickly. Picking up on his body language, my antennas immediately went up.

"Nephew, what's good witchu?"

"Ain't shit, just came by to check on the house before we go live." I looked at the steel door and then back at him. His eyes never left mine.

"Oh, okay. How does it feel to be taking over the reins here, looking after things for your brother? I'm glad to have been relieved of my duties."

I knew a shot when I heard one. "I can't call it. I guess you can call me a natural. Seeing as I'm part owner, the change just made sense. How's everything looking in there?" I nodded toward the money room.

"Shit, money almost to the ceiling. You know how it is."

"That's what I like to hear. Aight, Unc, let me go finish making my rounds." I gave him dap and a hug. "Oh, and since I'm here now, you don't need to check on the money. I got that. Enjoy your early retirement, old man."

"Fa sho," he replied before breezing off.

Wanting to be better safe than sorry, I made a mental note to let Truth know that the code to the money room needed to be changed asap. Unc had some underlying shit going on with Truth and our new change. What he needed to understand was that while this was a family business, it was me and my brother that had inherited it and our ideas that brought it to where it was today. I had no problem reminding him of that.

9

———

AMIKO

FINDING OUT THAT I'D DONE A LITTLE MORE THAN JUST LET MY HAIR down last night in the club had me annoyed because I didn't remember much of my turn up. The highlights, yeah, but not the overall night. That included my interaction with Truth. I could only recall meeting him and taking in how good he looked. The rest of the night was a blur — in a good way though.

"I'm never going out with you and Ming again. I don't know how to act, and clearly y'all don't know to watch me," I fussed at Jas over the phone while completing another job application on Indeed.

She giggled, already knowing what I was referring to. **"Boo, you was turnt up, and I lived for every moment of it. Don't try to front like you didn't have a good time."**

"I had a great time, but you know I don't have no business being in no man's face right now. No matter how cute I am, a bitch need to be worried bout a job and a job only."

"And a job you will find. Stop being so hard on yourself, Miko. You not one of these bum ass bitches. Oh, and for the record, you wasn't all in his face. You liked what you saw and so did he. But anyway, what you doing today?

"All that sounds good, and while I am a catch, I'm not in a posi-tion to be caught right now. And girl, I'm over here applying for

jobs on Indeed. I'm convinced they just collects resumes, and the employers pick the names out of a hat. I know for damn sure they don't look at the skills. You think they're hiring down at Tantra? Not shaking my ass or anything but bartending or waitressing."

"I'm glad you asked because I spoke to Truth about you."

"And?"

"And he wants to offer you a job. You should call and talk to him about it. I'm texting you the number."

Why did I need to call him to talk about the job? He could've just set up an interview like a normal employer. I didn't want to be alone in a room with his fine ass, but I needed a job like yesterday. It was as if the bills knew that I had gotten fired because they were coming in from everywhere.

"Thanks, boo. I appreciate it. So, tell me about this cousin of yours."

"Who, Truth? What's there to really tell? He's a really good guy, stays to himself outside of his circle, which consists of the family and a couple of employees he's close with. Very family-oriented and makes sure we're all taken care of. I think I've only seen him mad once in my whole life, and it wasn't good."

"Interesting. Anything I need to worry about?"

"Not really. I mean, he does kinda sorta have a girlfriend, but you don't have to worry about her."

"Oh, hell. I'm good. You talkin' 'bout don't worry about her. That's his woman, Jas."

"Technically, but shit, he barely even likes her."

I had to laugh at that one. Jas wasn't shit. Clearly, she wasn't a fan of this woman, but that wasn't my business. We continued our conversation until I heard Miko entering the house with Case.

"Aunty Miko, I'm hereeeee!" he announced.

"I'm in my room, nephew! Let me call you later, Jas. Ming and Case just got in."

"Okay, give him a kiss for me and tell sis I said hey. Make sure you text Truth."

"Will do." I hung up with her and went to greet Case as he rounded the corner and ran to my room door.

"Hey, nephew. I missed you, man. You just disappeared on me."

"I'm right here, Auntie. I missed you too." He gave me a big hug and made his way over to my snack fridge. Before he opened it, he looked over to me for confirmation.

"Go 'head, man. You can get whatever you want." Ming shook her head, and I giggled.

"You always giving him whatever he wants."

"And you don't?" I countered, making her laugh. "That's what I thought. How's Ms. Pat doing?"

"Great as always. Why when I got there, Chance opened the door?" I had no clue who Chance was, and the look on my face showed it. "Jas' other cousin. The one I told you I ran into a couple days ago."

"Oh, okay. Sis, that's meant to be. This is the third time y'all have run into each other. The universe is saying something." I winked my eye at her, and she frowned.

"Not in this case. I'm starting to think he got a damn tracking device on me."

"Ming, that man don't have no damn tracking device on your silly ass. He may just like you. Is that too far-fetched of an idea?"

She rolled her eyes. "Whatever. Whose night is it to cook?"

"That would be yours, Sister Soulja. And I'll have baked chicken over rice and spinach. Thank ya kindly."

"Okay, cool. C'mon, son." She held her hand out for Case, and he turned to me.

"I know she trippin', right? He don't wanna watch you cook. He wanna hang out with his auntie. C'mon, nephew."

"Forget y'all." Smiling, she left the room.

Running over, Case climbed up in my bed and cuddled up to me. I often thought about having kids, especially when he was first born, but that thought quickly vanished when I experienced firsthand what it took to take care of a child. Although I knew that I'd be a great mom, I wanted to be at a certain point in my life financially before I brought a child along for the ride. I also needed to be open to entertaining a man long enough to wanna have a child with. Truth came to mind, and I shook my head.

It was a shame he had a girlfriend. The man was fine as hell, owned a successful business, and overall had his shit together from what I could see. Who wouldn't want a man like that? Picking up my phone, I checked my texts for the number Jas had sent. I planned to give him a call today to see about setting up an interview. Going into the next week unemployed was not an option for me.

The thought of having to go through the whole hiring process again frustrated me. I didn't want to start over in a new position and possibly have to take a pay cut. Working at Tantra would be a different pace, and I was sure I would have to adapt to the new environment, but what the hell? An opportunity was an opportunity. I pressed Truth's number in the text thread and clicked the option to call. Waiting for the call to connect as it rang, I grabbed a comb and pulled Case over to me. He needed a break from the ponytail Ming had it in, so I was gonna hook him up with a couple braids.

"**Hello.**" Truth's smooth voice came through the phone, and my body got tingly.

"**Hey, this is Amiko, Jas' friend. We met last night at your club.**" I placed the phone in the crook of my neck and started to part Case's hair. The phone went silent, but I knew he was still on the line.

"**I remember your voice. What can I do for you?**"

I wanted to ask what the reason was for committing my voice to memory but kept it professional. "**Well, I'm currently in dire need of employment, and she gave me your number to discuss that.**"

"**Okay. What can you do?**"

His question threw me. "**What can I do?**"

"**Yeah.**"

"**Ummm, I have five years of customer service under my belt. I answered phones at my last job. I may not have the qualifications for waitressing or bartending, but I'm a fast learner.**"

"**I can work with that. Meet me down at Tantra tomorrow at two and we'll discuss it further.**"

"**Okay, I'll be there. Thank you for the opportunity.**"

"**You're not hired… yet.**"

"**Oh, you're going to hire me. I'll see you tomorrow, Mr. Truth.**" I hung up and continued braiding Case's hair. I would be fully prepared for this interview tomorrow. Truth wasn't gonna have a choice but to hire me.

Thirty minutes later, I'd braided Case's hair into six French braids to the back. "All done, nephew. C'mon, let's go get something to eat."

"Thank you, Auntie. I like my hair."

"You look very handsome. Go head to the kitchen with Mommy."

As I got up to clean the hair up off my bed, my phone pinged with an email notification. Hopeful that it was a job reaching out already, I opened it, disappointed to see that it was an email from my previous employment.

Dear Ms. Adachi,

After your recent termination, we are reaching out regarding your last paycheck and your healthcare. According to our records, you borrowed a total of three thousand dollars from your 401k plan. Your remaining balance as of today is twelve hundred dollars. We will be deducting the referenced balance from your last paycheck, which is set to be mailed to you within the next week. You have thirty days remaining before your healthcare is no longer covered through the company. If you have any further questions or concerns, please feel free to reach out to our HR department.

I read the email twice and felt like steam was coming through my ears. It was bad enough that I was fired over some bullshit, but now they were playing with my money. My check was only fourteen hundred dollars, and that was before taxes were taken out. Suddenly, I'd lost my appetite. Throwing my phone on the bed, I sat down and put my head in my hands. I couldn't do this shit anymore. Tears burned my eyes, and this time, I couldn't hold them. I didn't want to hold them.

"You coming to…" I heard Ming speak then pause. "What happened, Miko?"

"Nothing, Ming. I don't wanna talk about it. You can put my plate in the microwave. Thank you." Thankfully, she didn't press the issue. Instead, she turned and left the room quietly.

I needed guidance before I had a breakdown. It was times like these where I sought out God and my mother. Although she wasn't here physically, I believed my mother could feel me in the spiritual realm.

Ma, give me a sign that everything is going to get a little easier. I know that life will have its ups and downs, but as you can see, we've had more downs than a little bit since you've been gone. I can't take any more bad news. Something good has to happen for a change. Send me a sign if I'm doing something wrong and which way I should go next.

Picking my head up, I wiped my eyes and felt a little better that I'd given the burden up to God and my mother. Now, all I had to do was continue to press forward while they did the rest.

10

MING

"You're exactly what we're looking for, Ms. Adachi. When can you start?" The hiring manager at Great Expressions Dental sat across from me with a welcoming smile and a job offer that I would not refuse.

"I can start right now if you want me to," I joked, and she laughed. *That's right, eat all this charm up*, I thought to myself.

"How about we start next week Monday? This way you get to meet everyone, and the office manager, Tiffany, will start your training."

"Sounds good to me. Thank you again for the opportunity. I won't let you down." I got up from my seat and shook her hand. I couldn't get out of the office fast enough before I took out my phone to call Miko.

"Bihhhh, I got the job!" I shrieked once the call connected.

"Yesss! I knew you could do it. I'm so, so proud of you, Ming."

Hearing my sister say she was proud of me meant more than words could explain. Outside of her and Jas, I had no other friends. I liked it that way. After finding out my so-called best friend was trying to fuck Karter behind my back, I was cool on homegirls.

"Thank you, sis. Thank you for seeing more in me than I've seen in myself. Now it's time for you to chill a little bit and let me work."

"**That sounds good, but two incomes are always better than one. I don't know about you, but I'm tired of living paycheck to paycheck. We've been struggling too long; we deserve to have our heads above water. That's why I'm getting ready to meet Jas' cousin down at Tantra to talk about working there.**"

That was news to me. "**Which one? Chance?**" I didn't know why his name came to mind first.

She giggled before replying. "**No, not yo' boo. I'm meeting with his brother.**"

"**Ha ha, you're real funny. Call me when you finish and let me know how it goes. I'm gonna go pick up Case and head home. It looks like it's about to pour down raining out here.**" The clouds had gathered together like a gang, so I knew it was about to come down.

"**Shit, let me hurry up. I would be so pissed if I get caught in that rain, and my hair gets poofy. I swear I'm ready to do the big chop.**"

"**Girl, you're talking crazy, talkin' bout some big chop. Let me get off this phone with you before I miss this bus. Love you and hit me up when you get there too so I know you're safe.**" She assured me that she would and disconnected the call.

The bus ride was faster than usual being that I was able to catch the limited one that skipped stops. I was geeked about my new job at the dental office as the receptionist. It was right up my alley too. With my organizational skills, previous clerical experience, and overall customer service, I had it in a bag. Ya girl had the gift of gab too, so that was a plus. I managed to beat the rain and made it to the daycare just as the kids were settling down for their last snack of the day.

"Hey, boo. How'd everything go at the interview?" Jas asked while placing the snack plates in front of the kids. I hung my head, pretending to be sad, and she walked over to hug me. "Aww, man, Ming. I'm sorry, sis. Them people don't know an ideal candidate when they see one." Snickering, I pulled back from her. "You got it, didn't you?" I shook my head with a goofy look on my face.

"I killed it, Jas. They hired me right on the spot!"

"Oh, my God! Yessss!" she yelled, making the kids look over in our direction. "Everything's okay, y'all," she assured, pulling me in for a hug.

"Why are you doing all that yelling, Jasmine?" Ms. Pat came out from the kitchen with Case behind her and Chance behind him.

"She got the job, Ma."

"Like I knew you would, girl. Come over here and give me a hug. Congratulations." I hugged her while Case held me at the legs.

"Congrats, Ma," Chance said, and I thanked him.

Again, there he was in all his fineness. It just didn't make any sense, and this couldn't be fate. Or at least I didn't want it to be. Stopping myself before I could think too much into it, I gathered Case's things.

"Shoot, I gotta get going, y'all," I announced, noticing that it had begun storming outside.

"I would drive you, boo, but I got a ride from Chance today. I took my car in to get detailed," Jas mentioned.

"It's okay. We'll manage."

"I can take y'all home," Chance cut in.

"We'll manage. Come on, Case. We gotta make a run for it." The booming sound of thunder hit and made Case jump along with the other kids. Scared of the sound, he jumped behind me, holding onto my leg. "Shit," I whispered to myself while Ms. Pat and Jas peered at me to see what my next move would be.

"Man, stop being so stubborn and let me take y'all home. You acting like I said come to my crib," Chance let out, his voice laced with frustration. "C'mon, Case." I looked on in shock as he grabbed at Case's hand and swooped him up in his arms. They walked toward the door, and I had no other choice but to follow.

"Get home safe," Jas let out, and I gave her the finger on the low.

IN THE CAR, he drove, and I kept my mouth shut as he and Case carried on with their own conversation. It was crazy that he answered all one hundred and two questions Case had about everything in the universe and didn't get frustrated. I knew my baby was tired because it was the only time he rambled off question after question.

"Ma, you like Chance car?"

"Yes, baby, I like the car. It's really nice."

"It's fast. Chance said he's gonna get me a car when I get older."

I looked over at Chance, and he shrugged his shoulders. Why was he even discussing future plans with my son like he was going to be a part of his life in any other capacity?

"Case, are you sleepy?"

"Yes."

Chance laughed at his response. I knew my son like the back of my hand.

"Okay, we're almost home. You can close your eyes for a minute." I looked in the rearview mirror, and as if I had just cast a spell, he was knocked out.

"Why'd you tell him that?" I questioned Chance.

"Tell him what?"

"You heard what he said."

"Oh, about the car? We was kickin' it, and he showed me the car he wanted on his iPad. I told him I'd buy it. No big deal."

This guy was a trip.

"First off, how you kickin' it with a four-year-old? Second, it is a big deal because you shouldn't be promising my child anything. Especially a car when he's older," I snapped.

"What are you mixed with?"

"Huh? Are you for real right now? I'm talking to you about something serious, and you're asking me what I'm mixed with?"

"I'm trying to change the direction of this conversation. Every time I see you, it doesn't always have to be beef."

"I don't have no beef with you. I don't even know you."

"Exactly, you don't even know me, but every time you see me, you give me the cold shoulder. I know I may have started off bad with the whole crossing the street thing, but it was harmless. So, now, it seems like you have painted this picture of me as an asshole. I'm really not a bad guy. Ask your son."

"What do you want from me?" I didn't know what his angle was. As much as I wanted to keep giving him the cold shoulder he mentioned, his persistence was slightly winning me over.

"How 'bout we start simple? What are you mixed with?"

"Half Black, half Japanese. And no, I don't know how to speak the language. My mom was born here as well as me and my sister."

"That's wassup. That's where y'all get them chinky eyes and that good hair from."

"What do you consider good hair?" I couldn't wait to hear the stupid shit that came out his mouth.

"Whatever texture that is that Case got back there."

"We gon' skip the hair conversation because obviously you don't know what you're talking about."

"I know that's a lace front that you have on. What y'all say, no lace, no case?" I was shocked that he was able to tell. "Yeah, I'm up on game."

"Hmph, that just means you've been with a lot of females to be in the know about these things." The car came to a stop before he answered.

"I'm not gonna lie and say I haven't, but it's not how I know. It just means that I pay attention. Just like I've noticed that you curl your lip whenever you get ready to say something smart."

"First off…"

"There it goes right there." He cut me off and laughed. "You're very beautiful, you know that?"

"Thank you and thank you again for the ride."

"No problem. I have no problem helping out. Here, let me get him out the backseat for you."

"Nah, I got him."

"There you go again. You do know allowing me to help you doesn't mean I'm asking for any type of commitment from you, right?"

"Yeah, I know."

"Alright then, so just let me help you out. It's not a big deal."

I dropped my shoulders and got out on the passenger side while he picked Case up from the backseat. He was knocked out, so I allowed him to help me upstairs and lay Case on the couch.

"Get home safe," I said while holding the door open for him.

"Since we're kinda sorta past your mean phase, do you think I can get your number?"

I wanted so bad to say no, but how could I after he'd gone out his way to get me and my son home safe? "Sure, but as you already know, I'm a single mom, and I don't have time for games. So, if I give you my number, you better have the best intentions when it comes to me and my son or leave me the hell alone." It was best to let him know what he was getting himself into out the gate.

"Again, I'm not asking for any type of commitment. Not right now at least. I don't know what it is, but it's something about you, and us running into each other the way we've been, that has to mean something. I mean, that's what I've heard. I'm just tryna explore that possibility, starting with your number."

I read off my number and watched him lock it in his phone. A second later, I heard my phone ring.

Placing his phone to his ear, he gestured to mine. "Go 'head and answer it."

"I am not doing that. We're not in no corny movie. Now that you know it's the correct number, make sure you text before you call."

"What about FaceTime?"

"Still text. Goodnight, Chance."

"Night, Ming. Text me before you close ya eyes."

He swaggered off, and I closed the door behind him. Maybe he wasn't too bad of a guy after all. Only time would tell. I wasn't standoffish because I was a bitch; I was this way because life had made it so. I didn't know what would come of me and Chance chatting, but today, he'd left a lasting impression on me for the first time in the four times we'd run into each other. I walked over to Case, who was still knocked out, and picked him up to take him to his room.

"Where's Chance, Mommy?" he asked in a sleepy voice, rubbing his eyes.

"He left, baby."

"He likes you. He told me to tell you that." I stopped mid-stride.

"What you know about somebody liking someone?"

"I got a girlfriend, Mommy."

"Little boy, you ain't got no girlfriend." I tickled him, and he laughed.

Any man that wanted to be in my life would have to be ready for Case too. We were a package deal, and I guess Chance was okay with that, seeing that he liked me and all.

11

TRUTH

I DON'T WANNA STOP JUST BECAUSE, PEOPLE WALKING BY ARE WATCHING US. I don't give a damn what they think, I want you now. I don't wanna stop just because, you feel so good inside of my love. I'm not gonna stop no no no, I want you. All I want to say is...

Janet Jackson crooned through the speakers as I pinned Nyema against the wall and stroked her from behind. We were three rounds in, and my dick, for some reason, wouldn't go down.

"Ughhh, Truth, baby, I don't have no more to give," Nyema whimpered, her breathing labored.

"One more. Cum for me one more time, Ny." I reached around and played with her swollen clit, lifting her leg a little farther up so that I could hit her g-spot properly. Her walls squeezed around my dick, and I felt my nut building up. Speeding up my strokes, I pulled out of her and bust all over her ass. "Fuckkk," I groaned, emptying what felt like liters of cum.

I knew I had tired her out because she just leaned up against the wall, breathing hard. She looked worn out. Turning off the music, I grabbed a warm rag to clean the both of us off then redressed myself.

"How's everything going at the Elite house?" she asked while fixing her make-up in the floor-length mirror she had set up in my bedroom.

"Things are running smoothly. Clientele has grown, and the girls are keeping up with the pace."

"Yeah, I bet they're loving you being there all the time. That was the goal of pushing me out in the first place."

"I'm not there all the time. They don't need around-the-clock monitoring, Nyema. They're adults. I only manage their dates and how they get their money. Anything else outside of that is on them. You know, that was their issue with you all along."

"Whatever. I'm not even going to get into it with you about your precious Elites. I do wanna talk to you about Tantra and some opportunities for change that have come up."

"I'm listening."

"I noticed that the employees are able to eat free during their lunches, and I think you should change that rule and discount their meals instead. Also, what do you think about having poles in the place rather than the aerial dancers? I think having the poles is less of a liability."

It sounded as if she was trying to change the way I ran things, and the last time I checked, that wasn't the reason for me bringing her in.

"Thank you for your suggestions, Ny, but your job is to manage the place, not to make changes."

"So, what's the point then of being the manager if I'm not allowed to make changes, Truth?"

"Let me correct myself. You can make changes. They just have to make sense. As far as the two things that you just mentioned, those are big, unnecessary changes. I don't charge the employees to eat because they work hard, and they make sure Tantra is packed out nightly. Strippers don't work at my lounge; that's why poles won't work. The aerial dancers are what sparks conversation. And they make just as much money, if not more, than your average stripper with their clothes on."

"Again, tell me what you hired me for?"

"I'm starting to ask myself the same question. It seems like you're not cut out for the position, and that's cool."

"Not cut out for the position, Truth? You're not serious right now. When you met me, I was managing one of the hottest clubs in Vegas."

"You're right, but this is New York, and the difference between here and there is you ran things in Vegas; I run things here, so follow my lead and we'll be good money. I gotta go." I kissed her cheek and let myself out.

It was almost two o'clock, and I had to get down to Tantra for my meeting with Amiko. The rain was treacherous as I whipped my Porsche down the expressway. Being punctual was important to me. I didn't like to keep people waiting and expected the same consideration in return.

Pulling up to the club, I noticed Amina's car in the parking lot. Besides me, Chance, Robin, and now Nyema, she was the only other person who had access to the building. My circle was small. Amina was amongst the few that I trusted with such access. Entering the club, I heard laughing and turned the corner to find Amina at the bar, teaching Amiko how to mix a drink.

"Okay, girl, Truth only uses top shelf liquor, so you have to try your best not to be heavy handed. We had another girl that was like that. She was out here practically giving the liquor away. I had to recommend her for waitressing duty immediately. That chick was about to have us all out of a job."

They both laughed, and I watched quietly as Amiko focused, listening to Amina's instructions.

"Is that the position you're applying for?" I asked, stepping into their view.

"I'm applying for whatever position is hiring," she countered smartly. "All except for the aerial dance. It would be very embarrassing to find me all twisted up in the air with no way to get down."

I envisioned her twisted up in the ribbon with me fucking her from behind. Amiko had a small frame with titties that naturally sat up, a small waist, and a round ass. It wasn't too big or too small but just right for palming. I called her from behind the bar and over to a table.

"You're still not speaking to me, Amina?" She had been giving me the silent treatment outside of business ever since Nyema started.

"Hey, Truth. I'm doing some inventory, and I'll be out your way."

"I still love you, Mina."

"Shiiittt, I can't tell. You set us up with the manager from hell, and we've been clashing every other day, but I'll talk to you about that at another time. Go 'head with your interview. I hope you hire her. She has a good spirit." If Amina was giving her blessing, then Miko had made a good impression on her.

Walking over to where Amiko was, I sat across from her. "Before we get into the interview, would you mind telling me a little bit about yourself?"

"Sure. My name is Amiko Adachi. I'm twenty-six years old, very goal driven, and a hard worker. My last job was as a lead customer service rep at a telecommunications company. I was there for five long years. Oh, here's my resume." She pulled out a folder from her bag that rested on the table and handed me her resume. She was organized. I liked that. "I could bore you with the jobs I've held since summer youth when I was sixteen, but what you need to know is with the right training, I can work either the bar or the floor."

She was confident in herself, another quality that I liked. I didn't need to look over her resume. She was already hired. I just needed a reason to keep talking to her, so I skimmed over the resume. She sat in silence with her legs crossed. The pencil skirt she had on went well with the collared shirt she wore tucked in. Her stiletto heels made her appear taller than she actually was.

"I think you'd be a good fit here… for six months."

The smile that once adorned her pretty face turned into a frown.

"Let me get this straight. You're offering me a job but for six months only? Like a trial period?"

"Yes. And then, I'll be personally training you for another position. We'll talk about it in more detail as the time gets closer. As far as your position here, you can start off waitressing, and Amina can cross-train you for bartending during opening hours when we're not so busy. The position is twenty-five dollars an hour. We are open from five to two a.m., Thursday through Sunday. Are you comfortable with the attire?"

She still looked as if she was trying to figure out if there was a catch. I didn't know if the six-month trial thing threw her off or what I was paying. I paid my team well because they brought in enough money for me to do so. I didn't touch their tips, and they made sure we always reached the quota I set every night, if not more. It was a win-win situation.

"Yes, I'm comfortable. I'm sorry if I'm a little taken aback. The whole six-month trial thing threw me for a loop. I need a guaranteed position," she expressed.

I leaned forward and grabbed her hand, placing it in mine.

"Anything with me is guaranteed. As crazy as it may sound, you're going to have to trust me."

"I haven't done that in a long time."

"I can tell. You start this Thursday." I stood and so did she. "I don't tolerate tardiness. You must be here at the start of your shift, which is five o'clock. There are no grace periods. Get here at five or fifteen minutes earlier. If for any reason you have to be late, reach out to Nyema, who's the GM, Amina, or myself."

"Oh, your girlfriend works here too?" Her hand immediately shot up to her mouth like she'd said something wrong. "That was so out of line, and whether she works here or not is none of my business. Thank you for the opportunity. I'll see you on Thursday." Grabbing her bag, she scurried toward the front entrance.

"You don't want your resume?!" I yelled out while smiling at the sight of her small waist and plump ass.

"You can keep it!" she shouted back before exiting the building.

"I see you lusting after the new girl." Amina clocked me from where she stood at the bar.

"I'm not lusting after nobody," I responded, still looking at the door that Amiko had already walked out of. "I need you to look out for her for me. She won't be here for long, but I wanna make sure she's good."

"I got you. I hope whatever plans you have for her that your intentions are pure," Mina warned before going back to her work.

I had pure intentions. Amiko was going to be known as the madam, and I planned to see to it that she didn't have to clock in under anyone. She'd be her own boss.

12

SIX MONTHS LATER

AMIKO

"Miko, can you take these two bottles of Casamigos up to the second floor? It's a group of women in the birthday section. Tell them these are on the house."

I accepted the bottles from Amina and went to do as she requested. The past six months at Tantra had been some of the best nights of my life. When Truth first offered the job on a trial basis, I almost said fuck it. I mean, who would want to work a job that wasn't guaranteed? Something in me said he was genuine though, and so far, he hadn't done anything to taint that image in my eyes.

I adapted quickly to my new job. and the ladies loved me as well. I didn't do much and stayed out of the way the first two months, not wanting to push myself on anyone. That approach worked because they gravitated to me all on their own. Well, everyone except for Nyema. She was another Sheila off the rip. When I reported to work on my first day, she seemed confused as to why I was there.

"Hi, my name is Amiko. Today is my first day, and I'm unsure of who was assigned to me for training." I held my hand out for Nyema to shake, and she looked at me like I wasn't worth shit.

"Truth told me he hired someone, but I wasn't aware that you'd be starting today."

"Oh, no worries. I can chill out while you get everything together, no rush."

Her face turned up like I had just cursed her. "And what would make you think I don't have it together?"

"I... You just said... You know what? Never mind. I'll reach out to Truth and find out from him. Thank you." I went to pull my phone from my purse, and she stopped me.

"No need to involve Truth. As he may have already told you, I am the general manager. Anything that you need help with pertaining to this job, you come to me. You can train with Shika for the next few days. Come next Thursday, I expect you to know the menu like the back of your hand, both food and drink." She didn't allow me to respond before she walked off.

That was my introduction to the GM, and if I must say so, she left a lasting impression on me, and nothing about it was positive.

Placing the sparklers inside of the bottles, I held them in the air and danced my way through the crowd and up to the second floor. The music was rocking, and the birthday section was turnt. The DJ spun the *Birthday Bitch* song just as the birthday girl got in front of me and dropped it low. This happened often, and I was thankful that Truth didn't require us to wear heels all the time. At first, I didn't like being danced on, but I got used to it. It was just harmless fun.

"One time for the birthday bitch, aye, two times for the birthday bitch, aye, three times for the birthday bitch, aye, fuck it up if it's your birthday, bitch!" Her entourage hyped her up as she twerked on me, and I did my own little two-step with the bottles in the air. When the song was done, she turned and gave me half a hug as I placed the bottles on the table, letting her know they were on the house. Someone in her entourage slipped a fifty in my bra strap, and I went on my way.

Tips were the shit around these parts. In fact, I had started a savings account with my tips alone. Things had definitely turned around at the Adachi house; that was for sure. As I walked out of the section, the hairs on my arms stood up. That had been happening a lot lately when Truth was in the vicinity. It was like, if he wasn't in my face, I could sense him around me. I started down the steps, back to the main floor, and there he was, standing at the bar in my direct eyesight. We stared at each other, and as corny as it may sound, it felt like sparks were flying.

"Ahem, excuse me, Amiko." Nyema interrupted the moment her man and I were having.

Ughh, I should be ashamed of myself. I was really sitting here lusting over this girl's man.

"Umm, hey, Nyema. Wassup?"

"Wassup is the toilet in the women's bathroom is stopped up."

I gave her a dead stare, confused as to what she wanted me to do with that information. "Ohh kay. You need me to get maintenance?"

"No, sweetie. I need you to go in there and take care of it. I just sent Raymond on lunch."

"Hol' up, you sent the maintenance guy on lunch knowing the toilet is messed up, and now you want me to go fix it?" I had to make sure I was hearing her correctly.

She crossed her arms on her chest tightly and grilled me. "That sounds about right."

"Girl, bye. That sounds about wrong. I hate to be the bearer of bad news, but janitorial duties are not in my job description, love. As a matter of fact, here comes Truth right now. He's the owner. Why don't you ask him if he can handle it?"

"Evening, ladies," he spoke to both of us.

"Hey, Truth, you seen Raymond around?" I questioned, ignoring the hard stare from Nyema.

"Yeah. I just sent him to handle something in the women's bathroom."

"Oh, well, that fixes your problem, doesn't it, Nyema?"

She forced a smile, and I smirked.

"Yep, it sure does. Thanks, babe." Standing on her tiptoes, she kissed his lips.

"No problem. Hey, you have a moment?" he asked me to which I smiled smugly.

"Yeah, sure."

"Aight, follow me to my office. She won't be gone long, Ny."

I switched off behind him, not even bothering to look back to see if Nyema had picked her face up off the floor. Punching in the code to unlock the office door, he stepped aside for me to enter before him.

"You can have a seat. So, you're nearing the end of your six-month trial. How are you liking Tantra?"

"I love it. So much so that I don't wanna leave. The staff have become like family in such a short amount of time. That's different for me because quiet as it's kept, I don't like nobody."

"We have that in common." We shared a laugh. "I hear you, but I have a better opportunity that I'm sure you're going to love." I sat back in the seat, waiting for what he could offer me that was better than this. "I want you to manage the Elite house."

"Umm, as soon as you tell me what that is, I may be able to give you a solid answer." I had no clue what the Elite house was.

"The Elites are a group of women I manage who live in a house that I own. Hence the name the Elite house."

"Stop right there. A group of women that work for you? Are you a pimp? Or are they whippin' up work for you?"

His face was straight for a few seconds before he burst out laughing. "I'm not into pimpin', and I ain't never whipped up anything in my life. The Elites are linked to powerful men whom they spend time with and get paid very well to do so. There are no pimps and hoes, and everything is confidential."

Still sounded like pimping to me, and I wasn't sure I wanted to be a part of it. "I'm not saying yes… yet. What exactly would the job entail?"

"You'd manage their client list, set up dates, and make sure they're good by keeping an open line of communication. Don't worry. I don't plan to just throw you in there. I'm going to walk you through the whole operation. As a matter of fact, go get changed. We're going to go by the house right now. That way you can meet the ladies."

Although skeptical, I got up and went to the dressing room to change back into my street attire.

"And just where might you be going?" Nyema walked in as I was pulling my shirt over my head.

"Ask Truth." I wasn't tryna be nasty. I really wanted her to ask him.

It wasn't my place to tell her the plans he had for me. That was her man.

"You think you can just walk out in the middle of your shift and still be employed? I don't have to ask Truth anything."

"Welp, I don't know what to tell you." Sidestepping her, I made my way toward the exit. "Hey, I'm going to give you a call later, boo," I said to Amina, who was busy behind the bar.

"Okay, love. Have a good night and get home safe."

I didn't have to find Truth because he found me as we met up at the exit.

"C'mon, we're gonna leave through my office."

"Okay. You may wanna shoot Nyema a text to let her know what's going on. I think she just fired me."

"Good. Now you don't have to worry bout quitting." With a sly smile, he helped me into the passenger seat of his car. "And since I'm the one who signs your checks, you're good on that too. You see how that all worked out?"

I grinned and shook my head. What was this man getting me into?

THE CAR RIDE was filled with the sounds of DJ Mustard's *Surface* featuring Ella Mai and Ty Dolla Sign. I bobbed my head to the music as Truth whipped his Porsche skillfully. We pulled up to a townhome a half an hour later where he parked and opened my door for me. The outside of the townhome was beautiful, but I wasn't prepared for the perfection on the inside. We were buzzed in, and my mouth fell open at the layout.

"You're back again?" a woman asked, coming from the back of the home. She looked comfortable in a lounge set and fuzzy socks on her feet. "Hi," she greeted me with a big smile.

"Damn, I can't come visit y'all?" Truth laughed and grabbed hold of my hand.

"Shut up. You know it's not like that. Who's this? And why are you holding her hand like we bout to steal her or something? I'm Kane by the way."

I chuckled and held out my available hand for her to shake. "Nice to meet you. Miko."

"Call everybody down for me, Kane. I want to introduce Miko."

"Nicole is out, but everybody else is here. Let me go get them. And let her damn hand go before I take her from you." She winked her eye and flicked her tongue out.

"Man, go 'head." He laughed, still not letting me go. "Don't pay her no mind. She has some female clients as well." He ushered me into a living room that looked as big as the three bedrooms in my apartment.

"They're making bank up in this joint. You sure you want me to manage the house? 'Cause I wouldn't mind getting me a client or three." My eyes scanned the room before landing back on him, and his face was tight.

"I'm sure I don't want you having any clients." I picked up on his demeanor and didn't ask him to expound on why he felt the way he did.

"Hey, hey," another young woman sang as she walked into the living room, giving Truth a peck on the cheek, followed by two others and Kane.

"What news are you about to drop on us now, Truth? You're just full of surprises lately," another woman stated.

"It's nothing bad. This is Amiko. She's gonna be managing the house. I wanted to bring her here to meet all of you." They all stared at me for a split second, and one by one, they introduced themselves, complimenting me on how pretty I was.

"You ladies are beautiful. I don't want Truth to speak for me when it comes to me taking on this new position. If you don't mind, I wanted to go over what it is that you do before I sign on the dotted line."

They all agreed to give me their own version of a day in the life for them. Kane grabbed a bottle of wine, and we sat on the leather sectional while Truth left us. If I was going to run the house, I needed to know how I'd fit in.

13

MING

I sat at my new vanity, putting on my lashes and getting cute for my date with Chance. Hitting my body with a few generous sprays of Viktor&Rolf Flowerbomb Tiger Lily perfume, I glossed my lips up nicely. He had called earlier and told me to be ready by eight. It was now seven, and I was still indecisive about what I was going to wear. This would be the third date we'd gone on since he dropped Case and I off during the storm a couple months back. If it was up to him, we would've had date night once a week. I wasn't at that point yet. I let my guard down a little, but I still wasn't 100% sold on the idea of Mr. Chance Porter.

He seemed to be smitten by me though, and that made me feel good. I wasn't making him chase me, but I hadn't made myself readily available either. Right now, we were going with the flow, and it felt good. We spoke every day all day —_well, except for when I was at work. I always made sure that I had my head clear at work.

I was so proud of the progress that both Miko and I had been making. She was bringing home bands nightly, and I'd reached the six-month mark at my job. We'd started a ritual where we celebrated each month I completed. It was a running joke between us that oddly motivated me.

"Alright, I'm headed out. How do I look?" I asked Jas and Case.

I had finally chosen my outfit at the last minute —_a mid-length sweater dress and my stiletto booties. The shoes were killing my pinky toe, but only me and God would know because your girl was gon' be high stepping.

"You look pretty, Mommy," Case said, running over to me.

I bent down and kissed his cheek. "Thank you, handsome man. What you think, boo? Is it over the top? I don't even know what we're doing tonight." Chance gave no other instructions other than the time to be ready. I figured since it was late, dinner would be the only option.

"You look perfect, boo. You gon' be a little cold, but it's a small price to pay because you look da fuck good. Excuse my language, Case."

Jas had come over earlier to visit and volunteered to watch Case when I mentioned my date. My phone vibrated, and it was a message from Chance.

Chance: I'm outside.

Me: Coming down now.

"Alright, gotta go. Case, be good. I love you." I kissed his forehead and gave Jas a hug. "Thank you again for watching him."

"Girl, bye. Don't do nothing I wouldn't do." She winked, and I laughed.

That meant I could do anything. Taking the elevator downstairs, I checked my reflection once again in the elevator door. I did look damn good. My hair was bone straight, and I opted out of baby hairs with this new unit. Shit, if I was Chance, I'd want me too. Pushing open the door to the lobby, I was met by a gust of wind. It was so fierce I had to close the door back. My phone buzzed again.

Chance: You got that cap glued on tight?

I knew he was referring to my wig, and even I had to laugh at that.

Me: Lmao 🖕 . You lucky I can't stand you up because you're already outside.

I closed my faux fur coat and got to speed walking to the car where he had the door already open. I gave him silent kudos for his chivalry.

"You betta stop talking about my hair."

He laughed. "I like your hair. Can I have a kiss?" I leaned over and pecked his cheek then sat back, smiling.

"Aight, I'll take that."

"Am I dressed appropriately for tonight?" Scanning his attire, he was dressed casually in a pair of jeans that I was sure were name brand and a Gucci sweater and sneakers. He looked over at me and licked his lips.

"The dress is nice. You may have overdone it with the heels, but you look good as fuck, so it don't even matter."

Ahh, hell. I was overdressed. I knew I was overthinking, but there was nothing I could do about it now. When he pulled up in front of the Sugar Factory, I wanted to die. My face twisted up because I knew I had overdone it.

"If you feel uncomfortable, we can see if there's a sneaker store close by and get you some kicks."

"That's very thoughtful of you, but I'm good. C'mon, I love this place."

He helped me out of the car and placed his hand on the small of my back, guiding me into the restaurant. Once we were seated, I immediately ordered the lollipop passion for my first drink. We snacked on bread, and the conversation just flowed. That was one thing I really liked about Chance. When we talked, the conversation was never forced. It happened naturally.

As always, he had me laughing at myself. He never missed the opportunity to judge my wigs, from how I took them off at night to how I set them up on the mannequin heads. He always had a wig joke ready. It didn't take long for our food to come, and I was happy because I couldn't do too much drinking on an empty stomach. Just like a woman, I ate a little of mine and his too. And he didn't mind offering his plate to me.

In the middle of the meal, my phone rang out loud. Thinking it might be Jas calling about Case, I connected my AirPods without looking at the phone.

"You have a collect call from an inmate at the Green Haven Correctional Facility. Press one to accept the call."

I sucked my teeth, dropping my fork when I heard the automation.

"Gimmie a second to get rid of this call," I said to Chance while standing up from the table and pulling out my phone, pressing one to accept the call.

"**Yo?**"

"**What, Karter?**"

"**Where you at?**"

"**Out minding my business and staying out of yours.**"

"**Word? I just got a kite that you been hanging tough with some nigga I don't know. Wassup with that?**"

"**What the hell is a kite, Karter? Speak English because I don't speak prison.**"

"**A message, Ming. I got word that you been hanging with some new nigga. Is that the reason you couldn't bring my son on a visit? You got dude out there playing daddy to my seed?**"

"**Look, tell whoever told you that to keep my name out their mouth. Don't worry about what I do. I gotta go. Like I said, I'm out.**" Not giving him a chance to say anything else, I hung up the phone. Taking a deep breath, I returned to the table.

"You good?" Chance asked, reaching over the table and rubbing my hand.

"Yeah, I'm alright. I'm sorry to ruin the night, but do you mind if we wrap it up? I lost my appetite."

"You got it. Here's my card to pay. I'ma head to the bathroom. Have the waiter wrap my food up please." He laid his American Express down on the table and walked off.

I felt shitty for ruining the date, but had I stayed with my attitude, it would only rub off on him. The waitress came over, and instead of handing her his card, I gave her mine. It was the least I could do. I went to text Jas that I was coming home early when I heard my name.

"Hey, Ming. Long time no see."

My eyes met my ex-best friend's face, and my hand balled into a fist. She had a little girl with her, and I had to do a double-take because she favored Case a lot.

"Tiara," I responded flatly.

"It's crazy seeing you here. You weren't on the family day visit."

I quickly surmised that this cum guzzler had been fucking Karter behind my back and had made a baby. I wouldn't give her the satisfaction of seeing me upset about it though. I was too playa for that.

"And don't look for me on any other family day visit either. Your daughter is very pretty. Congratulations. You got what you always wanted, huh?"

"It wasn't even like that. It happened one time, and Kasey was conceived from there."

To hear her confirm my suspicions and have the audacity to make her child's name similar to my son's was insane. It really be some of the bitches that you call friends that be wanting to secretly be you.

"Here are your to-go items, ma'am. Thank you for dining with us," the waitress cut in, handing me two bags as well as my copy of the receipt. I signed my name and stood to my feet.

"I would call you out your name, but you're with your child, and I'm not that kind of female, so I'ma just go."

Spotting Chance headed back our way, I was glad because me and Tiara were seconds away from having an uncivilized conversation. Stepping into view, he grabbed my hand, and Tiara curled her lip.

"What are you doing here with her?"

"What's good, T? What you mean what I'm doing here with her? This is my lady."

"Wow, really?"

I was just as stuck as her. I didn't know when I became his lady, but I was more interested in how they knew each other.

"How long this been ya lady? 'Cause we just stopped fucking around a couple months ago."

"Exactly. A couple, as in six. Stop playing with me." Holding onto my waist, he turned me toward the door. "C'mon, Ma."

We made our way to the exit, and he helped me into the car. During the car ride, it was dead silent. I didn't have anything to say. The fact that he had dealings with Tiara was burning me up inside. Of course those dealings may have been before me, but it didn't matter. Anything tied to her, I had a problem with.

"So, we're not gonna talk about what happened back there?"

"Nah, you don't owe me no explanation."

"I know. But I wanna put you on."

As if there was anything to put me on about. Obviously, at some point, they were fucking, then he may or may not have stopped when I started to open up.

"I really don't see the point, but I got ears, so I'll listen." We parked, I took my seat belt off, and turned to face him. This had better be good.

14

CHANCE

When I invited Ming out tonight, the last thing I thought we'd be talking about was the past. Unfortunately, we were, and I had too much respect for her to lie about the nature of my previous dealings with Tiara. Her face said she wasn't about to believe shit I said, but she was willing to hear me out. That was a start, right?

"I met her while I was moving around, and all we had was a situation based on sex. I ain't never laid up with her or nothing. I didn't even know shorty had a kid, so you know there wasn't anything serious going on."

"Okay," she responded with no emotion.

"Okay? That's it? That's your response?"

"Yeah, what else you want me to say?" The attitude was apparent in her tone and the way she twisted her neck.

"Tell me the history so I can understand why she got you so bothered." She sat forward and looked like she wanted to curse me out. *Dammit, choice of words, Chance.* "Not like that. I mean, you were on the phone having an unpleasant conversation, then I come back from the bathroom, and you and homegirl bout to get it rocking. I'm just asking. And tell me without all that rolling of your neck, Ma."

"I don't wanna talk about it."

"You need to though, and I'm all ears. I don't have nowhere to be." I took the keys out of the ignition and put them in the middle console. We sat silently for a good five minutes before she spoke.

"Tiara is my ex-best friend. We had been close since high school. I met Karter, my son's father, when I graduated. He was the love of my life, and I told Tiara everything about us. When I say everything, I mean everything, which was a big mistake. He used to tell me that she tried to come on to him, and I didn't believe him because that was my friend, my best friend. Anyway, fast forward a few years, he's locked up and calls requesting I bring Case up there for family day. Then adds he wants him to meet his little sister, who I now know is Tiara's daughter." I let her digest everything she had just said because from the look on her face, she had yet to.

"How do you feel?"

"About them having a child together?"

"Nah, about finally being able to put to rest your suspicions. You were right all along."

"I'm pissed, but I know I would have felt worse if we were together right now."

"I would've had to get locked up just so I could beat his ass for hurting you." That got her to smile, and she let out a little giggle.

"Oh, here's your card. I forgot to give it to you back at the restaurant." She went into her purse and handed me my black card.

"Did you tip? Or were you cheap on my dime?" I joked.

"I tipped on my card because I paid," she said matter-of-factly, and that shit was a turn on.

She had a card with no limit in front of her and chose to pay. Now that was some boss shit. I leaned into her, and she leaned back like she knew I was going for a kiss.

"You better get over here and kiss me before I snatch that thing off your head."

"And I'ma whip yo' ass. Stop talking about my hair." She slapped my open hand down, and I laughed at her facial expression.

I liked fucking with her about her wigs. It wasn't because I didn't like them, but her hairstyles changed every couple of days, and I just wanted to see what she looked like natural.

"Aight, I'll leave ya hair alone. Let me taste your lips though."

Leaning in, she pecked my lips, but being the greedy man I was, that wasn't enough. I palmed the back of her head and pulled at her bottom lip with my teeth. Deepening the kiss, she moaned into my lips, causing my dick to brick up. Her tongue wrestled with mine, and her small hand went to my shoulder, massaging it. Something so minute had never been so sensual to me.

She rubbed my shoulder like she cared, like she wanted me to feel her emotion through her touch. Heavy into the moment, I reached over and rubbed her thigh. She put her hands over mine, and I figured I may be going too far, so I moved it. Pulling my head back, I watched as she spread her legs a little and guided my hand to her pussy. I felt the heat coming from her sex as she grinded on my hand. Moving my lips from hers, I found my way to her neck.

"Mmmm," she moaned.

I was afraid that if my dick got any harder, it would bust through my jeans. Moving the thin fabric that covered her pussy to the side, I slipped my middle finger into her sweet spot.

"Sssss," she hissed, and I continued to assault her neck while she held my finger hostage. I needed her in the worst way.

"I need that, Ma," I whispered, my voice now raspier.

"It's yours," she whispered back.

That was all the confirmation I needed. I reclined my seat a little and moved it back, making as much room as possible. Seemingly down for the ride, she carefully climbed over the seat and into my lap. Staring at me intensely, she skillfully used her hands to unbuckle my pants. When she reached inside my briefs and grabbed hold of my dick, I made it jump in her hand to which she smiled devilishly. I knew she could feel the veins around that motherfucka.

Lifting a little, I helped her pull her dress over her waist and moved my dick to her opening. Looking to her again for confirmation, she leaned forward and kissed my lips softly before easing down on my pole.

"Ahhhh," I made my gratification for her tight walls audible. Her pussy was nice and snug, the way I liked it. I could tell she hadn't had no dick in a while.

"Don't move," she demanded as she got herself in a comfortable position and began riding me slowly. Her wetness dripped down my shaft as she clenched her pussy muscles.

"Goddamn, Ma. Ride that dick." I was mesmerized by her concentration.

Her eyes were closed, and her bottom lip was sucked in between her teeth. I let her do her thing, only spreading her ass cheeks so that she could feel all of me. My balls slapped against her ass as she rode me into submission. She continued contracting her walls, fluttering her eyes open.

"This dick is dangerous, but this pussy is like a lethal injection. It'll kill you slowly."

"You think so?" I countered while holding back a moan.

"I know so," she replied, lifting up a little so that only the tip was in before sliding back down slowly.

"Shittt." I slapped her ass hard, but that didn't stop her movements. "I got something for that ass." Reclining the seat all the way back, I grabbed hold of her waist. Without warning, I began thrusting in and out of her at a fast pace.

"Ughhh, ahhhhh!" she screamed out while I pounded her little pussy like it owed me money. "Fuck, don't stop!"

I didn't plan to. This pussy had some power. It was tailor made for me. She just didn't know it.

"Shit, Ma, I'm 'bout to bust!" My balls got full, and I knew I was to the point of no return.

"Ooouuu, me too, Daddy." As soon as the words left her mouth, we erupted together, both of us oblivious to the fact that no condom served as a barrier between us.

Fuck it though. If a baby was to come out of what we had just done, it would be worth it.

"Shit, I'm tired, and I think I caught a Charlie horse."

We both fell out laughing as I helped her back into the passenger seat. I watched as she removed her panties and threw them in her pocketbook. My dick twitched again, but I silently told him to behave and got myself together. The car became silent again, not an awkward silence but silent nonetheless.

"Let me get up here to Case. Thank you for a memorable night."

"You got that, Ma. Whenever you're ready, I can make every night memorable."

I leaned over and kissed her forehead, pulling a smile from her. I waited until she was safely inside the building before putting my car in drive and speeding off. Tonight was good, but it was hard to tell what tomorrow would bring. Right now, my balls were empty, and I just wanted to get home and hit the sheets. It was still pretty early, but there was nothing for me to get into right now. On second thought, a pop-up visit at the Porter House was due. Ever since I'd caught Unc in the money room, I was more on point than ever.

My phone rang in the console, and Tiara's name popped up on the screen. I was still blowed that she tried to make a scene at the restaurant. I put a stop to that shit quickly. I was far from a sucka ass nigga, and I wasn't gon' have no showdown with her about when we stopped fucking around when we both knew the truth. Where there was no audience, there was no play, so it was nothing. Against my better judgement, I answered the phone.

"Wassup, T?"

"Wassup, T? You are not serious. So, you fucking friends now?"

I had to laugh because that was a joke. **"Tiara, I ain't fucked not one of your friends. None of the chicks you hang with are my type anyway."**

"You know I'm talking about Ming. Don't play dumb."

"Oh, that ain't yo' friend though."

"Well, my ex-friend. You know what I mean. It's still fucked up. I know her."

"And that should mean what to me? You were never my lady, so who I choose to spend my time with is none of your concern. Plus, I stopped fucking witchu a minute ago. Let's not forget that fact. And on top of that, you got some shit witchu. Why you ain't mention having a kid?"

The line went silent, and I gave her a few seconds to get her lie straight before she spoke. **"It's not even like that. My daughter lives between me and my mom, and you never asked me if I had kids."**

"Oh, aight," I said like I was accepting of her answer. **"I got some shit to handle. You be easy."**

"Okay," she replied in defeat. **"Hit me up later. Maybe we can chill."**

"Nah, I'm good. I'm spoken for, and my girl don't fuck witchu. And if she say it's fuck ya, then it's fuck ya."

I hung up the phone and tossed it in the passenger seat. Parking in front of Porter House, I went inside and was instantly captivated by the smell of money. The house was packed as always, but you wouldn't know from the outside looking in. All patrons were to park in the back of the warehouse, and anyone that attended on any given night had to be on a pre-approved list.

"Hey, Chance. What are you doing here? I thought today was your day off," Robin said as she greeted me with a half hug.

"It is. I just wanted to come check in and see how things were running."

"Cool. I'll be in my office if you need me."

Nodding, I went straight to making my rounds before heading to the money room. Inside, I found neat piles of green bills that aligned the walls and felt good that nothing had been tampered with until I found a stack that appeared low. Upon further inspection, a stack of plastic wrapped money that read ten thousand dollars was short five thousand. My blood boiled. Somebody had sticky fingers, and I had a feeling of who that someone was.

15

TRUTH

I watched from the doorway as the women fussed over Miko, who was seated in front of a vanity getting done up for a gala we were all attending. They all had an opinion on how they thought her hair and makeup should be styled for the occasion. Like a good sport, she sat there and let them do their thing. The smile on her face told me she was enjoying every moment.

"I think she should go with light blush, add some lashes, and hit 'em with this Ruby Woo lipstick from Mac. What y'all think?" Jomary asked, holding the lipstick up for them to see.

"Nah, she needs to pop! When she comes through, her look should scream I'm that bitch. These people have never met her before, and tonight she is staking her claim as Madam Elite, honey." Nicole dramatically snapped her fingers, and Miko giggled.

Although she was right, my intentions weren't to put Miko on display like she was some show bunny. It was for her to get familiar with the clientele and see that I wasn't running a prostitution ring.

"Natural," I said, making all eyes dart in my direction. "She looks better natural. Light on the lipstick. Y'all have another thirty minutes before we can start considering ourselves late. And y'all know I don't do late."

"Natural it is," Olivia agreed before shooing me out of the room.

As I groomed Miko to take my place at the Elite house, I found myself being in awe of her. She was humble but had boss tendencies. In a little time, I was able to bring them out of her. Shit was sexy as hell to see her boss up into her full potential, and she wasn't done.

While waiting on the ladies, I took a minute to fix the cufflinks on the Versace suit I had on. Whenever I stepped out with the Elites, I always made sure to match their fly. Tonight would be no different. I was a boss ass nigga, and it was a must that I looked the part at all times. Just as I was about to call out to the ladies, they walked downstairs, one after the other. Each Elite wore a designer dress in black, each with their own style, but they still managed to blend together so well. The floor length minks were also a nice touch.

"Y'all look beautiful."

"Thank you," they all replied in unison.

"Where's Miko?" I asked, finally noticing that she hadn't come down with them.

"Wait for it," Kane cut in with a sly smile.

I turned back toward the steps, and my heart leaped at the sight of Miko, a feeling that was foreign to me. The black sequined pantsuit she wore was tailor made for her body. I was pleasantly shocked to see her in a suit when all the Elites were in dresses. Her wanting to stand out was dope. Her hair was in a low ponytail that reached the middle of her back, and the shoes she had on made her tall enough to reach my shoulder. I could tell the hair was all hers too.

"Yessss, Madam Elite. Come through and step on necks, honey," Nicole complimented while doing some snapping shit she and the ladies did when they were giving each other props. "Hold on, let me get your coat, boo." Nicole grabbed her waist length mink from the coat closet and draped it over Miko's shoulders. "Oh, they not fuckin' witchu, Miko!"

"You don't think it's too plain? Or maybe too out there for such a big event?" she asked me, awaiting my approval. She could've come down in a paper bag, and I still would've been stuck.

"You look perfect. Let's go, ladies. They're awaiting our arrival." I held my arm out for Miko to grab hold of, and she fell in step with me.

"Go 'head, Barack and Michelle," Kane joked, making us all crack up.

We piled into my Denali truck and rolled out. Tonight, I felt like driving. I didn't plan on staying at the gala long. I had been running all week and had yet to get proper rest. I listened to the ladies talk about what Miko could expect and people to be aware of. I hosted the gala once a year with the most prominent men and women in the city. I liked to rub shoulders with the posh folks because they spent cash when it counted.

Once we pulled up, the valet came over and helped the ladies out of the car. When he made his way to the front to open Miko's door, I stopped him. Miko gave me a concerned look, and I flashed her a reassuring smile, signaling that all was okay. Stepping out of the car, I went over to her side and helped her out.

"That's my job," I informed her, and she smiled cooly.

Handing the valet my car keys, I looped her arm in mine and followed the Elites inside. The party planner that I'd paid a pretty penny to did a good job putting the hall together for the event. The colors for this year were black, white, and gold. I nodded toward the Elites to go work the floor, and as always, they caught my drift. I could already sense Miko's nervousness, so I squeezed her hand, letting her know I had her.

"You want a drink?"

"Yes, please. I didn't think I'd be so nervous."

We made our way over to the bar, and she ordered vodka and pineapple juice while I ordered Henny and Coke. I wasn't a heavy drinker, so this one drink would be enough for me.

"You good with me."

"You know all these people?"

"Yeah, pretty much. Some are current clients of the Elites and some ex-clients who spend their money on my other endeavors."

She put her drink to her lips and sipped while taking in the room. She was already picking up my ways just from being around me.

"You see how the ladies are working the room?"

"Yeah. They have this poise about them, but when they're home, they get a chance to let their hair down."

"I wouldn't have it any other way. During these types of events, when you step into my position, you must pay attention. I provide a service, and although these people smile in my face and are very generous with their money when it comes to the Elites, to them, I'm still not on their level." She nodded, and I grabbed her hand to introduce her to a few people.

I needed the clients to know her face and that they'd soon be dealing with her directly. I noticed the female clients checking her out and so did she. I made it clear that this one was off limits. After an hour of rubbing shoulders with the who's who, we entered a private room for a four-course dinner.

"So, y'all were gonna have a party without me?" Nyema entered the room, dressed to the nines in a white off-the-shoulder gown with a long train behind it.

Her hair was pulled up in a high bun, so the smirk on her face was on full display. She wanted to make a statement. Nyema, of all people, knew I didn't play when it came to my business. I had to dead all that acting out shit tonight.

"They just let anybody in now, Truth? Isn't there a list of some sort to get in here?" Nicole griped, causing the girls to mumble in agreement.

Miko sat up straight, unbothered, and it was sexy as fuck. Not wanting to make a scene, I went to excuse myself from the table. Before I could fully stand, Miko grabbed at my hand, pulling me down by my neck so that I was face-to-face with her. She placed a soft kiss on my lips, shocking me and everyone else.

"Checkmate," I heard Nicole say.

"Go handle your business," Miko encouraged. "I'll be here waiting on you."

For a second, I forgot all about Nyema being present because I was stuck in the moment.

"Truth!" Nyema yelled, pulling my attention. "Are you kidding me? You've been fucking this bitch the whole time?!" She started toward Miko, but the look in my eyes and all the Elites, including Miko, standing to their feet made her stop in her tracks.

"Please try it. Oh, please. Roberto Cavalli would have to forgive me for ruining this piece of art I'm wearing, but it would be so worth it." Olivia went to step in front of me, but I placed my arm around her waist to stop her.

Whispering in her ear that I was going to take care of it, she shook her head and sat back down. The other ladies followed her lead, all but Miko. She remained standing, staring a hole in Nyema's face. I knew if I didn't defuse the situation, I'd have to shut the whole party down. Walking around Miko, I grabbed Nyema's hand and ushered her out of the room. I didn't want to alarm the guests, so we moved swiftly toward the exit.

"I can't believe you'd embarrass me like this after all we've been to each other, Truth. I don't deserve to be treated like a side bitch that won't go away!" Nyema was really showing her ass now that we were out on the street. I didn't do public spectacles, and as of tonight, I was no longer doing Nyema.

"Where's your car, Ny?" My voice was steady, but my tone was deadly.

"Fuck that car, Truth! Tell me what you got going on with that fried rice eating looking ass bitch."

I got in her face and towered over her menacingly. "You know this is not what I do. I already let you slide because you're in your feelings. You out here looking real crazy, and I'm not about to be a part of this melodramatic shit you on. Where... the fuck... is your car?" I asked again through gritted teeth.

It took a lot to piss me off, and right now, Nyema was trying to wake the beast that I tried my best to keep at bay. Without a response, she stormed past me, and I followed close behind her. I heard the chirp on her Lexus just before she opened the door and got in the driver's seat.

"We're really at this point, huh? First, you fire me from the Elite house. Now, you have someone trying to take my place. We've had our ups and downs, but this is on another level." Her voice cracked as she spoke, but knowing Nyema, she wasn't about to let me see her cry out of fear of being seen as weak.

"Nyema, you and I both know that the end of us has been a long time coming. We've basically been going through the motions lately.

I'll speak for myself and say I haven't been happy in the relationship. The demise of us has nothing to do with Miko and everything to do with you. And I didn't just fire you and leave you fucked up. I put you in another managerial position and made sure that you were still good by hiring you at Tantra." I could tell my words were going in one ear and out the other.

"So, she's Miko now? You're giving out pet names and shit?" she snarled. "You wanna be done, fine. I'm not gonna beg you to be with me. Just know you're losing out on the best thing you ever had. Please move from my car."

Shaking my head, I did as she requested. Slamming the door, she sped off into the night. I made my way back over to the valet and gave strict instructions to be notified if she happened to pop back up. By the time I got back inside, dinner had already been served, but no one was eating.

"Why y'all not eating?"

"It just got here, and we were waiting on you," Miko spoke on everyone's behalf. "I'll say grace. Everybody grab a hand." She placed her hand over mine and blessed the food. Miko was one of a kind for sure.

We ate in silence, and once we were all full, I was all mingled out. I gave instructions to Nicole to ensure the party planner shut everything down by one a.m. and ordered a private car service to take the Elites home once the night ended.

* * *

"You sure you're okay?" Miko asked on the drive to her house.

Picking up her hand, I kissed the back of it. I wasn't supposed to be falling for my protégé. Of course, I found her attractive initially, and I was sure she felt the chemistry between us, but I wasn't supposed to fall for her.

"I'm straight. You ready to take on this life fulltime? I know it may seem like a lot, but all you have to do is make it your own. You're going to touch a lot of money, and it's easy to get sucked into any life that guarantees a bag. A big one at that."

"I think so. I adore the Elites, that I can tell you for sure. I don't mind being there for them in any way I can. Tell me about the bad side of this thing though. I know everything ain't just making appointments, exchanging money, and nice galas such as the one we just left."

"Honestly, it's not. Believe it or not, this is politics as well. The Elites don't have your normal clientele, which is why I'm so big on exclusivity. They don't just meet these people off the internet. Any new clients are referred by people who've already been set up and have a long-standing relationship with us. We all know that what we do is not what people consider the most desirable job and even frowned upon by some. Still, we remain in business, and we maintain a level of integrity that's not to be compromised."

"I guess I'm ready then."

"I need you to be sure, Amiko. I can't move on a guess." I studied her face, and she mirrored my expression.

"I'm ready."

She was sure. I felt it. Without giving my next move any thought, I leaned in and kissed her lips. It was quick but good enough for her to know the timing I was on.

"Goodnight, Truth."

"Goodnight, Madam Elite."

Amiko was a beast in the making. And quiet as it was kept, mine for the taking.

16

AMIKO

I could still feel Truth's lips on mine as I opened the door to my apartment. I had walked slowly up to my building, looking for a reason to have to turn around and go back to the car. My pussy was drippin', and if he would've tried to go further than the kiss, I would've happily slid my thong to the side and let him work my middle. Ideally, I didn't want to mix business with pleasure, but tonight, I was willing to make an exception.

The gala turned out to be a great experience, minus Nyema showing up and acting an ass. I was so happy that Truth had us set up in a private room for dinner. Had she did the most in front of all those people, I would've been mortified. Her calling me out my name didn't faze me, but if she would've made it a few more steps toward me, I would've did her dirty in my expensive suit. I knew the kiss would get under her skin, and that was just what I wanted.

I hoped for her sake that we'd stay out of each other's way. With me changing job titles, I didn't see that being a problem. Truth had introduced me to some important people and seeing him in his element made him even more attractive. The way he commanded the room without having to be the loudest one in attendance spoke volumes.

The Elites prepped me before we stepped out, and being the observant person that I was, I watched how they moved and took notes. I had a presence all on my own, but this scene was different. My skepticism about the whole madam thing had slowly fizzled. Initially, I felt strongly that Truth was running a prostitution ring that just had a little more class, but after getting to know the Elites individually, my perspective had certainly changed. Each woman had their own story that didn't involve abuse, and Truth wasn't holding them hostage.

From what I was told, he encouraged them to do other things outside of this. They had chosen this life and had the choice to leave at any time. Another thing I learned was every date didn't end or begin with sex. Some men actually wanted companionship, whether it be accompanying them to a work event, dinner, or just needing someone to talk to. You had those dates, and you had the men who wanted sex. This wasn't sex in cheap hotels either. This was rich sex, baby.

Entering my place, I took my shoes off at the door and headed for my room. I could hear running water coming from the bathroom as I passed, letting me know that Ming was home. Between her working and me being with Truth damn near every day learning the ins and outs of the Elite house, we hadn't spent much time together. We were both getting our shit together, and it showed by the way we'd come up over the last six months.

"Oh, hey. I didn't hear you come in," Ming spoke, coming out of the bathroom.

"Yeah, I just got here from being out with Truth."

"I just came in a little minute ago myself. Me and Chance went on a date, but it ended early. You just missed Jas. She watched Case for me. I'ma 'bout to heat up my leftovers. Come to the kitchen once you change so we can catch up."

I noticed the funny walk she had as she headed toward the kitchen and would definitely be pointing that out as soon as I changed. Inside the shower, my mind drifted to the kiss that Truth and I shared. It was quick, but the feeling that went through my body was long lasting for sure. He was everything I wanted him to be for me —_for someone else. I admired the businessman in him, but I had become enthralled with the other side of him. The side that I watched make anonymous donations to charitable organizations without having been told to.

The side that made sure everyone around him was in a position to make money. He made me feel like I was meant to run the Elite house and stressed that when I was ready to step into my role, he wouldn't be too far from me.

"So, how was your date?" I asked Ming as I entered the kitchen. "I thought you were heating up your leftovers." In front of her was a bowl of mangos covered in Tajin.

She shrugged her shoulders. "Changed my mind. The date was good until it wasn't. The night ended very well though."

"Does the end of the night festivities have anything to do with that stank walk you got going on?" She smiled and put her head down. "Oouuu, bitch, you nasty. Was it good?"

"Too good. Almost good enough to make me change my mind about putting an end to what we have going on."

Now I was confused. "Let me sit because I'm almost positive I'm gonna need to be seated to wrap my head around this whole thing. What do you mean put an end to it, Ming? You just started warming up to the idea of giving him a chance. No pun intended."

"Yeah, and now, I changed my mind. I'm allowed to do that, right?" she snapped. Just that fast, I knew something had happened. "Up until a couple months ago, he's been fucking Tiara."

"Tiara? Our Tiara?"

"That bitch is not our Tiara. She used to be until she became friendly pussy. Not only did I find that out, but get this, she also has a daughter with Karter."

"Girllll, get the fuck outta here. You're lying to me."

"Miko, I swear on Mommy." My face scrunched up. "Exactly, so now you see why I can't pursue anything with Chance."

I didn't see why she couldn't though, especially if he didn't know the history and wasn't fucking with her anymore. "So, you're making him suffer based on who he dealt with before you and your own history with Tiara? Sounds pretty unfair to me."

"Welp, that's what it is." I wasn't going to go back-and-forth to change Ming's mind. I learned when we were kids that once her mind was set on the side of no, then that was it. "How was your night?"

"Really nice. I told Truth I was ready to step into the position at the Elite house."

"You mean ready to be a female pimp?" She laughed, and I slapped her shoulder. "I'm just playing. It's just funny to me how you're going from working at Tantra as an employee to getting ready to be the head bitch in charge. Teach me, sensei." She put her hands together and bowed, making me laugh.

"Shut up. I don't know why he feels that I would be a good fit for it. All I know is that he offered the job, and the pay at Tantra ain't fuckin' with this salary. If I gotta go to stuffy meetings and manage money all while making sure the Elites are straight, then I'm all for it."

"You're gonna have to start carrying yourself a different way then." I cut my eye at her. "I'm not saying that in a negative way. I mean, you are about to step into a whole different world. You're gonna have to put Amiko aside and step into your role as boss bitch." She hopped down off the counter and left me with something to think about.

THE NEXT AFTERNOON, I called Truth for a meeting at the Elite house. Last night, I gave a lot of thought to what Ming said, and she was right. I had to be a boss bitch if I was going to assume the role as Madam Elite. The clients had become accustomed to dealing with Truth and even Nyema in some capacity, but they needed to know me. He agreed to the meeting, and I got up with the perfect outfit in mind.

"You betta werk, Madam Elite!" Ming gassed me up as she entered my room.

I did a little spin for her to take in the red Givenchy pantsuit. I'd decided that this would be my signature look. I figured a dress would be too common. The pantsuit made a statement.

"You feeling it?"

"Yes, ma'am. Here, let me change the ponytail though. I'ma put it high up like Gabrielle Union had hers on *Two Can Play That Game*. You know, since you got the red suit on and all. You putting on any makeup?"

"Nope. All natural." I listened to what Truth had said last night about the natural look and just added gloss to my lips.

"Okay, you're good to go."

I swung my ponytail to the side before standing. Grabbing my fur, I slipped it on and opened my phone to order an Uber. Before I could hit request on the Uber Black, a text message from Truth came through.

Truth: I'm sending a car for you. It should arrive in the next ten minutes. You'll know if the driver is there for you by the car that pulls up.

Me: You didn't have to do that, Truth. I would've been fine taking an Uber Black.

Truth: From now on, there will be no more Ubers. If I'm not available to drive you, then you will have an on-call driver. Things have changed. I'll see you in a few.

I held the phone up to Ming for her to see the message.

"You goddamn right. Oouu wee, I can't wait to see the car. Go downstairs. I'ma be looking out the window."

I chuckled at her foolishness. My YSL pumps led the way as I walked outside. I could only smile at the car that sat in front of my building, putting all the parked ones to shame. The driver stepped out to greet me.

"Ms. Amiko I presume?"

"That's correct. And you are?"

"I'm Ralph. I'll be your personal driver, Madam Elite."

"Thank you for your service, Ralph. I promise not to be too needy."

"No worries. Wherever you need to go, I'll get you there." He opened the door and closed it once I was inside. I reached for my phone to text Truth once more.

Me: The Wraith is a nice touch. I guess this does say Madam Elite more than any Uber Black.

Truth: You should expect nothing but the best.

If I kept smiling like this, my jaw would start hurting. Truth had that effect on me. The meeting I had planned for the Elites today wasn't to change anything. I wanted to get acclimated in the new position and find out from the ladies what they thought could be different. I was only as strong as the people on my team. Using the key given to me, I sauntered inside the Elite house and started toward the library where I requested the meeting be held.

I was happy to see that everyone was in attendance and awaiting my arrival. In fact, I was five minutes early. I greeted the ladies with a silent hello and watched as they smiled and nodded in approval. Whether it had been approval of my attire or my demeanor, either way, it was a good thing. My eyes focused in on Truth first. He sat at the far end of the table, at the left of the head seat that was empty.

"Thank you all for your attendance. I won't be before you long. As you know, Truth has been in search of someone to take on managing the Elite house permanently. When he first came to me with the idea, I was less than sold about it because I didn't see what I could bring to the table. That is until last night. I'm here to partner with you to take the Elites global. And we can because you know what we possess?" I fixed my gaze on each Elite before continuing. "We possess what's called Pussy Power. And it makes the world go 'round."

I took my seat at the head of the table, and Truth gave a proud nod. I was about to take this Madam shit to another level of exclusivity.

1 7

———

MING

"You know yo' homegirl wanna fuck me, right?" My eyes shot open, and I lifted my head from where I laid on Karter's chest.

"Who you talkin' about?" I knew he couldn't be talking about Tiara because that was the only homegirl I had. He stared down at me with a smirk on his face.

"Tiara. Shorty be tryna throw me the pussy."

"First off, stop talking to me like you havin' a conversation with one of your homeboys. This is another bitch we're discussing, and you actin' real nonchalant about it. You need to be chalant as fuck right now. So, Tiara's been trying to fuck you? Why are you just now telling me?" I did not like what I was hearing, and the last thing I wanted to do was have to beat my best friend's ass and try to kill my man.

"I mean, I had it handled. It happened a minute ago, but I shut that shit down and let her know that this was your dick." Pulling me on top of him, he eased into me and just that fast, he had erased all the doubt I had of both him and Tiara doing me dirty.

I knew then that I should've went with my first mind and pressed Tiara about the situation. Maybe I wouldn't have had to explain to my son that he had a little sister.

It had been two weeks since my date with Chance and two weeks since I'd seen him. I had been avoiding a face-to-face in fear of what I was feeling. I couldn't lie and say that him having dealings with Tiara in the past didn't bother me. As confident as I was in myself, a part of me felt like she had one up, and that shit stung a little. The first few days after the date, Chance texted me and I'd answer, but I was always short, claiming to be busy with either Case or work.

I had convinced myself that we had no real shot at whatever it was he was trying to have with me. Yeah, he was a great guy, always included my son in plans, and very fond of me, but how long would that last? Subconsciously, I'd been looking for a reason to cut him off, but he had been doing everything right. I was fully aware that I was self-sabotaging, but it was the only way I knew how to protect myself.

"Hey, Ming, Dr. Patel has one more patient, and then we're going to be closing for the day," one of the dental assistants informed me as I entered the appointments for the upcoming week.

"Sounds good to me. The perks of having your own practice must be nice."

She laughed. "I know, right? The patient should be here in a few minutes."

I gave her a thumbs up and resumed scheduling. The door chimed a few minutes later, and I looked up to see Tiara walking in with her daughter. Reminding myself that I needed this job, I welcomed her as I'd done every other patient.

"Good afternoon. Are you here for an appointment?"

"Go sit down, Kasey, while I sign you in." The little girl nodded and went over to the play area that was set up in the office.

"Yeah, we have an appointment with Dr. Patel for a cleaning. I would have never guessed that Karter would have you out here working."

Ignoring her comment, I continued with my normal protocol. "You can have a seat, and the dental assistant will be right with you."

"You know, it's real fucked up how you won't allow Case to see his father or meet his little sister. Your son shouldn't suffer because of something that went on with adults."

And just like that, the whole *keep it professional* shit I had been reciting in my head went out the window. "Bitch, let me tell you something. I may really, really like this job, but you got me real fucked up if you think you bout to speak on my son like you crazy. Now, I don't know if you forgot, but I'm still that bitch that will dog walk yo' ass in these scrubs or out of em'. You know what typa timing I can get on, Tiara. Fuck a cleaning, they'll be wiring yo' shit up to keep your jaw in place!"

"Kasey," the dental assistant called out, making Tiara's daughter run over to us.

"Hey, little one. Are you Mommy?" she asked Tiara, who nodded.

"Okay, you guys can come on back."

Tiara glanced back at me, and I cocked my head to the side, letting her know it was whatever. Her visit lasted forty-five minutes, and the whole time, I watched the clock, hoping she came out on bullshit just so I could slide her wack ass across the marble floors. Luckily for her, she didn't even look my way when she left out. Scary ass ho.

THE DAY ENDED, and I hopped on the train and headed straight to the daycare to pick Case up. Out of habit, I checked my phone to see if I had any messages from Chance. Up until a week and a half ago, he would text me to see what I was doing, and we'd talk throughout the day. Now, my phone was dry except for a text from Miko or Jas. Suddenly, missing him had become a familiar feeling. Scrolling through my messages, I found myself in our thread that I had yet to delete. I started to text that I missed him but quickly chickened out, reasoning that if he felt the same, he would've called.

Why would he want to speak to me now after I'd let a whole week and change go by? I wouldn't be surprised if he blocked my silly ass. Maybe Miko was right. I was blaming him for what happened in the past. I couldn't help the baggage I came with. Getting off the train, my phone rang as soon as I hit the sidewalk. I rushed to answer it but was disappointed that it wasn't Chance calling. It was an unknown number, likely tied to Karter. Without a second thought, I declined it. I jogged up the steps of the daycare, and before I could knock, the door opened and out walked Chance.

"Uh, hey. How are you?"

He looked me up and down before chuckling sarcastically and walking away. I felt like shit. A part of me wanted him to understand me, forget about what happened, and just go back to how we were. The adult in me understood why he reacted the way he did, even though it hurt.

"Mommy!" Case yelled out while running toward me. I hugged him tightly and kissed his forehead.

"Hey, handsome. Go grab your coat and your bookbag." I gave Ms. Pat a tired wave, and she instantly caught onto my somber look.

"Come on in the kitchen and tell me all about it." I followed behind her, not wanting to talk, but I knew I needed to get a hold on these emotions. "Whenever you're ready, you can start talking. I can see it all over your face that something is wrong."

I put my head down, and she moved about the kitchen as normal, waiting for me to speak. "I'm broken," I admitted aloud for the first time in my life. "I've been broken for a while now, and it's likely the reason I can't accept love. And I like Chance, Ms. Pat. I really do. When I'm with him, I feel different. I wanna be open, but I can't help but to have my guard up. I'm afraid of loving someone only to lose them."

Ms. Pat placed her hand under my chin and lifted my head. "Hear me clearly. Some people are put into your life for a season and some for a lifetime. You can write your story now and choose who gets to spend the rest of your days with you and your son. Chance ain't perfect by far, but he's worth it. I know because I had a part in raising him. The same way you're in here pouring your heart out, what you think he just left from here doing?"

"I hope crying and telling you he don't wanna live without me."

"Sugar, I said Chance Porter was in here. I don't know what Chance you talkin' bout."

I giggled while wiping the tears that trickled down my cheeks. The way Chance dodged me, the last thing I thought he would've been doing was pouring his heart out about me. I gave Ms. Pat a big hug and decided that I was going to put my pride aside and reach out to him again. I was open to the possibility of being rejected because I knew he had every reason to ghost me. Boarding the bus with Case, I attempted to call but was sent to voicemail, so I followed up with a text.

Me: I'm not particularly good at apologies, but I know when one is owed. I'm sorry that I allowed my own issues to push you away. When you're ready, I would like to talk to you about us. If there is still an us to talk about.

I put my phone in my bag to avoid checking for his response. I meant every word that I typed and hoped that he felt it. The day had been a long one, and these were the times where I was thankful that Ms. Pat made sure that the kids who were picked up late ate dinner. Case had already started rubbing his eyes, indicating how sleepy he was.

We had finally reached our stop, and with a half block walk, I knew he wasn't gonna make it. Placing my purse inside his backpack, I threw it over my shoulder and picked him up. The whole time we walked, I prayed that my back and legs wouldn't give out. When we did reach the building, I leaned up against the lobby door to catch my breath.

"Yo, Ming." I heard a voice very similar to Karter's call out to me.

I turned slowly, and there he was, jogging across the street. I noticed he had buffed up a little as he had his arms wide open, awaiting my embrace. I didn't budge, not even to shift Case in a better position to alleviate some of the weight from my right side.

"When'd you get home? And why are you just popping up at my house?" I scanned the cars across the street to see who he had driving him around.

"If you had answered your phone earlier, you would've known that they let the bull out. Better yet, had you come to family day, you would've known I was granted early release. Let me see my boy." He went to reach for Case, and I shook my head.

Shady, I know, but my son didn't know him, and after the whole Tiara debacle, I didn't trust his ass.

"He's sleep."

"Aight, let me come up for a few. I wanna talk to you."

"Let's try again tomorrow. It's late, and quite frankly, I don't fuck with you like that." Using my key fob to let myself in the building, I made sure the door closed behind me.

He watched like he wanted to say something but didn't. When I got upstairs, Miko was sitting on the couch in her pajamas with her iPad on her lap and the TV off.

"Heyy," she greeted. "Here, let me take him."

She grabbed Case from my arms and went in the direction of his room while I went straight for the kitchen in search of a wine bottle. I didn't know why but seeing Karter had me in my feelings —not like I wanted to get back with him but I was feeling played all over again. And on top of that, my phone hadn't gone off with a response from Chance yet.

"He was sleeping too peacefully, so I just changed him into his jammies and put him in the bed. Oh, damn, you got the wine out. What happened? And what are we doing about it?"

I knew my sister was gon' ride.

"Karter is home."

"Ooh kay, and what else is going on?" She didn't like Karter from the first day she met him, so I didn't expect any other response.

"I had a talk with Ms. Pat, and she definitely gave me some gems about my situation with Chance."

"Oh, so there's a situation again? Okay, okay, and what did you do with those gems?"

"I called but was sent to voicemail, and then I texted him but still no answer. So, what I do next?" She pulled out her phone and started texting in the middle of me talking. "Amiko, sister in crisis here."

"I know. That's why I'm texting Truth to see where Chance is, so you can go get yo' man," she said matter factly.

That was exactly what I was going to do.

1 8

CHANCE

"We gotta run these numbers again, Robin, because something is off like a motherfucka." We had been in the money room for the past two hours, counting last night's take, and it was short by fifty bands. I paced the floor, but it did nothing to control my anger. My phone kept going off, but I didn't bother answering it.

I hadn't been in the best of moods the past two weeks. Ming had gone back into her Ming way. She barely had anything to say to me through text, and the calls had stopped altogether, so I decided I wasn't going to chase her anymore. It was too time consuming, and I had to throw in the towel, no matter how much I was feeling shorty.

"I ran them three times, Chance. The money is short," Robin said, enraging me.

"Well, keep counting the shit until fifty thousand dollars appears! How the fuck did all that money come up missing on your watch?!" I barked at her.

Her eyes turned to slits, and she held her hand up to me. "Whoa, I need you to calm the hell down and remember who you're talking to. We don't carry each other that way, and we damn sure ain't gon' start now. Now, come to my office and let's get this figured out."

Leaving out of the money room, we walked side by side and to her office.

"Sit down." She scolded me like a big sister did her little brother that was acting out.

I was tripping for real because I knew it wasn't her fault. "My bad. I'm bugging."

"Yeah, you really are. Let's put our heads together and think. You and I were both here last night. Who else has access to the money room that could've come in and swiped fifty thousand dollars and left out unnoticed?"

All roads led to the one person that I told his assistance was no longer needed. I slammed my hand on the desk, making Robin jump.

"It was fucking Unc, man! That motherfucka robbed us again!" Jumping up, I pulled out my phone, bypassing the unread messages, and went straight to my contacts to dial Truth. He answered on the first ring.

"Yo, where you at? Ming has been trying to reach you."

"Man, fuck all that. I need you to get to Porter House like yesterday on some code red type shit." The line went dead, and I knew it wouldn't be long before he arrived.

I had to put Ming on the back burner for the moment. I didn't even bother checking her text after he mentioned her name. Between not being on good terms with her and now finding out my own damn uncle had sticky fingers, my head was all over the place. I didn't wanna take my anger out on her if the message rubbed me the wrong way.

The next call I made was to Uncle Boss, and just like I thought it would, the call went right to voicemail. I blamed myself to a point because when I saw him coming out of the room the first time, I failed to mention to Truth that the code needed to be changed or even change it myself. Unfortunately, I'd put it at the bottom of my list of things to do, then the five bands came up missing, and again, I put that at the back of my mind.

"How you figure it was Boss who took the money, Chance?" Robin questioned.

I ran down the day I'd seen him coming out of the money room as well as the five thousand that went missing two weeks ago. She just shook her head and listened. It left a bitter taste in my mouth that I even had to see my uncle as an opp now.

"Damn, I don't recall seeing him last night."

Neither did I, but he was the only other person with access to the safe. Another fifteen minutes passed before Truth arrived. Robin and I put the rest of the money up, and I took it upon myself to finally change the code. I decided to give it to Robin because she had proven herself loyal on more than one occasion. She had our backs, and that was something that we never had to question. Crazy how we couldn't trust our blood.

<hr>

"Why would Uncle Boss steal from us? If he needed it, he had it, no questions asked." Truth stared off, something he often did when he was in deep thought.

I couldn't answer his question because in his eyes, Unc was just Unc. In my eyes, he was a grimy ass motherfucka that would be dealt with accordingly when I caught up to him. I told him the same story I'd told Robin, and I could tell he was having a hard time believing me. I was having a hard time digesting the shit myself, but I knew what I saw. I heard the hate in his voice when he spoke on Truth, and I had come to the conclusion that Unc felt like he was owed more than what was offered to him.

"What are we gon' do? That fifty bands won't affect our overall take home, but the disrespect is sure to fuck up my mental." I let Truth know in not so many words that the matter had to be handled quietly but handled nonetheless. "Yo, this silent thinker shit you doing is not gonna work for me, bruh. Not right now."

"I'm processing this shit, Chance. Chill the fuck out. This ain't no regular nigga in the streets. This is our family, bruh. We have to give him the benefit of the doubt."

"Benefit of the doubt, Truth? What you want the nigga to do, come in and steal right in front of your face? C'mon, bruh, you don't even believe that bullshit you just said. Let me get outta here because you talkin' crazy and not in your right mind. And people say Mama stood by the microwave when she was pregnant with me." I got up and held out my hand for him to dap. "Just know when I see the nigga, it's a problem, so you gotta figure this shit out."

This was some real bitch shit Unc had pulled, and it had me questioning every interaction I'd ever had with him. We'd put him in a lovely position, and we didn't have to. When my parents died, a clause in their will stated that Uncle Boss would run the Porter House until Truth turned eighteen. Once he turned eighteen, it was his to do as he pleased with it. Out of obligation and not wanting to put him out of the family business after he'd maintained it for years, Truth kept him on payroll. He didn't show signs of disloyalty, at least none that I picked up on. He was getting up in age, so I figured he would welcome early retirement. I was wrong, and he was a snake.

In my car, I finally decided to check the message Ming had sent me. Reading over it, I wasn't sure that I was convinced she meant everything she said. Ming was holding back, and I couldn't help her sift through her baggage to find out what was worth carrying. I would be there through it no doubt, but she had to allow me to do so. I sent her a quick text back to acknowledge her attempt to make things right.

Me: I appreciate you putting yourself out there. I'm sure that was difficult for you. On some real shit, a nigga feeling the fuck out you. Me and Case have even developed a bond. You gotta let me be there and allow us to grow without thinking or making me pay for the last nigga's mistakes.

Putting my car in drive, I drove in the direction of Boss' house. He lived in Queens and was a homebody unless he was down at Porter House. This man had practically helped raise us. I remember him and my dad being thick as thieves. Why he would wait till now to steal was wild. Wasn't shit sweet about me or my brother, so if he thought he was gonna get away with it, he needed to rethink that shit.

Parking my car in front of his duplex, I got out and jogged up to his front door. His car wasn't parked in the driveway, but it wasn't uncommon for him to park in the garage. I went to knock on the door, and my phone rang at the same time. Like I thought, it was

Truth calling. Declining the call, I proceeded to knock. He knew there was no talking me down once I was on go.

No one answered the door, and Uncle Boss being the private person he was, he never gave us a key. I knocked again, harder this time. I was persistent in finding where this nigga had lost his mind. Again, there was no answer. He wasn't home, and I half expected that. If I had taken fifty bands and knew niggas were gon' want my head, I would get ghost too. My phone went off again with another call from Truth. This time, I answered.

"**He's still alive. In the wind, but alive,**" I said before he could ask me any questions.

"**Get back to the house asap.**"

"**You found Boss?**"

"**Nah, but you need to see what I found on these security tapes. You ain't gon' believe this shit.**"

I hung up with him and took one last look at the door before jogging back to my car. I didn't think to check the cameras when I was there with Robin. I was still trying to wrap my head around the missing money. I was skeptical about killing Unc because he was family, but I'd made up my mind that I was gonna cripple him.

Loyalty was everything to me. It had been drilled into our heads since we were kids. What Boss had done was unforgivable, and he had put us in a fucked-up situation to have to deal with him accordingly.

19

TRUTH

I SAT IN MY OFFICE WITH ROBIN REVIEWING THE SECURITY FOOTAGE from last night. I was more disappointed about what Chance had revealed to me than anything. Boss was his own man, and never once did I make him feel like he was beneath me. If anything, we were a team, or so I thought. Had I known he held some type of hate in his heart for me, I would've cut him off with no hard feelings.

The video played the whole day from 10 a.m. to 4 a.m. when Porter House officially closed. I watched as the dealers worked the room and people spent their money freely. Nothing stuck out to me. I hadn't seen Boss come through the frame not once, but I did see a familiar face. I knew the body anywhere, and as much as the person tried to hide their face, it didn't work. It was Nyema. Dressed in a puffer coat, running shoes, and a baseball cap, she made her way through the casino, blending in with the crowd.

"Did you know she was here last night?" I asked Robin without taking my eyes off the screen. I didn't want to miss one move she made.

"I didn't. I was in the office most of the night. Damn, how the hell did I miss that?" She stood up and walked over to the screen to get a better look.

I wasn't blaming her. And I didn't need to voice it for her to know that. I continued to look on as Nyema pulled the cap down over her eyes a little more once she passed one of the noticeable cameras. What she didn't know was that every move she made was being recorded.

Had I not been studying the tapes, I would've missed her. When I saw her approach the money room, I sat up in my chair, leaning forward. My blood boiled as she effortlessly punched the code into the security system and gained access on the first try. The only person that had access to the room outside of Chance and I was Boss. *When the hell did Nyema have time to get close to Boss to get the code though? I* thought to myself.

"I always knew that bitch was a scandalous ass ho. Truth, you gotta let me shoot her now. After this, you got to."

I ignored Robin and kept watching. In the back of my mind, I wanted to believe that Nyema would think twice before she made her next move, but again, she did the opposite. Her slick ass slipped five pre-sealed bundles of ten-thousand-dollar stacks into the tote-sized bag she carried in with her.

She must've thought that we wouldn't miss the money because we brought that in plus more on a nightly basis. It was no longer about the money; it was the principle. I paused the video, and the still shot captured her face as she glanced up, unaware that she was on candid camera. Tightening her grip on the bag, she walked out as swiftly as she'd come in. The door buzzed, letting me know Chance had arrived.

"I'm here. What you need to show me?" he asked with a scowl on his face. I pointed to the screen, and he remained silent. "So, she's conspiring with this nigga, huh? And it seems that the one thing they have in common other than being thieves is you. When is the last time you spoke to Nyema?"

I thought back to the gala and the way she crashed it, only to be escorted out. Nyema had a lot of shit with her, and while I ended the relationship, the last thing I expected was for her to be so fucked up about it that she'd steal from me. Even worse, to still show her face at Tantra after doing so.

"We haven't really spoken since I had to put her out of the gala."

"Okay, so let me get this straight. Fifty thousand dollars is gone, and by the footage that just played, we can confirm that Nyema took it, and to your knowledge, Boss put her up to it?"

"He's the only person she could've gone to for the code."

Chance dropped his head. "Not shifting the blame from them at all, but this shit is part my fault, bruh. I should've changed the code to the room as soon as I sensed some funny shit. I should've went with my gut."

"Always go with your first mind. Pop taught us that. But we're not here to talk about what we could've done. Let's get down to what we're gonna do."

Sitting back in my chair, I thought about the last conversation I had with my father before he died.

My parents were getting ready to head into the Porter House for a party they were hosting for an up-and-coming boxer. As always, my dad let me and Chance stay up while he got dressed to leave. During these times, we would chop it up, and he would impart words of wisdom on us. We would discuss everything from politics, music, morals, and how proud he was of the direction the Porter House was moving in.

"If y'all don't adhere to anything else I've said all these years, please keep this as a mantra to live by. Snakes are always hidden by the very grass you water. Once you spot one, chop its fuckin' head off."

Somewhere along the line, I allowed Uncle Boss to get too comfortable in his position. I didn't think anything of it because he was my blood —_emphasis on *was*. Now he was dead to me. If you'd steal, you'd kill. And I couldn't let a nigga take me out.

"Truth, you good?" Robin placed her hand on my shoulder, pulling me from my thoughts.

"I'm good. I need you to send me a copy of the books for the past six months to my phone. I have a feeling that this shit has been going on longer than we know. And if it has, then I dropped the ball."

I knew my pops was rolling over in his grave right now. I also knew that he would want me to handle the situation the way I saw fit.

"Let me go pull these files for you. I'll have them forwarded to your phone in twenty minutes. Y'all gotta promise me y'all are not gonna go do nothing crazy. Your mother would rise from the dead and kick my ass if something happened to either one of you."

I chuckled, remembering how protective my mom was of us when she was alive. Robin hugged the both of us and left the office. I never took Nyema for the shiesty type, but I guess the breakup brought out the worst in her. I glanced at Chance, whose brows were furrowed as he focused on his phone. I knew he was thinking about all the ways he could hurt Boss without actually killing him. Though I shared those thoughts, I wanted to pay Nyema a visit first. Crossing me was like a death sentence, and being that I didn't put my hands on women, I planned to kill her financially.

"Everything will be handled," I assured him. "Boss can't live off fifty thousand dollars, bruh, and neither can Nyema. Not with their spending habits. Soon, he'll be back for more, and we'll be here, waiting on him. In the meantime, I'ma go pop up on Nyema. You straight?"

"Yeah. You need to let Robin box that ho. My first thought was to find her and shoot her in her hand, but I ain't know how you'd feel about it." He gave me a pound, and I pulled him in for a half hug before letting him go.

"You know Nyema is money hungry. I'ma 'bout to fuck her head up by shutting down the pipeline. Any accounts of hers that I fund will be closed within the next hour. I'm also going to hit Mina up while I'm on the way to the bank to change the access codes to Tantra. I'll hit you if I need you. Bruh, don't make a move without telling me. We need to be on the same page in order for this shit to be taken care of properly."

He sighed. "I ain't gon' kill him when I see him. I know that's what you're getting at. I got it." He walked out ahead of me, and I ran my hand over my face. Chance was a hot head and had been managing it well up until now.

LEAVING PORTER HOUSE, I made a quick run to the bank and closed the checking and savings account that Nyema had access to. Usually, I would deposit money into her account whenever I felt like it, which was probably more than twice a month. A few bands per deposit. She was my woman, so she was taken care of. Once that was checked off my list, I headed for her condo.

I used my key to get inside her place. The living room was empty, but I heard water running in the bathroom. Making my way to the back, I could hear her voice. From the hallway mirror, I watched her pace her bedroom floor. I stayed out of sight and listened to her bark into the phone.

"Boss, this is my fifth time calling you, and now I'm starting to get pissed the fuck off! I did what you asked me to do, and you're not keeping up with your end of the bargain. We were supposed to split that money down the middle, and now I can't even get you on the phone! Now, I've laid up with you plenty of nights as you pillow talked and told me all your dirty little secrets and how you really feel about your nephews, especially Truth. If you don't want me to air your shit out, you had better call me back. Asap!" Throwing the phone on the bed, she stormed into the bathroom.

I made sure to angle my body so that I was out of sight. From the conversation, I gathered that they'd been working hard at their plan. Unfortunately for the both of them, I hadn't played a game yet that I didn't win. Pushing up off the wall I leaned against, I quietly made my way to her living room.

"This old bastard think I'm playin' wit him. I'm not about to keep doin..." She stopped mid-sentence, freezing up once she saw me seated comfortably on her couch.

"Nah, keep talkin'. I'm sure you can dig this hole deeper than it already is. What you not bout to keep doin with my uncle?"

"Tru..."

"We got some shit to discuss, don't we?"

Her face became flushed. She knew she was caught up. And she didn't have long to tell me what I wanted to hear. I was fresh out of chances for her.

2 O

NYEMA

"Talk to me, Ny. What you not bout to keep doing with Boss?"

The blank look on Truth's face let me know that I needed to choose my words wisely once I got them together. Not being able to read him made me uncomfortable. He was known for being slow to speak and methodical. And I knew it would be easy for him to detect a lie in the smallest twitch of my mouth or if I swallowed wrong. I couldn't have that, so I recovered the best I could, refusing to let him see me sweat.

"You scared the shit out of me," I said, placing my hand on my chest. "And I'm not gonna keep calling him about the business we have together. Which is none of your business, by the way." I only realized how crazy I sounded after the words had left my mouth.

"Oh, word? You got business with Boss now? That's news to me."

"I don't know why you're concerned about who I speak to or what business I have. You don't fuck with me, remember?" I attempted to flip the script in an effort to buy myself more time to come up with something else to say.

"You're right, but since when did you start fucking with Boss?" His brows were raised, and I faked like I was insulted.

"First off, I don't like what you're insinuating. If you must know, he borrowed money from me a few weeks ago to settle a gambling debt. He has yet to repay me, and I've been looking for his ass ever since." I rolled my neck after each word, hoping it made me more believable.

"How much did he borrow?"

"Why you wanna know all that?"

"I wanna know, so I can pay you back. My family shouldn't be owing you anything."

My mouth clamped shut, not expecting him to say that. The money hungry bitch in me couldn't pass up the thought of more money passing through my hands —_money I didn't have to work for. What Truth gave me on top of what Boss had me take from Porter House made my pussy wet just thinking about it. "I let him borrow ten thousand," I said, lying my ass off.

I didn't wanna give a high number, but I didn't want to go too low either.

"You sure?"

"Yes, I'm sure. Why would I lie?"

"I don't know. Why would you?"

"Whatever, Truth. Like I said, I gave him ten thousand dollars."

"Aight. Come down to Porter House tomorrow, and I'll have that for you."

He got up and took a few steps toward me, towering over my five-foot four stature. I panted, taking him all in. Truth was a beautiful man, and his aura was intoxicating.

"I have somewhere to be. I'll see you tomorrow. Come around eleven."

He kissed my cheek, and the kiss felt cold. I was used to my pussy acting a fool whenever his lips touched any part of my body. This kiss felt final, almost like the kiss of death.

I knew going down to Porter House was suicide, being that I had just snatched fifty thousand dollars the previous night, but money was the motivation. Keeping my eyes on him as he headed for the door, I walked slowly behind him. On the way, I spotted my keys on the kitchen counter. Shaking my head, I felt myself getting pissed. It was really over and for reasons I couldn't understand other than it having to do with that Jhené Aiko reject, Amiko.

"The least you could have done was put my keys in my hand and look me in the eyes when you did it. This," I held the keys up, "was some real coward shit. Similar to what you pulled at the gala." I still wasn't over the embarrassment of that night. I even cried on my way home, but I'd never let him know it. I was past the hurt and just pissed that he had dismissed me for a bitch he only knew for five minutes. "I think I at least deserve that kind of decency."

"It's no hard feelings, Nyema. I felt like putting the keys in your hand would have only added salt to the wound."

I didn't bother responding. Opening the door, I motioned for him to get out. He smirked and nodded, getting the hint. Stopping short of the elevator, he turned around and left me with parting words.

"Always remember, you can become the company you keep. And their transgressions can make you guilty by association." The elevator doors opened, and he stepped inside, cracking another smirk as it closed.

Rushing back into my apartment, I made sure to lock the door and put the dead bolt on. I dialed Boss' number again, only for it to ring once and go to voicemail. This motherfucka had me confused with some other bitch. Not letting the voicemail deter me, I dialed the number again. I could do this shit all day because I knew once he picked up, I was going to let him have it. Just as I went to hang up, the call connected.

"What the hell is yo' problem? Why you blowing up my phone like you crazy, woman?!" His voice boomed through the phone, shocking me. Boss had never so much as raised his voice at me before. His reaction was new, and I wasn't feeling it.

"Well, excuse the fuck outta me. That 50K got you acting brand new, huh? Brand new enough to not feel like you have to answer your phone when I'm the one that made it possible for this shit to happen!" I refused to let another Porter play me after all I'd done. **"Truth just left my house, and it wasn't a pleasant visit. Where the hell are you?"**

"Nyema, this ain't the first time fifty grand has graced my palms, and it won't be the last. I'm out here making moves so that

we're secure, baby. Don't worry about Truth. I'ma take care of him." His tone was now calmer than before.

"**I'm sure you will,**" I replied with much sarcasm. "**You still haven't answered my question.**"

"**I had to make a run. Relax. I'm not tryna stick you for your money. We're better than that.**"

"**That's what I thought too. And now, I'm having to track you down on some bounty hunter shit for what's rightfully mine. Make your way to me as soon as you're done with whatever it is that you're doing, Boss. Don't fucking play with me. I will air all your shit out and let the chips fall where they may.**" I hung up in his face, not waiting for his response.

This thing with Boss and I kind of just happened. One minute, he was consoling me, and the next, I was riding his dick and telling him all my business. The Porter men just had it like that.

"Go find you something to do, Nyema. I'm done going back-and-forth witchu. This is what lame ass niggas do, which I'm not." Truth scolded me outside of the club before getting in his car and speeding off into the night. I stood in front of Porter House, seething and embarrassed.

"You're too fine to be treated average, Nyema. I thought you knew your worth, little lady." I looked to the right of me, and Boss was nearing closer, dressed in a three-piece suit and a pair of Stacey Adams on his feet. He had a cigar in his hand and a smirk on his face. *"He don't know how to handle a woman of your caliber."*

"Oh, and you do?" I countered, fanning the smoke rings he made from my face.

"There's only one way to find out." He pulled out a phone and held it out for me to take. *"My number is already programmed."*

Seeing that I wasn't going to take it from him, he slipped it into my purse and swaggered off. Boss was probably pushing fifty but didn't look a day over thirty-five. He reminded me of Truth in a lot of ways. Ignoring his slick talk, I made my way to my car and put both the conversation and the phone to the back of my mind.

At three that morning, I found myself horny, and Truth wasn't answering his phone. It was one of the things I hated about him. When he went silent, it was almost like he was a ghost. There was rarely any making up, and that shit irked me to no end. I looked over at my purse that sat on my dresser and thought about the phone that was inside. Thinking, what the hell, I retrieved it and let my fingers navigate to the one contact that was saved.

Hitting the green button to connect the call, I nearly jumped out of my skin when it started ringing. Everything in me said to abort mission, but I proceeded anyway. Boss answered on the second ring, as if he knew I would call. He rambled off his address without so much as a hey and hung up the phone. It was evident that that cocky shit ran through the Porter bloodline. I second guessed my next move once I arrived in front of his duplex. All of the what ifs went through my head as I sat inside my car, tapping my stiletto nails on the steering wheel. Dialing Truth again, my call was sent straight to voicemail, and the bitch in me took over my decision making.

I opened my car door, and my Valentino booties hit the pavement with much sass. Making my way up the two steps, I stood in front of Boss' door. He opened it before I could knock, shirtless with the same smirk from earlier on his face. For his age, he was fit, and the hair on his chest laid where it wasn't too much. I wasn't a fan of a hairy chest, but I didn't mind it on him. No matter how hard I tried not to be, I was definitely turned on.

"You can come in. You're already here."

I stepped inside, and the beginning to a torrid affair began.

And here we were, still at it and making plans to take over Porter House right under Truth's nose. Only I didn't plan on having to deal with him head-on so soon. Money and power made my world go 'round. Truth knew this, and Boss would soon learn. At a point, I did love Truth. Hell, I still loved him, but he diminished me to nothing and devalued what I thought I was to him.

Yeah, I was fucking his uncle, and he spent a pretty penny on me, but he made me this way. I was a woman scorned; at least that was how I justified my actions. No longer feeling like sitting around the house, waiting on something to happen, I decided to get dressed and do some retail therapy. My bank account was still sitting lovely thanks to Truth and his generosity.

Knowing the weather was less than appealing due to the frigid temperatures, I opted to dress down. Forcing my juicy ass into a pair of jeans, I put on an oversized sweater and my combat boots from my new favorite shoe designer, Jennifer Le. Pulling my hair back from my face with a headband from Chanel, I grabbed the matching bag and threw my mink coat over my shoulders.

Not in a driving mood, I ordered a car service to chauffeur me around for the day. When the black Tesla pulled up, the driver got out to open the door for me. I was supposed to go into Tantra later tonight for work, but after Truth's visit, I thought it would be best to stay out the way. I was sure I wouldn't be missed. Amina could hold it down as interim manager like she'd been doing.

"I need to stop by Chase bank first if you don't mind, sir," I said to the driver.

"Sure, no problem."

Night had fallen, and the bank was set to close soon, so it wasn't too packed inside. I made it to the teller with a big, bright smile on my face. Money did that for me all the time. Just the thought of it passing through my fingers made my pussy wet.

"Hi, how can I help you?" the young girl asked with a smile as big as mine that matched her chipper tone.

"Hi, love. I'd like to make a withdrawal from my checking account." I handed her a withdrawal slip from my purse that was pre-filled with the amount I wanted.

"Okay, we're withdrawing five thousand dollars today. And how would you like the money to be dispersed?"

"One-hundred-dollar bills only please."

She nodded and got to typing on the computer. I waited patiently, checking messages in my phone, while she got everything together.

"Oh," I heard her say, causing my head to shoot up.

"Oh? I don't do well with ohs, sweetie. What's going on?" My body went from relaxed to real tense in a matter of seconds.

The girl's face turned a shade of red before she got it together to speak. "Umm, Ms. Rose, this account, along with your savings account, has been closed."

I put my ear closer to the glass to make sure I heard her right. "Umm, come again."

"Uhhhh, your accounts... Both of them have been closed." She repeated what she stated the first time, and I lost it.

"I don't know what kinda games y'all playing up in here, but you should know I'm not the one to be played with. So, what I suggest you do is run along and get your supervisor before I lose my shit in here today!" Just that fast, my looney ass went from sweet to sour.

Without thinking twice, she scurried away to do as I demanded. A line started to form behind me, and I was sure people were looking at me like I was crazy, but I didn't give not one fuck. I was gon' act a special kind of crazy if I didn't get the answers I wanted.

"Ms. Rose?" a white woman dressed in a skirt suit and pixie haircut called out to me. I assumed she was the supervisor.

"That's me. Tell me what the hell is going on with my accounts."

"I'll be glad to go over that with you, Ms. Rose. Do you mind stepping into my office?"

Backing away from the glass, I waited for her to come from behind the counter. "Lead the way." I walked behind her, fuming, as she guided me. The fact that I even had to go through this bullshit had me on a thousand. Taking a seat in front of her desk, I did my best to calm myself down.

"Look, Ms…" I paused, waiting for her to give me her name.

"Gulliard."

"Ms. Gulliard, that account has over $20,000 in it. So, come on and just tell me it was y'all's mistake so I can go about my day."

"Ms. Rose, I've taken a moment to look over this, and it looks like the accounts were closed at the request of the account holder."

"Okay, maybe we're not on the same page, or my words are not reaching your ears. I am the account holder! I didn't request for shit to be closed!" By now, I was seething, and I knew no one other than Truth could have done this bullshit. Had he been in front of me right now, I would've gouged his eyes out. "So, you mean to tell me anyone from off the street can come waltz in here and close an account that's in my name? Is that what you're telling me?"

"No, not at all, Ms. Rose. With Mr. Porter being the primary account holder, only he has the power to close the account." She slid a piece of paper in front of me and sat back.

I snatched up the paper and held it up to my face. Sure enough, my name was set up as an authorized user only. Slamming it back down, I pushed the chair out to stand.

"You'll be hearing from my lawyer!" I belted out, making sure to slam the door behind myself.

I knew damn well I wasn't contacting a lawyer because there wasn't shit I could do. Back outside, I didn't even wait for the driver to open the car door for me before I snatched it open myself. Truth had really outdone himself this time. It was one thing to break up with me, but this was a ho ass move. And yes, I may have been wrong about some shit —_well, a lot —_but again, he pushed me here. This shit wasn't cool, and he was gonna bring out the worst in me. I knew things, and if I had to use what I knew as leverage to get my money, I would.

21

TRUTH

If I wasn't so pissed off, I would've fell out laughing at Nyema's facial expression as she stormed out of the bank. She was heated, and I had accomplished my goal. I knew that closing her accounts would fuck her head up. Technically, the accounts were mine. I just let her think she had control of them. Sitting in her living room, listening to her spew different lies, I wanted nothing more than to yoke her ass up. I knew my mother would haunt my dreams if I laid my hands on a woman though.

As soon as her car pulled off, I made my way to Amiko's crib. It wasn't in my character to just pop up unannounced, but for some reason, I felt like I needed to see her. It didn't take long before I pulled up in front of her building. Picking up my phone, I dialed her number. She answered quickly, putting a smile on my face.

"**Hey, boss,**" she spoke, and I could tell she was grinning.

"**Hey, Madam.**"

"**Uhn uhn, don't call me that. It don't sound right when you say it.**"

"**And it don't sound right when you call me boss, so let's stick to what we know.**"

She giggled. "**That's fair.**"

"**Cool. What you up to?**" I tried to make small talk before mentioning I was outside.

"**Nothing much. Just watching you trying to blend in with the other cars on the street. It's not every day that you see a matte black Porsche 911 coming down my block.**"

I looked up to see her standing at her window, waving her hand. "**So, you're a people watcher?**"

"**No, not really. I just happened to walk by the window and peeked out. Park and come up. I know you didn't come by just to talk to me over the phone.**"

I really wanted her to come downstairs. Judging by the way these folks had their cars parked, my car was bound to be fucked up.

"**Ain't nobody gon' hit your precious car, Truth,**" she said, reading my mind.

I laughed and let her know I'd be up in a second. A text came through with her apartment number, and as luck would have it, someone pulled out of the spot across the street from the building. Parking, I put my phone on vibrate and entered the building. Stepping off the elevator, she stood at the door with her arms folded and a smile. Dressed comfortably in a pair of oversized sweats and t-shirt with a picture of Chris Brown on it, I nodded my approval of her chill attire.

"Come in before you let the hawk all in my apartment." Pulling me by my coat once I was close, she closed the door behind me.

"Who the hell is the hawk?" I asked, laughing.

"The cold, fool." She laughed along with me while walking farther into the house. Following her lead into the living room, we sat on the couch. It was comfortable and looked inexpensive. I was digging her style though. Leaning my head back, I closed my eyes and sighed. "That bad, huh?"

"You don't even know the half. Shit is real crazy right now."

"Well, I'm a good listener. I'll even let you talk." I opened my eyes and looked over at her as she giggled. "You know those people who say they're good listeners but somehow end up making the conversation about themselves. I'm not one of those people, so go 'head and lay it on me."

I smirked and leaned back, closing my eyes again. This time, it was because I was laying my burdens on her, and I wasn't used to doing that. I was used to being the one people brought their issues to. "I found some snakes in my grass today, and it has me questioning my judgement. I've always been able to spot bullshit from a mile away and weed out the real from the fakes. Now, I don't know." I was a confident man and damn good at what I did. This shit with Nyema and Boss had me twisted. My eyes opened when I felt Miko put her hand in mine.

"Don't ever question your judgement over someone else's disloyalty. Sometimes you don't know who's bad until they actually show themselves as such. You're a solid dude, and I know that just from being around you in a short amount of time."

"I appreciate that, Miko. You're not too bad yourself."

She blushed, and I reached up and ran my hand down her cheek. Her skin was smooth, and her lips made my dick hard. Her humbleness turned me on. Having been around her the last few weeks, I'd seen a change in her that she may not have picked up on yet. The change was subtle but there. Amiko was stepping into that boss bitch that may have been lying dormant in her for some time.

I watched as she closed her eyes and sucked in a breath when my hand went from her cheek to her neck. I wanted to explore her in the worst way.

"Truth," she whispered my name while sensually kissing the palm of my hand. The small gesture made the hairs on my arms stand up.

"What are you afraid of?" I questioned, moving closer and kissing the nape of her neck.

"The unknown," she answered. Seeing that she wasn't stopping me from going further, I pulled her by her waist and onto my lap.

Locking eyes with her, I tenderly caressed her back. "I want to assure you that there's no fear needed for the unknown between us. It might seem unexpected, but having watched you from afar as we've worked together, I appreciate what I see. And I want to delve into these feelings that have emerged."

Her eyes said yes, but no words were spoken. Instead, she leaned in and kissed my lips. Rubbing her booty while we explored each other's mouths, I felt my dick brick up more. Pulling back, I lifted her shirt over her head, and she was bra less. My mouth watered at the sight of her erect nipples. Her areoles were a perfect shade of brown.

"Promise me this won't change our business relationship." Her eyes held a longing that matched the fire in mine.

"You are my business." I circled her nipple with my tongue, causing a gasp to escape her lips. The other hardened as I used my free hand to toy with it. "Miko, can I taste you?"

Her eyes were so low that it looked like she was high. She bit down on her bottom lip and nodded. Lifting her up, I helped her out her sweats, and again, she had nothing on underneath. I placed kisses along her waistline and licked the outline of the butterfly tattoo that sat just above her pussy. I wanted to take my time and get to know every crevice of her body. Switching places, I made her lay down on the couch. Spreading her legs, I slid two fingers down her slit just to see how wet she was. The way her pussy was dripping, I could tell she was ready for whatever.

Latching onto her clit, I slurped it into my mouth, making her thrust her hips upward. I licked all over that pretty pussy as she threw it in my face. The scent of coconut coming from her body was intoxicating.

"Shit, Truth," she moaned while thrashing her head from side to side.

"Mmmm, this pussy good, Ma. You been holding out on a nigga? You a squirter?"

"Uhhh, I don't knowwwww."

I didn't need her to know. I was gonna find out in the next few minutes. Sliding two fingers back in her pussy, I used my thumb to apply pressure to her asshole.

"Oohh, wait, shit, I'm cummin'."

I kept the pressure the same until she burst. With a devilish smile, I drained her of all her good juices. Once she was done, I gave her pussy a wet kiss. Her chest heaved up and down as she came down from her orgasm.

"If that's what the head is giving, you can keep the dick. You won't have me sitting outside your house at night."

I cracked up laughing as she stood to her feet, picking up her sweats and disappearing to the back of the apartment. Feeling my phone vibrate in my pocket, I retrieved it, and there was a text from Nyema on the screen. Before reading the message, I went into the text settings and turned on my read receipts. To fuck with her, I wanted her to know that I had seen her message. I was getting a kick out of Nyema, and I hadn't done half the shit I planned to do to fuck her up for stealing from me.

Nyema: That's some bitch ass shit you pulled at the bank. Closing my accounts, really, Truth? All that money you're sitting on, and you're worried about the measly couple thousand in my account. It's cool though because remember, I was a go getter before I met you. I'll bounce back. You believe that, bastard!

The message was filled with a lot of hostility, which only made me chuckle. If Nyema knew like I knew, she had better get to poppin' that pussy to make that money back. A few moments later, Miko reappeared in a different outfit than what she had on earlier. Instead of sitting in her original seat, she sat on the loveseat across from me.

"Why you so far?" I asked, fucking with her.

"I'm comfortable here. At the moment, I'm too tempted to throw this pussy on you, and right now is not the time."

"Says who?"

"Says our new business venture. After that performance, I think it's best we slow it down."

"No problem. I can respect that. Just know that if you ever have an itch that needs to be scratched..." I paused and licked my lips, still tasting her before continuing, "I got you." I watched as she crossed and uncrossed her legs. I wasn't trippin' behind no pussy she was gonna gladly give me when she was ready.

"Anyway, what you have planned for the rest of the day?"

"Damn, you kicking me out already after I made that pussy speak in tongues?"

"Shut up." She threw a pillow at me, and I caught it in my hand. "On a serious note though, what do you think about me setting up a meeting with the Elites' main clients?"

My eyebrows rose, trying to figure out why she would want to call such a meeting. "I can tell you more about what I think once you give me more insight. What direction are you trying to go in?"

She got up and reclaimed the seat next to me. "Here's the thing. I've had individual conversations with the Elites regarding their client list and those that have become regulars. I haven't been cemented in my position more than two weeks, but I know that we're not trying to make love connections. Our objective is to get the bag, correct?" I nodded in agreement while smiling inwardly at the way she went about breaking the organization down to a science. "Okay, so there's no room for love. I've been researching, and I want to start an app where the ladies can go on virtual dates and build their clientele outside of the US."

"I put you in position for a reason. I like the idea, and I can see how it'll be lucrative. I'll play the background, but know I'll be close by in case shit goes left."

"You got it. Now get outta here before I change my mind about putting this snapper on you. Just sitting next to you got my little hot ass in my feelings." I moved toward her to accept the challenge, and she held her hand up to my chest to stop me. Giggling, her scary ass backed away from me. "I'm just playing."

"Aight, well, gimmie kiss at least." Leaning forward, she tapped my lips. That wasn't enough for me, so I sucked her bottom lip into mine, tongue kissing the shit outta her. Tapping her thigh, I nodded toward the door. "Come walk me out and lock up."

As I made it to the door and went to open it, she stopped me. "I wanna explore this feeling too, but right now is not the time. I need to stay focused in order to accomplish what I've set out to do with the Elites."

"Ain't no rush, Miko. We got a lifetime ahead of us, Ma. I'm here whenever you're ready, Madam Elite." I winked and walked out. Miko was already mine. I could show her better than I could tell her.

22

AMIKO

I swayed my hips in the mirror while getting dressed for my meeting. Summer Walker's lyrics made me think about Truth. He was such a vibe and in a class of his own. I loved the way he made me feel when I was in his presence. It was also a feeling I knew I couldn't succumb to. Not at the moment at least.

I meant what I said about exploring what I was feeling —when the time was right. We had already established that what he had with Nyema was a done deal. For now, I had plans to keep the Elite house running smoothly and more money coming in. As I checked myself out in the mirror, I had to admit I looked damn good. The black slacks I had on held me hostage at the hips and flared at the bottom, covering my Casadei pumps. While working at Tantra, I had picked up a slight shopping habit that included a lot of pricey things. And it went well with my boss bitch aesthetic.

Buttoning my black silk shirt, I tucked it in my pants. From head to toe, I gave THAT BITCH. Removing my scarf, I made sure not to disrupt the bun that sat on the top of my head. The hawk was no joke in December, and I didn't want to have to keep moving my hair from my face, hence the bun that made me look every bit of my Japanese heritage. Using my phone, I sent a text to Ralph, letting him know I was ready. I'd taken the time to get to know my driver, and he was cool as hell. We never rode in silence because he always had me cracking up, laughing. Whether he was talking about his kids or his wife, I always got a kick out of his stories.

Fully dressed and equipped with everything I would need for my meeting, I headed downstairs. "Hey, old man," I joked, walking toward the open car door.

"Ain't nothing old about me. I'm seasoned, woman." He winked and closed the door behind me.

At forty-seven, Ralph was a charmer for sure. Taking out my iPad, I opened it to skim over the profiles of the five men I'd be meeting with — Judge Jake Sims, Judge Christian Kimes, Mayor Delonte Ellis, Senator Ronald Bell, and Kenneth Combs. These men all had their very own special Elite that they catered to often. All of the men were well known too, all with the exception of Kenneth Combs. He was a mystery man with a bigger bag than the government officials.

I was most intrigued by his relationship with Jomy. While the others met with Elites twice a week at most and for occasional events, Kenneth and Jomy got together daily, excluding Sundays. According to the ledger, he dropped five thousand for the day and ten for overnight stays with no problem. If that wasn't love or something along the lines of it brewing, then call me crazy.

"I'll be here for about an hour, Ralph, two tops," I announced as we pulled up in front of the Italian restaurant Truth suggested.

I arrived a few minutes earlier than the time I had given so that I could have my thoughts together. Truth had gotten the place closed for the duration of the meeting. It was boss shit like that that made me want to drop to my knees and suck him up until my jaw cramped up.

"I'll be right here reading my paper, arguing with Stephanie about what we're having for dinner and whose turn it is to cook it." He parked and got out to open my door while I laughed.

"You do know the saying, *happy wife happy life*, right?"

"Darling, I've been married twenty-six years, and that saying didn't mean shit then and don't mean shit now."

The straight look on his face let me know he was so serious. He may have been onto something though. Twenty-six years married when the relationships these days couldn't last the duration of a two-hour movie was definitely a blessing. Patting his shoulder, I grabbed my bag and stepped out of the car.

As always, the streets of Manhattan were buzzing with people all in a hurry to get somewhere. Even the people who really had nowhere to go were on the move. I felt my phone vibrate just as I walked down the steps to go inside the restaurant. I knew it was Truth because I felt my body heat up. After his performance yesterday, my senses when it came to him were even more heightened.

Truth: My man, Brock, is inside waiting for you. The guys will be entering from the back entrance for obvious reasons. Brock is there to watch your back. He has strict instructions to set anyone straight that disrespects you or seems like they're not on board with your vision. Have a good meeting, love.

Me: That was very thoughtful of you. How'd you know I'd be here early?

Truth: You learned from the best (wink).

I blushed and put my phone away. He sure had a way with words. Gathering myself, I kept on stepping, and before my heel could touch the last step, the door was opened for me. A muscular man with a scowl was on the other side of it. His gazed started from my feet, and when it landed on my face, his scowl turned into a slight smile.

"Hello, Madam Elite."

"Brock?"

"That's right. It's a pleasure to meet you." He held his hand out for me to shake, and I accepted it. "Right this way. Truth had everything set up for you."

I took in his attire as I followed behind him into a private dining area. He had on a pair of brown slacks and a brown turtleneck that was halfway rolled up, exposing his detailed tattoos. It reminded me so much of Truth's laidback style. I could appreciate the swag. There was a long table with three chairs on either side of it and a chair directly at the head, which, of course, was for me. I took off my coat, and Brock stood at the side of me with his hand out to take it. As I went to take my iPad out, there was a knock at the back door. I looked over at him, and he gave me a nod that let me know that the men had arrived. I closed my eyes and took a deep breath while rolling my neck in a circle.

"You ready?"

"Always," I said with confidence.

He smirked and nodded again. "Yeah, Truth knew what he was doing."

I didn't know what he meant by that, but it seemed like a compliment. He went to the door and opened it, shaking hands with the men as they filed in with all of their testosterone in tow. What I enjoyed was that the men in attendance were Black. It was something about a Black man in power that was bomb as fuck. Brock stopped the last man and said something in his ear. The guy smirked before pulling out a gun and handing it over to him. I swore my heart stopped for all of five seconds, but I didn't show it.

Once everyone was seated, I spoke. "Thank you for coming out to meet with me today. I'm sure you all have pretty busy schedules so know that I appreciate your presence. I recognize some faces from the gala, but I would like to reintroduce myself for those not familiar. My name is Amiko, but to you, I'm Madam Elite, the new head of the Elite house. Now, I know that you gentlemen are not used to a woman being involved in the day-to-day dealings, at least not in the capacity in which I will be. It's very important for you to get with the new program." I checked to see if there were any disgruntled facial expressions or any objections. Seeing none, I continued. "The reason I called this meeting was to let you know that the availability of your special friend will be changing within the next few weeks. Meaning, there are going to be in-house changes to the Elites' schedules."

"What does that mean for us? I mean, my two days a week schedule I have set with Nicole works just fine for me," Judge Kimes pointed out from where he sat to my left.

"And how is that working for Mrs. Kimes?" I rebutted. "How does she feel when you go on your mini excursions that don't include her or your two children?"

He gave me a blank stare, and I knew I had caught his attention. I had done my research on each man, and the only one who didn't have a significant other was Kenneth. All of the political figures, however, had wives or a hidden fiancée. Although their dealings with the Elites were confidential and there were official ADAs signed and sealed, my first thing was to ensure the security of the ladies. There was nothing like a woman scorned, but a woman of a certain stature was worse than anything.

"Go ahead." He nodded for me to continue talking.

"With your political status, you are being watched, and quite frankly, you've become predictable as far as your frequent meetups with your special friends. My job is to ensure that the Elites are never in the line of fire. Just as it is the job of those who help you keep your affairs in order. What we'll do going forward is schedule meetups on these." I handed them each a new iPhone 15 from my bag. "These are the phones you'll now need to use as your only point of contact. The number of your Elite is pre-programmed as well as mine. Dates will still be scheduled as usual, but the place will be picked by the Elite. Any questions?"

"Excuse me, Ms. Madam Elite." I turned to my right just as Kenneth spoke. "This whole change shouldn't even apply to me, seeing as I'm not tied down to anyone, unless you consider money a person." He smirked, and I could see what kept Jomy out on overnight stays. The man was a looker for sure.

"I'm aware, Mr. Combs, and that's what I'm leery about. Out of everyone here, you seem to have developed an exceptionally close relationship with Jomy."

"I have. She's like my best friend, and unlike these dudes, in the business I'm in, you don't get a lot of them. If you do, they don't stay around for long, if you know what I mean." I was picking up what he was putting down, but that was a conversation for a different time.

"We can talk outside of this meeting if you'd like."

By his response, I knew that my first mind was right. He was in love with Jomy, and I would have a talk with her about it. I mean, who was I to stand in the way of that? By the time the meeting ended, I felt like we were all on the same page as the guys filed out.

"You sure this was your first meeting?" Brock asked as he helped me into my coat.

"Yep. How did I do?"

"You're the female Truth in my eyes."

I smiled and so did he. "Now that's a compliment." He walked me out to the car where Ralph was waiting for me with roses. "Awww, Ralph, this is so nice. I don't sleep with married men though."

He chuckled. "Good because Stephanie would kill me and you both. These are from Truth."

This man was just too good to be true. I said my goodbyes to Brock and got in the car, clutching my roses. There was a note attached to it.

I already know you did a great job, Ma, and I'm proud of you. You wear the boss role well. Hit me once you're settled in at home.

Yeah, I did my thing. Now, following through was the next step.

23

MING

I threw my phone back on my bed after reading the fifth text from Karter today. He had been trying to see Case since he showed up in front of my door days ago. I called bullshit because he wasn't checking for my son this much when he was locked up. He had me confused with Tiara's silly ass if he thought he was gonna try and sneak off and play family with my damn child.

I didn't know what Karter had done to get released early, but I was not feeling him being home at all. Another person I hadn't been feeling was Chance. His ass hadn't bothered to reach out to me. I'd poured my heart out in the text message I sent him. He responded that he understood, but it sure as hell didn't feel like it. I missed him something terrible, and I had been a mean ass grouch lately because of it. It didn't help at all that he had fucked my head up with the sex we had in the car. I could only imagine what damage he could do to a bed.

"Sistaaaaa," Miko sang my name while entering my room. I unglued my eyes from the TV and looked over at her.

"You're mighty happy. Wassup?" I took in her new glow and loved what I saw. Happy looked good on my big sis.

"Nothing, I'm just having a good day. Why you sitting in here with ya face all long and what not?" I handed her my phone and stared straight ahead. I knew her response was gonna be anything but positive.

"Hmph," was all I got before she handed the phone back to me.

"Yeah, that sounds about right. I still can't believe he's out. He's been blowing my phone up so much I had to put it on DND. I think I'ma just have him meet me somewhere, so he can see Case."

"Hmph."

"Oh, uhn uhn. You not about to hmph me to death. What else do you think I should do?"

"I mean, I just don't like him, and you know that. Shit, he knows that. I understand too that he needs to be a father to his child and needs to be given the opportunity to do so. Ughh, you don't know how much it pained me just to say that."

I giggled at her smacking her lips like she had a bad taste in her mouth. "Oh, trust me, I know. Anyway, how's everything been going with Truth ever since he ate you like the last supper?" Sucking her teeth, she shoved me playfully. "Hey, your words, not mine."

"Everything is good except for the fact that I haven't seen much of him. We communicate daily though. It just would be nice to see his face. Ever since this whole thing with his uncle went down, he's been trying to move things around to get that taken care of."

"What happened?" I was clueless being that I hadn't spoken to Chance.

"Girl, his uncle was on some undercover snake shit and was stealing from them."

"You lyin'!"

"Nah, real shit. Both he and Chance have been on the hunt for him. Wait, you still haven't spoken to Chance?"

Sadly, I shook my head no. I wanted to be selfish and say to hell with him, but I knew he was probably not in the best of spirits right now. Chance was big on the little family he had, and loyalty was everything.

"No, I haven't. I was giving him space and figured he'd just come around." I shrugged my shoulders like it was no big deal, knowing damn well I was checking my phone every few minutes to see if I had missed a text or call from him.

"Aww, pooh, that's why you got the long face. Sis, get dressed and go to his house."

I swung the covers off me to get up. "Nah, I'm good on that. When he's ready, he'll reach out. Right now, I'm gonna hit Karter back up and tell him to meet me at the park or something so that he can hang out with Case." My pride was a motherfucka, and I had already put myself out there when I reached out to him the first time.

"Okay, well, let me know if you need me to do anything. I'm gonna be headed out soon. I have some stuff to do over at the Elite house."

"Alright, love you."

"Love you too, sister."

I watched her walk out and took a deep breath before responding back to Karter's last text. I let him know that he could meet me at the park which wasn't too far from my house. It was chilly outside, so I didn't plan on having Case out for long. He texted back that he'd be there in an hour. Dragging myself out of the bed, I went into Case's room to find him stretched out at the foot of his bed, watching cartoons.

"Hey, handsome guy. You wanna go to the park?"

He jumped up excitedly, rushing over to me. "Yesss!"

Smiling at his excitement, I pulled out a quick outfit for him to wear. After getting him situated, I went to do the same for myself. While getting ready, my phone went off, and when I looked at the caller ID, I froze. Chance's name flashed across the screen. My heart palpitated as a wave of nervousness washed over me. Figuring this would be my only chance to speak to him, I dove on the bed and answered before the ringing stopped.

"**Hey,**" I spoke nonchalantly.

"**Wassup, beautiful? What you up to?**" His response was so regular, and that pissed me off.

"**Nothing.**"

"**I miss you.**"

Unlike me, he was straightforward with his feelings. That was another thing that I loved about him. I mean, liked. Another thing I liked about him. I wanted to act tough, like I didn't miss him, but I couldn't.

"**I miss you too. I heard about what's going on with your uncle. How are you dealing with that?**"

"**Shit, I'm still trying to figure that out myself. What I do know is that nigga ain't no kin to me, and when I catch up with him, shit gon' get real ugly. Enough about that though. Just thinking 'bout that situation gets me hype. How's my young bull?**"

My face lit up when he asked about Case.

"**He's good. He's been asking about you a lot. I'm about to take him to the park for a little bit.**"

"**Oh, yeah? You could've hit me up and told me he was looking for me. I would've come by to hang with him. You know that's my lil' man.**"

"**Umm, I've been looking for you too,**" I said in a low voice.

"**I know.**" Here he go with this cocky shit. "**Let me come scoop y'all and we can go out to lunch.**"

I almost said yes, immediately forgetting about Karter.

"**Hey, before we make that plan, I gotta tell you something.**" I paused, not really wanting to tell him Karter was home in fear of his response. "**Case's dad is home. He was in front of my building when I came home a couple nights ago. He's been trying to meet up to spend time with Case, and today, I agreed. We're meeting up at the park in a little bit.**"

"**Oh, that's cool. Just hit me up when you're done. I still wanna see y'all.**"

"**You sure?**"

He chuckled. "**Yeah, Ma. You think I wouldn't want to see you because your baby father home? That don't change nothing for me as long as it don't change nothing for you.**"

Before I could respond, Case came in, fully dressed, with his coat in his hands.

"I'm ready, Mommy."

"**Yo, put me on speaker real quick,**" Chance requested, and I did. "**What's good, youngin'?**"

"**Chance!**" Case yelled out while practically snatching the phone out my hands.

I shook my head as they spoke while I continued to get dressed. I heard Chance say to call him when we were done at the park and disconnected the call once I agreed.

"Alright, baby boy, let me help you with your coat, and then we'll head out."

I texted Karter again, letting him know we were on our way to the park, to which he confirmed he wasn't too far away. It felt good to know that Chance wasn't insecure about Karter being home. It felt even better to hear his voice. I couldn't wait to see him later and kiss those full lips of his. Just thinking about him made me shiver a little.

"Mommy, I'm going on the swing."

"Okay, baby, I'm going to watch you from here."

I sat on the bench and watched him struggle to get in the swing. I didn't bother getting up because, lately, he had been telling me he was a big boy, so I would let him figure it out. After a minute of trying, he had managed to make it work and gave me a thumbs up like he knew that I was seconds away from coming to his aid. The park was unusually scarce for it to be a Saturday, but that was fine with me. The less kids I had to worry about monitoring when my child was around the better.

"Wassup, Ming?"

I rolled my eyes hard at the sound of Karter's voice. I knew I was going to be able to be an adult about this whole situation, but I didn't know how I was gonna hide my disdain for Karter. Turning around to see him walking with a little girl by his side, I was steaming when I saw Tiara bringing up the rear. What really had me through with the whole look was the fact that Tiara and her daughter had on fur coats. Who the fuck brought their child to the park in a damn fur coat?

I wanted so bad to be disrespectful, but I was a parent before anything, and I wasn't going to show my natural Black ass in front of their daughter. Up close, I had to admit that the little girl was beautiful. She had a wide smile like she should have been on a Toys "R" Us commercial. It was so infectious that before I knew it, I was smiling back at her. However, mine quickly dropped to a frown when Tiara linked her arm in Karter's. He looked uncomfortable, but I wasn't stunting either one of them. I planned to address this fake family meet up at a later time.

"Case, baby, come here real quick please."

He ran over to me at full speed. "Did you see me, Mommy? I pushed myself on the swing."

"Yeah, baby. I saw you, big man."

"You was out there doing that shit, man," Karter added, making my head whip in his direction.

"Excuse me? Watch your language around my son please," I snapped.

"My bad, my bad."

"Hey, handsome," Tiara spoke, and I could just envision my fist colliding with her eye. She was clearly trying to get a reaction out of me. Case waved at her, and this was one of the times I wished that I hadn't taught my son manners.

"Case, this is your dad, Karter." I pointed at Karter, who had a smile on his face.

"And this is your sister, Kacey," Tiara butted in, and I just about blew a gasket.

She was really playing with me. My eyes bore into Karter, and when he said nothing, I knew I had to check this ho.

"Case, why don't you take Kacey over to the slide and play? Mommy's gonna be right here watching you. I need to talk to your dad real quick."

He hadn't even acknowledged Karter but seemed happy when he took Kacey's hand in his. Once they were out of earshot, I sidestepped Karter and got all up in Tiara's space.

"You really fucking trying me out here like you don't know who the fuck I am. You know I will lay yo' ass out right in this park, and this nigga right here would have to pick you up off the ground. I don't even know why his simple ass brought you here in the first place.

Keep pushing your luck if you want to, and I'ma wear yo ass out in this park."

"What you not about to do is think you about to sit here and punk me, Ming. You and I both know that I ain't pussy."

"Yeah, you can say what you want, but you heard what the fuck I said. And I know your track record, but you just remember mine."

"Ay, come on. All that is unnecessary. We came here in peace, Ming." Karter's interjection only further infuriated me.

"You call showing up here with her and her daughter peace? You're even dumber than you look right now," I scoffed. "Shut up talkin' to me."

"Look, it was the only way I could ensure that he was able to meet his sister. If I left it up to your petty ass, he would never see her. I'm just here for my son, man. That's it."

"You done? Because I'm not buying nothing that your sneaky ass is selling. I'll be in this park for thirty minutes tops, so you go 'head and enjoy."

Leaving the two of them to stare at each other, I reclaimed my seat on a bench away from Tiara while Karter walked over to where the kids were. I was boiling and needed to talk to someone that could calm me down. Pulling my phone from my coat pocket, I dialed Chance's number.

He picked up on the first ring. **"How's it going?"** was the first thing he asked.

"I'ma 'bout to find my ass locked up; that's how it's going. Can you believe this bastard had the nerve to bring Tiara and her daughter here without even giving me a warning? What type of clown ass shit is that?"

"You feel uncomfortable?"

"Did you hear anything I just said? Because if you did, then that can't be your response." Chance was about to make me hang up on his ass since he was talking stupid right now.

"I heard exactly what you said, and my question is still the same. Do you feel uncomfortable?"

"I feel like I'm being betrayed all over again. Like they're throwing in my face that they have a child together. I could give a

fuck about the two of them; it's the disloyalty that's getting me." I blinked back tears of frustration.

"That's all I needed to know. Drop yo' location. I'll see you in a minute."

The call disconnected, and I moved the phone from my ear to drop my location as he requested. I didn't know what to expect next, but our call didn't do anything but leave me feeling stuck when I called him to put me in better spirits. I looked over to where Tiara was, and she was so busy in her phone that I knew she didn't come to actually watch her daughter play. Messy ass bitch.

I watched as Karter chased the kids around the slide, and they were having a ball. I had never seen this side of him. It was cute and all, but not cute enough to make me wanna fuck with him. Glancing down at my phone to check the time that had elapsed, a message came through from Chance.

Chance: Yo man here, baby.

My head shot up in time to see him stepping out of his Bentley truck. Tiara must've felt his presence as well because she craned her neck in the same direction. I stood and crossed my arms on my chest, watching him stroll into the park like he owned it. I could tell Tiara wanted so bad to say something, but she and I knew that Karter's mean streak was something serious. He was possessive about his women, and he would be on her ass like white on rice if she even waved hi to Chance. He bypassed her, beelining straight to me. Scooping me up in a bear hug, he placed kisses on my neck, making me squeal.

"Damn, I knew I missed you before I got here, but now being in front of you is something different."

"I hope that's a good thing."

"It's a damn good thing, shorty." Without warning, he planted a wet kiss on my lips, and I laughed. "Them shits is juicy as hell. Where lil' man at?" I was so caught up in the kiss that I drew a blank for a second but recovered quickly.

"He's over there by the slide." He grabbed my hand, and we walked over to where Case was still running around. I looked back at Tiara, and I could've sworn I saw steam coming from her head. Salty ass ho.

"Case, look who's here." I knew it was petty of me, but since Karter and Tiara wanted to tit, I was tat out this bitch.

Once Case realized Chance was present, he ran full speed ahead into him.

"Wassup, youngin'?" Chance picked him up, tossing him in the air before placing him back down on his feet. "Hey, man, I'm Chance," he said to Karter, who looked him up and down like he wanted beef.

"Who dis nigga, Ming?" Karter questioned disrespectfully.

"My name is Chance. I just introduced myself on a peaceful type vibe."

I knew I was going to have to step in before things went left.

"This is my man. And he told you his name, so out of respect, address him as such. Again, your language around my child."

"It's cool, baby. He heard me, and you ain't gotta speak on my behalf." Grabbing me by my waist, he pulled me back into him.

Case stood beside me, looking up at Karter.

"Why the fuck he so comfortable tossing my son in the air and shit?"

"Oh, no. See, let me go because you gon' make me show out in this park. Come on, Case." Taking Case's hand in mine, I went to walk off.

"Gimmie a second, bae," Chance said before addressing Karter. "We know each other? 'Cause you seem like you got a lot of animosity. Like you wanna do something."

"What you tryna do, my nigga?" Karter wasn't backing down, and I knew it was about to get ugly.

"Do your homework on me, Karter Stone, because I sure did mine on you. I value family, mine above all else. And since I consider your son family, I'ma act accordingly and let you have today. You might wanna thank youngin' cause niggas like you get put on t-shirts fuckin' wit killas like me. Enjoy the park, Karter."

Chance grabbed my hand, picked Case up, and we walked to the exit. I knew Karter was pissed, and going forward, he would be on bullshit.

24

CHANCE

I GRIPPED THE STEERING WHEEL WITH ONE HAND AND HELD ONTO Ming's hand with the other as we drove away from the park. I was still laughing at the exchange between me and her baby daddy. I did my homework on any new person I came in contact with, especially a nigga that just came out the bing. From my connections up top, I found out that Karter was a grimy nigga who started out as a stick-up kid. Eventually, he graduated to moving a little dope. It was nothing big enough for his name to ring bells, maybe a little chime. He was also known for putting in work in the field. Which was where the nigga could meet me with all that tough guy shit he was poppin'.

I glanced over to find Ming gnawing at her lip, and her leg wouldn't stop shaking. "You gotta pee, bae?" I joked, trying to lighten the mood. She had been silent since we pulled off.

"No. I'm trying to calm myself down. I'm sorry about what happened back there. Had I known Karter was going to be a dickhead, I would've never agreed to meet up with him." She looked back at Case when she spoke to make sure he wasn't listening. He was in his own world, watching *Spiderman* on the TV that was set up in the headrest.

"You don't have to be sorry that your baby daddy is a clown, Ma.

You're not a reflection of him. Don't sweat the small shit. How do you think Case did with him today?"

"Okay, I guess. This was his first time meeting him, so he didn't have much of a reaction. He was excited to play with Kacey though."

"That's good. Youngin' back there deserves a father. He's a dope ass kid. Shit, he acts like one of my homies." We both got a good laugh at that statement. Case was one of those kids that you didn't mind watching because he would do his own thing and didn't get into shit. "Y'all wanna go to my crib, and I can hook us up some burgers and fries?"

"I want a cheeseburger!" Case shouted from the backseat.

"I don't want burgers and fries though." Ming pouted and crossed her arms.

"We'll pick you up a steak then, Mama. I gotta stop by the supermarket anyway." That made her smile, and I chuckled. She was getting her way already. I had plans on spoiling this woman and her son for as long as she let me.

Arriving at Whole Foods, Case got out with me, and Ming waited in the car.

"You like turkey burgers or beef burgers, little man?" I asked while picking up a small basket.

"Iono." He shrugged his shoulders. "I just like burgers."

I cracked up at his facial expression. I had to constantly remind myself that he was only four.

"Aight, beef it is. You can get whatever else you want. Like snacks and shit." He put his hand to his mouth and smirked. I turned to act like I was looking for something so that he wouldn't catch on to the fact that I had cursed.

"I heard you." He laughed, and I nudged him.

"Oh, yeah? You know snitches get stitches, right?" I put the basket that I was holding on the floor and lifted him up to tickle him. He fell out in a fit of laughter. I just knew the white people were staring at us, shaking their heads.

"Alright, alright. I won't tell." He squirmed to get down, and I released him.

He had to learn the no snitching code early. For that, I let him load the basket with whatever he wanted. I knew he thought he was getting over with loading a bunch of candy into the cart. Little did he know, I was on to his ass. One hundred dollars later, we were walking out of Whole Foods with two bags each. I had his candy bag stashed in the inside of my coat pocket, so Ming wouldn't call him out.

"My bad, bae. It was a little packed in there," I said, tryna cover for me and Case. I helped him in the backseat and quickly picked up on her silence. I figured she may have had an attitude because we took so long.

"Mommy, I'm gonna help Chance cook."

"That's nice, baby. Sit back and put your seatbelt on," she responded, her voice cracking, putting me on high alert.

I got in the driver's seat, and she handed me a folded piece of paper. Unfolding it, the message written had me heated. *I'll be seeing you soon, nephew. Love, your favorite uncle, Boss.* The only thing I could think about was breaking this nigga's neck. Ming didn't even make eye contact with me. She did let me hold her hand though.

It ain't no telling what his punk ass said when he gave her the note. Not wanting to ask while Case was around, I drove off. I was so pissed off that I wasn't even mindful of Ming and Case when I swerved into my parking spot and hopped out the car. Doubling back, I opened Ming's door and helped her out.

"My bad, Ma."

"It's cool. C'mon, Case." She held his hand while I grabbed the bags from the trunk.

Ming had never been to my crib, so she stood off to the side while I gathered everything. We took the elevator to the penthouse floor where the doors opened to my foyer.

"Wow, this is so cool," Case marveled before taking off.

"Uhn uhn, Case. That's what you're not gonna do," Ming snapped at him, making him stop suddenly before retreating back by her side. I took her by the hand, letting her know it was fine.

"He's good, Ma. As a matter of fact, c'mon, man. Let me show you something." I led him to my game room where there was a seventy-five-inch flat screen on the wall with both a PlayStation 5 and Xbox One connected. There was a basketball hoop that had a scoreboard above it. I even went as far as setting up a Ms. Pacman machine. I knew he could keep occupied here with no problem. I turned the PlayStation on and handed him the controller. "Make yourself at home." I headed back to the front where Ming had taken the bags into the kitchen.

"What happened back at the supermarket?" I inquired. She tried to avoid the question by focusing on unpacking the bags. I walked up behind her and put my head in her neck. "Ming, you gotta tell me what happened, Ma."

"One minute, I was on my phone, texting Miko, and then, there was a knock at the window that scared the shit outta me. I saw a man in a suit who resembled you and Truth. He was puffing on a cigar and motioned for me to roll the window down. When I shook my head no, he smacked a picture against the window." She stopped talking, and I could hear her sniffling. I held her close, letting her know that I had her without speaking. "It was a picture of Case on the playground. This bastard had a picture of my son, Chance. I rolled the window down, and he threw the paper inside that I gave you and casually walked off."

To hear her crying the way she was fucked with my heart. My first thought was to find Boss and put a bullet in his fucking skull, but I knew Ming needed me here. This was another line he had crossed that he couldn't come back from. Knowing that he'd been watching Case had me seeing red. Turning her around, I cupped her cheeks and kissed her lips.

"I'm not gon' ever let anything happen to you or my lil' homie back there. You understand me?" She nodded, but her words would give me the confirmation I needed. I wanted her to understand that once I confessed my loyalty, I was willing to go to the end of the earth behind what and who I deemed important to me. "I can't hear you."

Her eyes bore into mine, and I felt like our souls were getting acquainted with one another. "Yes, Chance. I understand."

"Cool. I want y'all to spend the night. We can go swing by your place to get clothes after we eat. You can save any excuse you've already thought of in your head as to why y'all can't stay. Case has already made it clear that he ain't tryna leave."

She rolled her eyes, and I caught a hint of a smile. I was going to do everything I could to keep her smiling.

"Okay," she conceded without a fight.

We made dinner together and before I knew it, day had turned to night. We retired to the living room after eating where we built a fort with Case. Although my body was physically here with them, my mind was elsewhere. I wanted to body Boss so bad that my trigger finger was itching.

"Hey, you good?" Ming looked up at me, and I moved a strand of hair from her face. I could stare at her pretty ass all day long.

"I'm straight. Case knocked out though." At the bottom of the fort, he was stretched out with his arm wrapped around a bowl of popcorn. Ming snickered before reaching down to pick him up. "Here, I got him." I grabbed him from her and motioned for her to follow me toward the back. My place had three bedrooms and two and a half bathrooms. The shit was lavish as fuck and more than enough room for just me.

"No offense, but are these sheets new? I'm very picky about where we lay our heads."

"You good. You two will be the first guests that actually stayed the night since I got this place." With her okay, I laid Case down on the queen-sized bed that sat in the middle of the bedroom. "Bathroom is to your left. There's fresh rags and towels in there too."

"Thank you. Are you heading out?" she asked, already knowing the answer to the question.

"Yeah. I don't plan on being gone for long though." I kissed her cheek and headed for the front door before she could ask any more questions.

"Make it back here tonight." Her voice was filled with concern.

I nodded because the plan was to always make it back home. It was even more important now that I had the two of them here waiting on me.

I WHIPPED my truck through the streets of Manhattan, anxious to get to Boss' house. All that kept playing in my head was the same man that had raised Truth and I to be men had it out for us. Right now, he was treating us no different than a nigga he had beef with in the streets. I pulled my phone from my coat pocket to connect it to the Bluetooth. No sooner than the phone connected, a call came through from Truth.

"**Yo,**" I answered. In my head, I already knew he was calling to throw a monkey wrench in my plans.

"**Abort mission. Meet me at Auntie's crib.**"

"**How you know what the hell I'm about to do? You tracking my car or something, bruh?**" Truth had a tendency to overdo it when it came to protecting me. I had to remind him that I was a grown ass man.

"**Ming called Miko; Miko called me. I'll see you in a few.**"

He hung up, and I grinned. Shorty was concerned about me; I liked that. Turning my car in the opposite direction, I jumped on the Westside Highway to Aunt Pat's. Truth and I arrived at the same time. It was late, so if she was calling us out to her house, it was important.

"Aunt Pat, where you at?!" I yelled through the house, knowing it would piss her off.

"I know you better stop hollering like that in my damn house like you don't have no sense." She emerged from the back in her house-coat, and her hair was in a roller set. Aunt Pat was the definition of an old school auntie.

"What you call us out here for, Auntie?"

"Come in and have a seat so I can talk to y'all." Her face got serious quick, and I wasn't sure if I wanted to sit. Truth must've sensed my hesitation because he hadn't moved either. "If y'all don't come in here and sit y'all asses down. I ain't dying or nothing."

I breathed a sigh of relief at that revelation.

"Aight, but I can't stay long. Ming and Case are at my house." I took a seat on the La-Z-Boy while Truth sat next to her.

"Well, it's about damn time. I was getting tired of her moping around here when she comes to pick him up."

"No disrespect, Auntie, but can we get to the reason we're here? I feel like you're stalling," Truth cut in.

She looked back-and-forth between the both of us before speaking. "I called you two here because I wanted to talk to you about Boss." I balled my fist up at the mere mention of his name. I wanted to bug out, thinking he had come here and threatened her, but I held my composure and let her finish talking. "Boss and I dated for about a year when your parents first opened Porter House. Only our inner circle, which consisted of us four, knew about it because at the time, he was heavy in the game. Let him tell it, he kept me a secret for my protection. It was all bullshit though. He didn't want me to find out about the multiple girlfriends he had. Anyway, during the course of our relationship, I started to pick up on how envious he was of your father. He would say that Porter House was his idea that your father ran with, getting rich without him. I can't tell you how many times he'd lay up with me and express his disdain for his own blood brother."

"Why you telling us this now?" Truth took the words right out of my mouth. While it was shocking to learn that they fucked around, I didn't too much care. I needed to know the relevance.

"The reason I'm telling you now is because he reached out to me today. He says that the two of you are in danger and that it has to do with the Porter House. Now, y'all know I don't get into your business when it comes to that, but I'm concerned. I know what happened to my sister in that place, and I just..." She paused and took a deep breath. My mom was a sore subject for us and even more so for my aunt. Aunt Pat was the eldest of the two of them. "Y'all need to keep a close eye on Boss. My gut has always told me that he may have had something to do with your parents' murder."

Now that took the wind out of me. Could Boss have set my parents up to be murdered over some jealousy shit? I was gonna find out if it was the last thing I did.

25

TRUTH

The last thing Aunt Pat said really caught me off guard and further confirmed the theory I had in my head at the same time. I noticed years ago how vested Boss seemed to be in Porter House and how he always had an issue when I made an executive decision. It was like he couldn't grasp the fact that the business had been left to me. Now hearing that he did hold a grudge with my pops only made things a little clearer.

"Did he say anything else to you, Auntie?"

"That was all, but he didn't need to say much for me to know that there was some bullshit in the air. My number hasn't changed in ten plus years, and now he's reaching out? I knew something was fishy as soon as I heard his voice."

"Aight, well this info was definitely needed." Although I didn't involve her in our dealings, I needed to put her up on game so that she knew how to handle herself should a situation arise. "Recently, we found out that both Nyema and Boss were in cahoots and got away with a nice chunk of change from the Porter House."

"Well I'll be damned. Didn't I tell you I didn't trust that girl when she came here? I told you from the day I laid eyes on her that she was no good."

"She did tell you that, bruh. I was there," Chance cosigned.

"Yeah, well, now I have to play the hand I was dealt. Auntie, I'm going to be sending Troy over here to make sure your security system is good, and I'm sitting someone on the house to ensure your safety."

"Oh, uhn uhn. Just because I ain't out there like y'all don't mean I can't take care of myself. Who you think taught yo' mama to be the pitbull in a skirt she became? I just chose not to indulge in the street life as much as she did. Trust me, baby, I got me."

"I'm sure you do, OG, but I'm still going to have someone check in daily." I stood to hug her and kissed her on her cheek. Aunt Pat didn't know it, but she gave me a whole new outlook on how to go about getting to Boss.

"Can you believe this motherfucka?!" Chance barked once I closed the door behind us. "All these fucking years, bruh. All these years, this bitch ass nigga sat in our faces, plotting. He's been plotting since forever. This some bullshit!"

"Get in my car real quick." I walked ahead of him and got in the driver's side. It took him a minute, but he followed and got in on the passenger's side.

"You're way too calm for me. Wassup? What we doing here?"

I felt the same hurt he was feeling, but unlike him, I was in control of my emotions.

"This shit has just taken on a whole new meaning. Now, I know for sure that him coming at us is no coincidence. He's been planning for the right time to take us out so that he can have control of Porter House. If he wants it bad enough, he can come get it."

"Again, what we doing here? 'Cause I'm not just gonna sit back and wait for this nigga to push my shit back."

"When have I ever not had a plan? Boss had plenty of opportunities to take us out, but he hasn't. That tells me there's something else he wants. He wants us to come looking for him. Why you think he reached out to Aunt Pat? He knew she'd warn us. Right now, I need to find out more info surrounding our parents' death. Don't move without me, Chance."

"He's been watching Ming and Case, Truth. He approached her earlier while I was in the store. This nigga on some bullshit. We gotta figure this shit out asap. I can't promise you that if I see him, I'm not

gon' do something to him. I can only promise that I won't kill him."
He dapped me up and got out.

I sat there for a moment, watching him get in his car and drive off.
I knew Boss had to die; I just didn't know if I had the heart to kill him
—_at least not until he admitted to my face that he was behind my
parents' murder. I needed a stiff drink and a fucking nap. Glancing
down at my phone, a 911 text flashed on the screen from Amina.

Starting my car, I pulled off in that direction. When I arrived,
Amina was standing outside, pacing back-and-forth, yelling into her
phone. What stuck out to me was the fact that the parking lot was
empty with the exception of her car. That was odd seeing as the club
didn't have a scheduled closing.

"You just get your ass here asap, Troy!" I heard her yell into the
phone just as I got out. "Oh, my God, Truth, I'm so glad you're here."
Her eyes were wide and alarming.

"What's going on? Why it look so dead out here?"

She kept pacing and talking to herself instead of me. "What
happened was you stuck ya dick in the wrong bitch and then gave her
access to your business!" she barked, shocking the both of us. "My
bad, Truth. I'm just so pissed I could spit right now."

I knew who she was referring to, but I was stuck on what Nyema
had to do with us being closed. "You good but back to my first question." I excused her outburst, knowing that whatever the problem was,
it had to be big. Amina and I didn't handle each other any kind of way.

"Shit is bad. You gotta see it for yourself." She walked off, and I fell
in step with her. When I crossed the threshold of Tantra, I saw red.
The main level had been destroyed. Tables were flipped over, along
with the custom couches and chairs. Glass littered the floor, and with
each step I took, the sound of glass crunching under my boots was
deafening to my ears. "Look at my bar, Truth." Her voice cracked
when she spoke.

"Motherfuckas," I growled in a low tone. I didn't know which was
worse, the bar or the main floor. The plexi glass that lined the counter
was shattered, and all of the top-shelf liquor had been swiped off the
shelves. Or what once was because the shelves were now hanging off
the wall. "You run the cameras yet?"

"That funky bitch pulled the tape. That's why I called Troy so that he could come and pull the back-up footage. I swear I'ma stomp Nyema out when I see her, and it's nothing you're gonna be able to do about it. We've been in the business going on three years, and we ain't never had no shit like this happen. I know she's behind it even if she didn't do it herself!" Amina had been with me since the beginning. So like Tantra was my baby, it was hers as well.

"Was anybody here when it happened?"

"No. I came in earlier than my normal time today. I don't know why, but when I left last night, I had an uneasy feeling. And you know when something is off, I can't shake it until I find out the source of that feeling." Amina was very spiritual and took that shit seriously. Often, she came in and burned sage throughout the club to ward off bad energy.

"I'ma take care of this. Your bar will look like new. Give me three weeks, tops. Anything else I need to know?" She shook her head no. "Aight, once Troy gets here, send him to my office, and you head home and get some sleep. I'm sure you've been screaming your head off since you got here."

That got a little laugh outta her. "I'm not leaving. I wanna see the cameras too. They must've gotten tired from what they did down here because the lazy bastards didn't touch upstairs."

I nodded before heading to my office. I knew Nycma would be pissed from me closing the accounts. I also knew that she wasn't capable of doing this on her own. This had Boss written all over it.

I had come to the conclusion that the same man I had looked up to after the death of my father was really bitch made. He orchestrated this to send a message, and the only thing he succeeded at was further pissing me the fuck off. Everything that was ruined was easily replaceable, even the custom shit. My money was long, and this was a small thing to a giant. But since his bitch ass wanted to play, I decided to go out on the playground with him. This shit was chess, not checkers. Pulling up his number, I called him on FaceTime, and the call connected immediately.

"Nephew, you look like you're having a rough day," he taunted while puffing on a cigar.

"You're just full of surprises, Boss. First, you conspire with my ex to steal from me, then you threaten me through Aunt Pat. And now, the ultimate bitch move, you tear up my place of business. You can't be from the Porter bloodline. We don't breed bitches."

"Nigga, I am the Porter bloodline!" he spat, getting closer to the camera. "You and Chance wouldn't be shit but some little niggas living off their daddy's trust fund if it wasn't for me."

I had already gotten under his skin, and we hadn't been on the phone two minutes. I snickered at the veins popping out his forehead and sat on my desk.

"You betta calm down before you fuck around and stroke out. I'd hate to see you die before your time. Which is coming sooner than you think, by the way."

"Ohhh, big dawg, Truth." He laughed heartily. "You know it's okay to be real with your Uncle Boss. I know what you're capable of. Killing me is not one of those things. You have the same qualities as your father. You act like the big dawg when in all reality, it's a nigga like me behind you putting in the work."

I could see the envy in his eyes when he spoke on my father. Boss was the kind of snake he warned me about growing up. I had unknowingly allowed the hate he had for me to fester, which allowed him to recruit Nyema to push his agenda, taking over Porter House. They were cancers that spread and had now become so infectious I had to do major surgery to rid myself of them. In this case, I knew it would end up with someone being dead; it wasn't going to be me or anyone close to me though.

"The difference between my father and you is he was a thinker. You, on the other hand, have a habit of acting on emotion. While you're sitting back mad that me and Chance control the Porter House, I bet you haven't thought about going out and starting your own shit. Nah, you've sat back and reaped all the benefits of my hard work. Make no mistake, old man, you've been able to do that because I let you. He that giveth can and will taketh away."

"Make no mistake about it, nephew, I'm coming for what's mine. We are at war."

"Indeed, bitch ass nigga," I spat and disconnected the call just as

Troy walked in. I held out my hand to shake his. "Thanks for coming, man."

"No problem. I ran some footage from my phone on my way here, and this is what I was able to pull up." He handed me his phone, and I watched a hooded figure type in the code to our security system and gain access to the building within seconds.

Not a few minutes after, two other hooded figures carrying steel bats came into view. My eye twitched as I watched the trio go crazy with the bats to my shit. They knocked over tables and had gone so far as to pull out pocketknives to destroy the chairs and couches. I watched the full video until they made their exit back out the same way they came.

Handing Troy back his phone, I swiped my hand over my waves. I could only wonder if the people knew whose place they had targeted. Both Nyema and Boss had dug a hole so deep for themselves that there was no getting out. Using the intercom, I called for Amina to come to my office. After the conversation I just had with Boss, I needed to put my immediate team up on game.

"Call Brock for me, T."

Amina entered at the same time Troy's phone connected, and Brock's voice came through the phone.

"Hello."

"Brock, it's Truth."

"What's the word?"

"I needed to put you all up on game and let you know that both Boss and Nyema are excommunicated effective immediately. Y'all know I don't control what people have going on outside of the business, but if you fuck wit them, I know where you stand."

"Family feud or should we be gearing up for war?" he asked for clarification. I stood and made eye contact with Mina and Troy before looking back at the phone.

"We are past the point of family feud. They stopped being family the moment they plotted against us. So, to answer your question, a war is evident." Some shit was just inevitable.

BOSS

I THREW MY PHONE ACROSS THE ROOM, SMASHING IT ON IMPACT WHEN IT hit the wall. I was sure the staff at the Hyatt would be charging my card for any damage left. Right now, I could give a flying fuck because I was pissed. That fucker, Truth, had gotten too big for his britches. I taught him and Chance everything they knew about business, and he had the nerve to talk to me like I ain't shit? I was gonna make him eat every fucking word.

Hearing the door to the bathroom open, I turned my head to find Nyema standing in the doorway in a black lace teddy. The see-through lingerie left nothing to the imagination, and that worked for me. It wasn't until my eyes met her face did I notice that she mirrored the way I felt.

"That whole interaction didn't sound like anything we discussed, Boss," she said, rolling her eyes. "While you're over there having a pissing match with him, he's onto us, and that little bit of money we have is not enough to get off his radar."

"Who said anything about getting off his radar? I ain't no ho ass nigga. Can't nobody scare me off. Especially not a motherfucka whose nose I wiped as a child. Why you listening to my conversation anyway when you're supposed to be in there washing yo' ass?" Nyema had a mouth on her, and at this point, if my dick wasn't in it, her opinion wasn't necessary unless asked for.

"We're supposed to be a team, or am I tripping? The last time I checked, I was in this shit just as deep as you. Plus, I'm the one doing all the fucking dirty work if you wanna be technical."

"That's because you want to, and your ass is compensated very well. We're a team, but I run this shit, and you follow my lead."

"Well, excuse the fuck outta me. All I've been trying to do is help. You need to direct all that right there," she motioned in a circular motion, "to the motherfucka who's running yo' shit. And since you run this shit, make sure you pay my cousins for the job they did at Tantra."

She plopped down on the bed, pouting. I wasn't coddling no grown ass woman, so that shit didn't faze me. Grabbing my spare phone from the dresser, I made my way to the living room. Now was the time to reach out to my insurance plan. Going to my text messages, I started a new text thread.

Me: I might need you sooner than I thought.

Insurance: Prices have gone up, and I have a problem of my own that relates to you.

Me: We'll talk more in person. Meet me in the morning at The Row uptown.

Insurance: I'll be there.

I learned early on that you had to have a back-up plan for your back-up. Now, I knew people would look at this situation thinking I wasn't shit for turning on my family. Probably even thought I didn't have any loyalty. But this wasn't about loyalty. This was about principle.

Growing up, my brother, Tim, and I were thick as thieves. We had the same father but different mothers. We made money together, got fly together, and bagged plenty women together, amongst other things. I was his go-to guy, and he was mine. Things changed once he met Tammy. Tammy with the big ideas —_all except for Porter House. That was all me. I remember bringing up the idea of opening the gambling spot while we were packaging bricks to be driven down to Miami. The drug game was our shit back then.

"Bro, this flipping bricks shit is getting old. We're throwing rocks at the penitentiary daily," I stated while stuffing the empty Enfamil cans with dope.

"We're so good at it tho'," Tim responded while laughing.

"Yeah, that's all good, but we need to take this shit to a whole other level." I knew I had piqued his interest because he stopped packing and gave me his undivided attention.

"Talk to me."

"Aight, so boom, what you think about opening a gambling house?"

"Nigga, I thought you was talking about making some money. They got gambling spots all up and through the five boroughs, bro."

"Nah, you not hearing me. I'm talking about some official shit, like Vegas. Crap tables, Blackjack, Ceelo, all that shit. It'll be a place where the white businessmen can come and spend their money and the corner boys alike. We'll have Vegas in New York."

Tim rubbed his goatee and nodded. "Let's do it, bro!" He slapped fives with me, excited about the plan.

That night, we mapped out the look of the place and finalized the name. Imagine my surprise when we met up the next day and Tammy was alongside him with some ideas of her own. Somehow, our duo became a trio. I sat back and watched them execute what Tim and I had planned while only asking my input when they saw fit.

Once the monies were paid for the space, I played the background while Porter House was built. When I mentioned how I felt like Tim had said fuck me, his response was, "This is for all of us. Your vision made this shit happen. I just did the leg work." That was all bullshit. Yeah, I may have been a partner, but the fact still remained that when Porter House was mentioned, Tim and Tammy Porter were the faces associated with it.

I was only brought in when it was convenient. Naturally, there was a lot of built-up animosity for both my brother and his new wife. Only when Tammy got pregnant with their second son, Chance, did he step back, allowing me to step in. I was fine with him wanting to play family man because it gave me a chance to run Porter House how I saw fit.

Things went even more left when I got access to the books. We were bringing in more money than I thought, and I got paid crumbs compared to what Tim paid out to himself. The only logical explanation was Tammy had gotten into my brother's head and made him believe that Porter House was *theirs alone. I didn't like that bitch, and she needed to go. I was fed up and went by their house to confront the both of them.*

Pulling my car into the driveway of their Jersey City home, I puffed on my Cuban cigar in an attempt to calm myself down before I exited the car. I knew if I went inside all riled up, there would be no calming me down. And the one thing that neither me nor Tim tolerated was disrespect from anybody. I knocked twice on the door and waited impatiently for one of them to answer. I heard Tammy ask who it was from the other side.

"Me!" I answered, my tone laced with animosity.

"Me who?" she snapped with an attitude.

"It's Boss. Open the door, Tammy." She knew my voice, and I wasn't in the mood to play. Once the door opened, I pushed past her.

"Oh, hell no. You don't walk up in my shit like you pay bills around this motherfucka!" she shouted while following close behind me.

I walked into Tim's mancave where he was known to hang out at. The game was playing loudly as he sat comfortably in his recliner.

"You better get your disrespectful ass brother before he sees another side of me, Tim. I'm not gon' put up with his shit for much longer."

Turning around, he looked at the both of us before speaking. "What's going on, Boss?"

"I just came from Porter House, and some shit is off." I knew by the tone of my voice the conversation would go left.

"What you mean off? Money is missing?" he asked, now standing.

"Yeah, money is missing. The funny thing is it's only affecting my pockets."

"Bro, stop dancing around the issue. Fuck you mean money is missing from your pockets? You get paid just like everybody else."

"That's the fucking point. I ain't like everybody else!" I barked, getting in his face. He had me fucked up, talking to me like I was a worker. "Ever since this bitch came along, you've been moving like this y'all shit. Forgetting that it was my idea to get this shit crackin' in the first place!"

Before I could continue my rant, he tapped my jaw, and it was on from there. I could hear Tammy in the background, yelling for us to stop before we woke the kids, and that halted any further blows from him. I stumbled a little when I stood and could feel my lip swelling. Other than that, I was good.

"Don't you ever in your fucking life call my wife out her name! You have

an issue, you take that shit up with me. Tammy, leave the room so I can holla at him real quick." She shook her head at the request and glared at me with disgust before walking out.

"I don't know what you asked her to leave for. Ain't shit for us to talk about. Clearly you're the boss, and I'm just the fucking worker."

"What are we, teenagers, my nigga? You know we're equal partners in this shit. What the books say and what has been put into a separate account for you are two different amounts. And the same woman you just called out her name suggested that shit as a way to help you. You think I haven't noticed the gambling habit you've picked up since Porter House opened? I ain't never been no grimy ass nigga. The fact that you would even think I would cheat you outta some fucking money knowing we came from the same ball sack shows exactly where we are. I'll write you a check for what's being held in that account. We'll handle everything separately from now on."

He turned his back and unpaused the TV, dismissing me. If he wasn't my brother, I would've put a bullet in his head and called it a day. For the sake of him being my family, I walked away. The moment I left his house, things had changed. Long gone was the brotherly bond. In my eyes, we were on two different teams. While he had Tammy, I just had Boss.

As the years went by, I developed an intense hate for both Tim and Tammy. When the opportunity presented itself to take him out, I jumped at the chance. I knew it couldn't be me, but it was nothing to hire someone to do so. Seeing him bring Truth and Chance around more, I noticed he was showing them the ropes. With the way they soaked up the information, I knew he was grooming them to take over.

I couldn't let that happen. Fortunately for me, there was a crew of wild ass stick-up kids from Queens that were willing to body the mayor if the price was right. I linked up with their leader and offered 20K if he agreed to take care of my brother and Tammy. With no hesitation, he was on board. Time flew by that week, and before I knew it, the day of reckoning had come. I didn't go into Porter House that day because I knew what was set to go down. I had not one ounce of guilt.

After the deed was done, I played the role of grieving brother who vowed to kill anyone involved. I did that for two weeks straight while secretly solidifying myself as the head nigga in charge. I even went so far as to send some of our people out in search of the killers. No one ever suspected me. Not that I would've noticed anyway. I was too busy making changes that would benefit me. My new income was top priority. I took my nephews in and let them study under me and made sure to share old stories of their father and I growing up.

Unfortunately, even in death, my brother had found a way to fuck with me. In his will, he gave Truth and Chance sole ownership of Porter House when they turned eighteen. Truth thought he was doing me a favor by keeping me on board and letting me move how I saw fit while still keeping my pockets lined. It wasn't enough then, and it damn sure wasn't enough now. That was why we were here today.

"Are you done being mad now? This pussy ain't gon' play with itself." I smirked at Nyema's straightforwardness. This was one asset of Truth's that I enjoyed daily. She made her way over to me and picked her leg up, placing it over mine. "I'm sorry about earlier, Daddy."

Running her tongue across my lips, she grinded her pussy in my lap. Even though I knew her apology was bullshit, I had no intention on turning down the wet box she was offering. Smiling at me as if she had just gotten over, she raised her hips and pulled my dick from my briefs. It stood at attention, awaiting the feeling of her sugary walls. Lowering her pussy onto my dick, she made sure to keep eye contact with me. Nyema had mastered the art of seduction while I, on the other hand, had mastered how to mind fuck a woman. Having good dick gave me an edge up.

"Ughh," she groaned while biting on her bottom lip. I didn't give her a minute to adjust to my size like she normally did. Instead, I grabbed hold of her waist and pushed upward so that she was able to feel all of me. "Ohh, fuck, Boss." She pressed her hands against my chest in an attempt to halt my strokes. I planned to show her who was boss around this motherfucka. I thrusted into her, making sure to put a hurting on her g-spot.

"You like how I do this pussy, huh, Nyema? Ride this dick." I palmed her ass cheek and wrapped my hand around her neck, tight enough not to hurt her.

"Ooh, ooh, shit, Boss. Make me cum, baby."

Not wanting her to cum yet, I pulled out and laid her on her side. Positioning her in a way where I could see my dick slide in and out of her, I went to work. Seeing her wet up my pole made me nut faster.

"Ooh, wee, this pussy is something else." After she drained me, I pulled out.

"You know you remind me of your age every time you say that shit, right?" She chuckled, and I smacked her on her ass. Too tired to go to the bathroom and clean myself up, I slid my briefs back on and laid back on the couch. She cuddled up next to me. "Can I ask you a question?" I looked down at her and nodded for her to speak. "Do you really plan on killing your nephews?"

Her question made me look at her sideways. Nyema was with me, but as I got to know her, it became apparent that I was a means to an end. And just by her question, I could tell her feelings for Truth were still there. That was cool with me too. I knew this thing between us wasn't for the long run. I chose my words carefully before answering.

"I can't tell you what may happen. Plans change every day. You don't worry your pretty little head about that though. All I want you to do is pick a side and stay there." Kissing her forehead, I turned her around so that her ass was pressed against me and slid into her from behind.

"Sssss, I know what side I'm on," she moaned while throwing her ass back at me. For her sake, I hoped that there was truth in her words.

I SAT in the back of The Row restaurant, making sure the front door was in my direct line of vision. You could never be too careful, especially with all that I had going on. Not only was I warring with my nephews over Porter House, but I also had a debt that I had yet to pay off in full from some years ago. Tim didn't know that my part of the money to start Porter House was borrowed from our old mentor, Don Gates. I needed full access to Porter House in order to pay back the remainder of what I owed along with the interest. Taking a sip of my Hennessy, I watched my insurance policy bop through the door.

"Boss, what's good, old timer?"

"Nice to see you, Karter. Have a seat." I gave him a firm handshake, and he sat down across from me. The last time I'd seen Karter, his pants were sagging off his ass, and untamed dreads were all over his head. The man that sat before me today was clean shaven, and the dreads were long gone. "How you feeling about being home?"

"Shit, I can't call it. Right now, I'm tryna make some moves to secure my kids and keep my baby mamas off my back."

"I hear you. I'ma get right to it. I have two problems I need dealt with, and you're the man for the job."

"Is that right? I wonder why."

I took a sip of my drink and set it back on the table. "You already took out the parents. It's only right that you lay the children to rest with them."

"Well, then, I don't have to beat around the bush. It seems we have a mutual problem." He handed me his unlocked phone. A picture of Chance was on the screen. "This the nephew you talking about, right? Well, he's one of them."

"It is. That's Chance. What's your beef with him?"

"He has a thing going on with my son's mother, and I'm not feeling that shit. Once my pussy, always my pussy until one of us steps through those pearly gates."

That got my wheels turning. The only woman I knew about Chance seeing was some chick who had a son in his aunt's daycare. This was getting more interesting.

"I see you like your women young too, huh?"

"I like 'em legal. Are we in agreement?"

I held out my hand for him to shake. "An enemy of my enemy is my friend."

27

———

AMIKO

feasted on my kitty.

He had been down there for the last fifteen minutes and showed no signs of getting tired. He detached his mouth from my clit, but his fingers still dug into me, causing me to squirm. The feeling was so euphoric. It felt like I was in another world.

"This pussy gon' do whatever I tell it to do. Ain't that right, kitty?" he spoke to my pussy before swiping his tongue down my slit, causing me to erupt. "Mmmm, what a sight." My chest heaved up and down, and my hair was all over my head. We were supposed to be having a business meeting, and my hot pussy ass ended up sprawled out on his desk with my skirt above my waist.

"This is crazy," I said with my hands covering my face.

"What? The fact that your pussy does what I tell it to, or the fact that you haven't let my dick meet your happy place?" He smirked while pulling me up by my arms and kissing my lips. Out of habit, I licked all over his, wanting to taste the sweet nectar that had him so gone.

"We were supposed to be discussing the Elites, babe. C'mon." Although we still hadn't made things official, I still had a pet name or two for him. Right now, we were going with the flow, but to the outside world, we were an item.

"Go 'head and talk. I'm not stopping you," he claimed while kissing along my jaw line.

"Ssss, yeah, but I can't focus with you kissing and licking on me. To add to that, my pussy is exposed." He chuckled and stepped back, allowing me to fix myself. Hopping down off the desk, I pointed toward his chair for him to sit down. Smirking, he licked his lips when I sat across from him. "So, I have Troy working on the app for the Elites. That should be up and running by next week. When I leave here, I'm gonna be meeting up with them just to reiterate the new set up and address any concerns."

"Sounds good. Have you spoken to Jomy yet?"

"I haven't. I plan on doing that today. I can tell you now though, Kenneth Combs is truly in love. And if she has that spark in her eyes like he did when I spoke her name, we can forget it."

"An Elite falling in love is not a bad thing. Will the terms of business change, yes, but we're not here to deter that in any kind of way."

"I completely agree, which is why I've been on Instagram scouting new potential Elites." His eyes showed he wanted to object immediately. "Now, I haven't contacted anyone because I wanted to run it by you first. I have three women in mind that I want to put through a vigorous interview process that includes meeting with the Elites. They're between the ages of twenty-five and thirty and not video hos or Instagram thots. They already have their own lane."

"Okay. Like I mentioned before, this is your thing. Run it how you see fit. If and when I need to step in, I will."

"Alright, well, let me get out of your hair and get over to the house." Standing up, I smoothed out my skirt and walked toward him. "The remodel is coming along well."

"For as much as I'm paying, it better be. I think I like the skirts on you better than the pants."

I kissed his full lips, and he grabbed a handful of my ass. "Uhn uhn, I gotta go." I giggled, moving out of his embrace.

Blowing another kiss, I left out and made my way up the steps. I smiled, noticing Mina wiping off the countertop of her newly built bar. "Look at you. How many times you gonna wipe this bar down, lady?"

She chuckled and came around to hug me. "I'm too hype, boo. Yo' man did his thang. It looks even better than the last time." I smirked at her referring to Truth as my man. Thinking about what he did to me back in his office made me bite my bottom lip. "Umm, eww, don't be having an outer body experience with me standing right here, nasty. Where you headed?"

"The Elite house. As a matter of fact, I'm running late. I'm gonna call you this week, and we can do lunch." Time was getting away from me, and I prided myself on being on time wherever I went.

"Okay, boo. I'm down whenever. Be safe." I gave her a quick hug and peck on the cheek before heading out to my car.

"You're late," Ralph let me know while opening the door for me.

"And you're old." I stuck my tongue out at him, and he laughed. "You can drop me off at the Elite house and then get home to your family. I know your wife is sicka me."

"She sicka me too, so join the club."

Grinning, I pulled out my phone from my purse to text my sister. Ming had visited Chance one time, and he had been holding her and my nephew hostage ever since. Even though I was barely home myself, when I was there, I missed both of them, especially Case.

Me: I know you practically moved out and all that, but can you bring my baby by to spend the weekend with me? I know he misses his auntie.

Sissy: Lol, you wanna see me too, right?

Me: I guess you can come if Chance lets you out. I miss y'all. Come stay the weekend and I promise to send y'all right back.

Sissy: Oh, shut up. We'll be there later today. Love you, sis.

Me: I love you too, Mingy. See you later.

We parked in front of the Elite home, and I let myself in using my key. As always, the house was lively, and music could be heard from the living room. I removed my jacket and sat my Fendi tote bag down on the arm of the couch. Summer Walker's music could be heard from the kitchen.

"Baby, I'm talkin' crazy. I need you right in my space, but I still can check in with you. I..." Everyone had some kind of utensil in their hand, using it as a microphone. I couldn't help but join in, using my phone as a mic.

"Know that I need my space, but I wouldn't wanna leave. You know I wouldn't wanna plead, but my heart, my mind, and my body sayin'..."

"Yes!" they shouted in unison, making me crack up laughing. I serenaded them for the remainder of the song.

"Y'all got me in my feelings playing my good sis." We slapped fives, and I took a seat at the breakfast bar.

"Hey, girl, what you doing here?" Olivia asked while handing me a mimosa. I took a sip and savored the taste of the refreshing drink.

"I needed to have a quick meeting with you all about some changes I plan to make."

"Alexa, pause," Joi called out to the Bluetooth speaker.

I had everyone's attention, so I got right to it. "Okay, ladies, so as you know, when I first came on board, I expressed that I wanted to work on expanding the brand. I made it a point to sit back and observe how things in the Elite house worked as well as the business aspect. During that time, we've also had private one-on-one conversations on what has been working and what would make the Elites more successful. I found a way to see more money as well as more stamps on your passport courtesy of your clients." Going into my purse, I produced a phone for each of them as I had done the men during our meeting. "These phones will be your way of communicating when it's anything Elite related. As soon as next week, there will be an official app for your services. You won't be as accessible to your old clients as you'll be taking on new ones. The great thing about that is you'll be chatting through the app until you are comfortable enough to meet in person."

"Uhhh, this sounds good and all, but how much of an increase we talking? I can't speak for anyone else, but I make good money with Judge Sims and my other clients as well. To add to that, the dick that the good judge serves me with is splendid." We all laughed at Kane's revelation.

"Well, since I'm looking to take the Elites beyond New York, you can expect double of what you're seeing now. The way you market yourselves will be different. Lastly, I wanna bring in three new potential Elites. They'll be going through a strict trial period, and they won't be living here. They will also go through you during this trial period to determine whether or not they make the cut."

Olivia stood and spoke. "As long as it makes me money, you can count me in. If we're done here, I need to go see the good Mayor Ellis. I know he's just torn up that he won't be able to access his chocolate kitty at least three times a week." I slapped her on the ass as she walked past me.

"If there are no further questions, I'm gonna go 'head and get outta here. If you need me, you know I'm just a phone call or text away." Everyone stood and hugged me before going off in their separate directions. Everyone except Jomy, who remained seated. Her face held a look of uncertainty, so I asked her to walk me to the door to talk privately.

"Everything okay?" she inquired.

"Everything is good. I wanted to ask how you really feel about the changes?"

She looked down at her feet that sat comfortably in a pair of Ugg slippers. Bringing her eyes back to mine, she spoke. "It's cool. A great business move." Her slumped shoulders didn't indicate she was okay with the way things were set to proceed.

"I spoke to Kenneth."

Her eyes shot up to mine. "Oh, you did?" She began to fidget like a teenager that had been caught sneaking around.

"I did, and he adores you, boo. Do you love him?"

She paused and stopped fidgeting. "I need the money, Miko." It was almost as if she was pleading with me to not make her admit her true feelings. That alone tugged at my heartstrings, and I knew right then it was best that she be with the man she loved. I held my hands out for her to hold, and she did.

"Do you love him?" I asked again.

"Love won't feed my family in Colombia. Thank you for what

you're trying to do, Miko. I really appreciate it, but I can't do much with love."

I felt myself getting teary eyed. Blinking them back, I pulled her into me, hugging her as tight as I could.

"Allowing that man to love you will put you at peace and let you know that you are doing all you can for your family. You deserve that, Jomary. We all do." I kissed her cheek and let myself out. Closing my eyes for a second to regroup, I opened them to find Truth's car parked in front.

"What I tell you about being exposed, Miko?" he quizzed while stepping out of the car.

"I'm not exposed, Truth. I gave Ralph the rest of the day off because I was headed straight home once I left here. I was just about to order an Uber, but I guess I'm riding with you."

"Beauty and brains. Come on and get in." He held the door open for me with a smirk, and I giggled. Pecking my lips, he helped me inside. "You are exposed if Ralph is not with you. I have to run upstairs real quick to get some papers from Nicole. I won't be longer than ten minutes."

"Take your time. I'll be here when you get out."

He closed the door, and I went to text Ming to find out what she wanted to do for dinner later on.

Before I could complete the text message, gunshots rang out, making me drop my phone. Just as I went to open the door to run out, I felt a burning in my side and shoulder. The shooting ceased, and I heard tires skid off. Determined to get to the house before the shooter made a decision to spin back around, I got out and did the best I could to walk. My vision started to blur, and I could feel myself slowing down as I took steps, but I kept going. Finally reaching the door, I reached up to ring the buzzer, and the door opened.

"Fuck, Amiko!" I heard Truth yell out. "God, don't do this, man. She got peoples, dawg. She got peoples. Her sister, her nephew, Jas, Aunt Pat. She got me. Don't let her go out like this. I'ma murder whoever's responsible, WHOEVER!"

THE LAST THING I could remember was Truth praying and vowing harm to whoever was responsible for shooting me before I woke up the next morning. On the side of my bed, I could see Ming asleep, holding my hand and Case at the same time. I didn't want to wake her, but I was thirsty and seeing my shoulder bandaged up, I didn't want to take the chance of moving it. Squeezing her hand lightly, she stirred before popping up, causing Case to hit his head lightly on the railing.

"Ouchh," he cried out while rubbing his head.

"Damn, heffa, watch my baby!" I scolded her, making Case laugh.

"Oh, shut up. Sorry, son." She kissed his head and then focused her attention back on me. "You become a madam to get shot at? What part of the game is that?"

"You're aggravating," I said, smiling.

"No, forreal though, Miko. I lost it when Truth called Chance saying you had gotten shot and to get down to the hospital immediately. I would die if I lost you." She was getting emotional, and that was so unlike her. I cracked a joke to lighten the air.

"I know you lost it, bringing my nephew in here in pajamas like we ghetto and shit. I know it was urgent, but he could've put some sweats on. Ain't that right, nephew?" He nodded while giggling. Ming laughed too, and that made me feel good.

The door creaked open, and Truth entered with Chance behind him. Truth had a teddy bear and flowers in his hand.

"You're up."

"That I am. You know they can't keep a real one down."

"Word," Chance added, making me giggle.

"You know you on leave, right?" Truth stated matter-of-factly.

I wanted to protest, but it would be of no use. If he said it, that was what it was. The pain in my side had started up, reminding me of where I got shot.

"I need the meds for pain. Ssss, my side is hurting."

"Let me get the doctor," Ming offered while handing Case to Chance.

She returned a couple minutes later with the doctor in tow. After going over my condition with me and everyone in attendance, I was given pain medication through my IV that knocked me out. I didn't know who shot me, but Truth assured me that he would handle it. He reminded me that I was his, and it was his job to protect me. I had no doubt that he would.

28

MING

I stood by Miko's bedside all night once I arrived at the hospital. I was still in disbelief that my sister had been shot. My sister, that didn't bother a soul, had been shot twice. I already knew that the bullets weren't for her, and that was the worst part. The other part of me was laying in that bed with a bandaged side and shoulder.

"You wanna go back to the crib, so you and Case can shower? I'll bring you right back," Chance offered while handing me a coffee cup from Starbucks.

"Thanks, but I'm not going anywhere until she's released."

"Oh, yes the hell she is. She gotta get outta here funking up my room," Miko blurted out from the bed with her eyes closed. "I know you wanna be there for me and all, but you can be here and be fresh, so go 'head on. And take Case with you. I don't want him to see me like this no more. I already called Ms. Pat, and she said you can bring him by."

I swore she got on my damn nerves sometimes. She didn't have to say all that. Chance was trying not to laugh, and I hit him in the stomach. He went to grab Case, and I went over to Miko. Her eyes were now open, and she was smiling. Who the hell felt this jovial after getting shot?

"First off, heffa, I don't stink. I may be a little tart under the arms, but I don't stink." I mushed her in her head. "I'll be back in two hours." We left out, and Jas was walking in with a bag from Red Lobster.

"Hey, where y'all going?"

"I'm taking them home, so they can shower. We'll be right back."

"Whose home, hers or yours?" she teased.

"Mind yo' business and go feed yo' friend," he answered for the both of us. Securing Case in his car seat, I got in the passenger seat, and we drove off. "You alright?"

"I don't even know honestly. I mean, my sister was shot, and she's in there cheesing it up while I'm over here losing it internally. What if I had lost her? That's my twin, Chance. You and Truth are brothers, but that is my twin. We shared a womb together. She is me, and I am her." I felt myself getting emotional all over again. He grabbed my hand and held it tightly.

"Just because we're not twins don't mean I wouldn't feel the same way if it were Truth laying in that hospital bed. Have you thought that maybe she's being strong for you? You can't possibly think she's not going through her own emotions during the moments she has alone."

"That's not what I'm saying!" I snapped out of nowhere, neck rolling and all.

"So what you saying? And you can stop all that chicken head shit too."

With my arms folded, I turned in his direction. "Chicken head shit?"

"Yeah, that rolling your neck." He imitated my neck rolling, and I couldn't help but laugh. "I'm glad you laughing at how crazy you look when you do that shit. Look, I'm not telling you how you should feel. I'm just trying to get you to see it from another point of view."

"I hear you, and I'm sorry for being a chicken head. Gimmie kiss." I leaned over to kiss him, and he dodged it.

He smirked while I pouted. "Nah, I'm straight."

"Okay, you lucky Case back there sleep, or I'd make you pay for that."

"You was gon' gimmie some sucky sucky?"

"Shut up and drive."

I reached for my phone to check my messages. The last thing I was concerned with was my phone after finding out about Miko. I had missed calls from Ms. Pat that I would return once I was en route to her house. I also had a few messages from Karter. I knew it wasn't nothing that important that he needed to text me five times. After reading over them, I shook my head. The messages went from do you think I can pick Case up to spend time with him to me being a shiesty ass bitch for not responding to the first few messages. Being that it was my first time seeing them, I replied back.

Me: I don't know how far you think you're gonna get talking to me like you don't have a mama, but that's a fast way to get yo' ass blocked. It wasn't even a minute before the dots came up on the screen, indicating he was responding.

Deadbeat: I ain't tryna hear all that shit you saying. You got a nigga in yo' face, now you tryna keep my son from me, and I ain't having that shit. You know me well enough to know that's not gonna fly with me, Ming.

Me: First off, what my man gotta do with you, Karter? Second, I had a family emergency, which is why I didn't respond. With the way you coming at me sideways, I'm regretting even doing this. Your question was can you spend some time with Case, correct? Where would you like to meet?

Deadbeat: So this what we gon' be doing? Meeting up for me to see him? I can't come see him at your crib?

I didn't bother to respond. Instead, I turned on my read receipts so that he would see I read his dumbass message. Karter was far from slick. There was no way he was coming in my apartment. And it would be a while before I allowed him to be alone with Case as well. Call me what you want, but I wasn't gonna play with anyone about my son —_his father included. We pulled in front of Chance's place, and he got out to get Case before I could.

We had yet to have a conversation about how long we'd been at his place. Every time I mentioned going home, he would come up with a reason why we should stay. It was way too soon to talk about moving in together. I hadn't even experienced living on my own yet, and although I had the money, I didn't think I wanted to, especially now after the last twenty-four hours.

"You can bring him to the bathroom. I'm gonna give him a shower first."

"Aight, I'll grab his clothes."

Doing for Case was like second nature to Chance. For the last week, he'd been getting up early to make him breakfast and would drop the both of us off before going about his day. He had even offered to watch him for me when I worked late, but I declined. I didn't want to do too much, and everything was still fresh. While in the bathroom bathing Case, my phone went off.

"Baee," I called out to him. "Can you grab my phone? It's in my bag."

"You want me to answer it?"

"Yes, please." I thought nothing of it. He came in and handed the phone to me.

"Here, it's his father." His tone was flat, and after placing the phone on the towel I had laying across my lap, he walked out.

I put the phone on speaker and let Karter know that his son was in front of me, hoping that he wouldn't say no off the wall shit. They spoke for the remainder of Case's bath. My son was uninterested as Karter spoke about a whole bunch of nothing. I didn't know if he was bullshittin' or just genuinely didn't know what to say. Either way, I was over the conversation and so was Case.

"Alright, handsome. Tell your dad you'll talk to him later."

"**Talk to you later,**" Case said, not bothering to look up at the phone.

I took it off speaker and placed it at my ear.

"**Alright, I'll have him give you a call tomorrow. I'm about to step back out.**"

"**Why that nigga answering ya phone?**"

"**Stop questioning me, Karter. You no longer hold that right and haven't in a while. Goodbye.**" I hung up and helped Case out to dry him off.

"Mommy?"

"Yes, handsome?"

"Is Auntie Miko okay?"

"Yes, baby, she's okay. She's just a little banged up right now. I'm gonna go back to the hospital and check on her, and you're gonna go hang out with Ms. Pat, okay?" He nodded. "How 'bout you get dressed, and while I shower, you can make Auntie Miko a get-well card?"

His face lit up. "Yesss! Chance can help me."

"Sounds good." I kissed the top of his head and watched him get dressed. Once his teeth were brushed, I set him up with his coloring book and crayons while I got myself together.

Chance still had yet to return to the room, and I wanted to know what kind of exchange he and Karter had. The shower was imperative though. After thirty minutes, I was out of the shower and feeling refreshed. I even took the time to wash my hair. Since I had been at Chance's place, he had me wearing my natural hair. It felt good to have the air hit my actual scalp, but I was over having to mess with it every day.

With my weave, I wrapped it up at night and was ready to go in the morning with little to no brushing. Opening the door to the bathroom, I found Chance laid across the bed while Case sat on the floor, coloring. At first, I thought he was sleep, but upon further inspection, he was coloring as well.

"You mind if I go in your room and get dressed?" He didn't answer verbally but gave a head nod toward his room that was across the hall.

Disregarding his attitude, I picked up my clothes and headed to his room, closing the door behind me. I quickly threw on a pair of Adidas jogger pants, a t-shirt, and hoodie. I had towel dried my hair and wrapped it up in a messy bun. Opening the door, I ran right into Chance, who pushed me back a little and closed the door behind himself.

"You have any feelings for that nigga, Karter?" The look on his face was serious.

"Would I be here with you if I did?"

"Don't answer my question with a question, Ming."

"You should already know the answer to that. You not so sure about it now?"

"Nah, honestly I'm not."

"Wowww, really, Chance?" I went to walk away, and he pulled me back. "Alright now, you keep pulling on me, and we gon' have to move some furniture around this bitch. I don't have time for this. I have to get back to my sister."

The question was stupid, and the fact that he was questioning me about my feelings for Karter was pissing me off. There were no feelings. He was a man I had a child with, nothing more.

"I just need to hear you say it."

"No. The answer is no and would be no if he was the last man on Earth. Can we go now?" He pinned me against the wall and tongued me down so good my legs instantly parted. "Mmm," I moaned into his mouth. I was all hot and bothered when he pulled away, fucking up the mood.

I could see the annoying smile on his face. "We gotta get back to the hospital and drop off Case. I got you later." He smacked my ass and kissed the side of my mouth before opening the door and walking out. "Come on, C. Let me help you with your shoes." He turned quickly and winked at me. I gave his stupid ass the finger.

<hr>

Back at the hospital, Miko was sitting up, talking with Jas and Truth. Well, Miko and Jas were doing most of the talking. Truth, on the other hand, was too busy staring at her like she was the last woman on Earth. He was so into her, and it was too cute. I cleared my throat, making my presence known as Chance walked in behind me, placing his arms around my waist.

"What happened to I'll be back in two hours? You were a little stronger smelling than you thought, huh, sis?" She and Jas snickered, and I gave them both the finger.

"Girl, fuck you. I got caught up talking to Ms. Pat." We all sat around, talking and laughing while waiting on a nurse to come change her bandages.

"Hey, Ms. Adachi, I'm here to change your bandages. Do you mind if everyone steps out for a minute?" the nurse asked, standing at the door and waiting for the okay to come in.

"You can come in. The guys can step out, but the girls can stay."

Watching the nurse change the dressing, I had to close my eyes a couple times to keep from squirming. Once she was done, the doctor came in, along with the guys. "Hey, Doc, do you have an idea on when I'm going to be able to go home?"

"Yep, and I wanna give you an update on your condition. The good news is the bullets went straight through, and you will be cleared to go home in two days. I just want to monitor everything to make sure no infection develops, and then I can release you to your family. Any other questions?"

"Nope, I guess that will work. Thank you."

"No problem. Let me know if you need me."

"Two days is not so bad," I said to keep her spirits up.

"You're not the one in the bed, Ming. I wanna go home and lay in my own bed."

I couldn't argue with her on that one.

"Well, look at the bright side. I'll be home with you."

"You plan on being at my crib then? Because that's where she's going," Truth spoke up on Miko's behalf.

"And you're coming home with me," Chance added. Before we could check the both of them, my phone rang. Shaking my head, I answered when I saw Karter's name displayed on the screen.

"Yes."

"Since you don't wanna bring my son to me, I'm outside of this Ms. Pat's daycare waiting to go in and get him. Now, you can either come and talk to me about visitation or I can just take him. I'm on the birth certificate, and unfortunately for you, I have rights."

"Take my son somewhere if you want to. Jail will be the last place you have to worry about going." I hung up the phone and rushed out of the room abruptly.

"Yo, slow down, Ma. Wassup?" Chance called out, catching up to me.

"I need to go get Case. Karter is outside of your aunt's place." Surprisingly, I wasn't hysterical. I was eerily calm. I knew Karter wasn't pulling off the curb with my damn child.

"I'ma end up murking that nigga on some real shit. Nigga ain't been home a month and already becoming a pain in my ass."

I stayed silent because I was feeling the same way. It was always some shit with Karter Stone. What he failed to realize was that I wasn't the same young girl that he left years ago. I was a grown ass woman who would take on an army behind her child.

29

KARTER

It was a damn shame that I had to threaten to take my son in order for me to get some act right out of Ming. By now, I was sure she was hauling ass from wherever she was to get over to the daycare. I hadn't even arrived there myself yet. I just said that to fuck with her. That shit was funny as hell too. On some real shit though, Ming was fresh out of passes with me. I had given her too much power when it came to how I was able to access my kid, and that shit was over with today.

I knew she was only putting me through this shit just to spite me for fucking with Tiara. To be real, I felt like she was more upset with me than she was her own homegirl. Last I checked, it took two to tango, and right now, I was the only one being punished for the dance. I could say that I didn't mean for it to happen, but niggas always said that shit. The honest truth was Tiara was throwing it, and I was catching.

I even presented Ming with the opportunity to check her friend, only for her to get mad at me for being honest. It was like she gave me the thumbs up to fuck on her homegirl, so, I did. There wasn't anything special about the box T was throwing my way either. It was just something to do when there was nothing to do. It didn't mean I loved Ming any less. Contrary to what she may have believed, I loved her mean ass to death.

It wasn't my intention to get Tiara pregnant either. It was kind of hard to deny someone that held you down when you were behind the wall. So, when I was able to stick it to her again, I did without hesitation, and boom, Kacey was born. From there, we formed a relationship naturally. Now, did I really want to be with Tiara? No.

My plan when I got out the pen was to link back up with Ming, apologize, and start over. What I didn't expect was to come home to this new Ming playing house with my son and the next nigga. That shit had me .38 hot. And it explained why she'd been ducking my calls and acting as if I had to schedule an appointment to see my child. I had to remind Ming of who I was. En route to the daycare, my phone rang with an incoming call from Tiara.

"**Yo.**" I answered in a flat tone.

"**Where you at?**" she pressed.

"**On my way to pick up my son. Wassup, Kacey need something?**"

"**No, and I'm good too. Thanks for asking.**"

I wanted to say get off my line then, but I fell back. "**That's wassup.**"

"**Mmhmm, so she's finally letting you watch your child by yourself?**"

"**We're still getting that figured out.**"

"**You know what's grinding my fuckin' gears?**"

I sighed and hooked the phone up to the Bluetooth as I got on the Westside Highway. "**Nope, but you bout to tell me, right?**"

"**Ya damn right I am. I find it really crazy that you're on my back about any decision I make when it comes to Kacey, but Ming is playing yo' ass like a Nintendo Wii.**"

"**First off, ain't nobody playing me. How I handle Ming is none of your concern.**"

"**It is my business when it starts to affect the dynamic of my household!**"

"**Man, if you called me to argue, you can hang this shit up. And if you called to talk about Ming, don't.**"

Prepared for her to challenge me, I went to hit the call end button, but she beat me to it. Shrugging my shoulders, I pulled in front of the daycare and waited to see how long it would take for Ming to get here. I went to spark up a blunt when I noticed the same car Ming got into at the park pull up behind me. Chance's clown ass hopped out of the driver's side and went around to open her door.

I couldn't wait to put a bullet in this nigga's forehead. All that cocky shit he was on, I couldn't rock with. And then he had the nerve to try and pull my card like I was some ho ass nigga. He didn't know that I was the one behind his parents being murked. I wanted so bad to say something when he was talking that hot shit about doing my research. Fuck nigga betta do his research on me. I was a lot of things, but a pussy wasn't one of 'em.

Ming didn't know what kind of car I drove, so I was able to watch her as she went inside the daycare while he waited for her. Wanting to egg things on a little longer, I got out and leaned against my driver side door. He stared at me, and I waved.

"Don't go getting no ideas about playing family with my little man, aight? That daddy shit, I got that covered."

The smug look on his face made my trigger finger itch. "Yeah, that's the problem, my nigga. Any man can be a daddy. It's the fathering part that's hard for a bitch such as yourself to get right. But don't worry. **I** got that covered."

"Fuck you say to me?" I stood up from my car and put my hand on my hip. I didn't know who this pretty boy motherfucka thought he was talking to, but shit was about to get real spooky around this bitch.

Planted in the same position, he continued. "You heard what I said, nigga. You got ya hand on your hip like you wanna get active. Let's pop, nigga! I'll expedite your trip to your final resting place."

"Chanceee."

I turned my head, and it tripped me out to see my own son barreling toward this nigga with open arms.

"Wassup, youngin'?" he spoke while reaching down to ruffle Case's hair. The sight before me was enough to make me risk it all and send a shot Chance's way. "Go 'head and speak to ya pops," he encouraged, and that blew me.

"I don't need you to have my son do shit. Come over here, Case! Ming, get ya nigga before I push his shit back."

My son's head darted back-and-forth between me and his mother like he was scared to come to me. That shit made me want to yoke Ming's ass up.

"Get in the car with Chance, Case." Ming instructed.

Without giving me a second thought, he grabbed Chance's hand and got into the car. Chance then returned to Ming's side.

"Word, Ming? So you making our son choose? That's crazy as fuck. And it's only out of respect for him that I won't splatter ya man's shit and have you crying over his body. You don't want me being in my son's life, cool. Just know when he's of age, he's gonna have questions which will lead to him looking for me. Keeping him away from me only makes you a deadbeat ass mama," I spat venom, wanting every word to cut into her.

"Karter, the only deadbeat ass mama is the bitch that gave birth to you." She stepped to me like a nigga that wanted to fight, and the fuck boy grabbed her by her waist.

"Yeah, get yo' bitch, nigga." I laughed, watching Ming gnaw at her bottom lip but stop abruptly when I heard the cocking sound of a gun.

"Get my what?" Chance spoke menacingly, pulling Ming behind him.

I'd been so into my taunting that I'd gotten caught slipping. On any other day, I would've gone toe to toe with him, shooting it out if necessary, but no matter how fucked up people perceived me to be, I didn't want my son to see that.

"I'ma see you. You can bet that shit."

Hopping back in my car, I peeled off. Hitting the steering wheel as I sped through the streets, I called Boss. The worst mistake this nigga could have ever done was back out on me and not kill my Black ass. "Yo!" I barked into the phone.

"I was just about to call yo' ass. You fucked up!"

"What you mean I fucked up?"

"I mean you fucked up! The one opportunity you had to hit Truth and you missed it. Did you even confirm he was the one you hit?"

"I ain't have to. I saw the car, and I lit that shit up. One plus one equals fucking two."

"What the fuck is this, amateur night at the Apollo? You hit his woman!"

"Well, sometimes there's casualties in war." I could care less that I popped his woman.

"Yeah, well, you might care that it's ya ex's sister. And for your carelessness, Truth is about to be even more on guard than before."

The phone clicked, and I was left stuck. It didn't take but a few seconds to put it all together and figure out that I had shot Amiko.

I felt bad for all of a second before I shrugged my shoulders and kept driving. Had Ming and I been together, then I would've had a reason to give a fuck. While heading in the direction of my crib, I made a detour and went to Tiara's instead. She was going to be in on my plan to get at that nigga, Chance. And I wasn't gonna miss.

"Who is it?" Tiara called out from the other side of her door.

I had been knocking for the past three minutes, and she had finally turned the music down enough to answer me.

"Me."

"Me who?"

"Stop playing and open the damn door, Tiara."

I heard the locks twisting, and she snatched the door open with a scowl on her face.

"What, Karter?" Her hands were on her hips, giving me a peek of the bra and panties she had on underneath her robe.

"Man, watch out and let me in." I moved her to the side and walked in the apartment, helping myself to a seat on the couch. "Close the door. I wanna talk to you about something."

She made sure to slam the door closed before taking her time coming over to me.

"Oh, you wanna talk? Because when I wanna talk it's an issue."

Knowing she was looking for a fight, I ignored her attitude because what I had to say next was gon' humble her ass.

194

"How long you been fucking with that nigga, Chance?"

Her mouth clamped shut, and her face went blank. I already knew how Tiara got down, and I didn't expect her to be on no faithful shit while I was locked up. I only expected her to hold me down, which she did.

"Didn't nobody fuck around with…"

"Aht aht. Before you finish the lie, please remember that I will come across this couch and be on your ass within seconds. If I'm asking, it means I already know. Now, you can continue."

"I… I only hung out with him twice. It was nothing crazy."

"Hung out as in fucked, right?" She nodded her confirmation. "Aight. Hit him up and tell him you want him to come over."

"He's not coming over here. In case you forgot, he's with your other baby mama." She rolled her eyes hard and sucked her teeth, salty as hell.

"Get ya phone and do what I asked you to do." She snatched her phone from the coffee table to make the call. "Tell him something that make sense and make it believable." The phone rang four times on speaker before it connected.

"Why you calling me, Tiara?"

"I, umm, I was reaching out because I need to talk to you about Ming's baby father."

"You mean yo' dude?"

Even I had to look at her silly ass sideways.

"We don't need to discuss nothing, especially if it has anything to do with homeboy."

"Not even if it affects the safety of Ming and Case?"

There was a pause, and the phone went silent.

"What you say?"

"I figured that would get your attention. I'd rather not talk to you about this over the phone, so can you come over please?"

"I'll be there in thirty minutes, and you better not be on no bullshit either."

I nodded for her to hang up, and she did. Clapping at her ability to think on her feet, I went into plan mode.

"Now what?" she asked, throwing her phone back on the table.

"Now we wait. When he comes in, you get him nice and comfortable. Shit, you can even throw the pussy again. It'll be the last piece he remembers before I dead his ass."

3 0

CHANCE

I HUNG UP THE PHONE WITH TIARA AND KNEW SHE WAS UP TO NO GOOD by the sound of her voice. She didn't sound sure of what she was saying and was hesitant when she spoke. I had already dropped Ming and Case off at my crib and made sure they were straight. Seeing my reaction to that fuck nigga, Karter, Ming tried her best to get me to stay inside, but there was no convincing me.

I thought it was comical that he called himself trying to play the daddy card when he saw the interaction between me and Case. This nigga was a joke, and he was still alive off the strength of his son. My patience was starting to dwindle though. If I was a betting man, I could bet that he put Tiara up to reach out to me. The difference between the two of us was I always planned two steps ahead.

While en route to her apartment, I put a call in to a clean-up crew. I intended to return to Ming the same way I left —_in one piece. I thought about calling Truth to put him up on game about what was going down but quickly changed my mind. The first thing he would've said was to wait on him. In this scenario, there was no wait-ing. I had to move so that Karter thought he had the upper hand. By me agreeing to come over, in his mind, he had already completed phase one of his plan. I almost felt sorry that I was going to have to ruin that.

I texted Tiara to let her know I was parking my car and for her to come downstairs. Five seconds didn't pass before she was texting back an excuse as to why she couldn't. I smirked at the text before agreeing to go up. Making sure the silencer was screwed on my gun, I secured it in the front of my pants and walked toward the building. While I rode up on the elevator, my phone chimed with a message from Ming telling me to be careful. Putting the phone away, I cleared my head and stepped off the elevator onto Tiara's floor.

Not one for games, I took my gun out and held it at my side. This wasn't no friendly visit, and I wanted —no, I needed —Tiara to know I wasn't above airing her whole apartment out if she said the wrong thing. Knocking on the door, I stood back and waited for her to answer.

"Hey, Chance," she spoke nervously.

As soon as I saw her face, I thought about her little girl briefly. "Is your daughter here?"

"No."

"Cool." I sidestepped her and walked inside. "What you wanted to talk to me about? And let's make this quick. I got shit to do." She walked around me and toward the living room. Noticing I wasn't following behind her, she stopped short and turned around.

"Why you standing by the door, and why do you have a gun?!" Her voice went up an octave, switching from nervous to scared.

"You can never be too careful. And like I told you, I got moves to make, so what is it that you wanna tell me about Mr. Karter?"

"Oh, umm, well, you know how…"

"You nervous?" I asked, cutting her off.

"You have a gun pointed at me, Chance. Hell yeah, I'm nervous."

"Is that why you keep looking toward the back?" Along with her demeanor, I picked up on her wandering eye. "Karter, you can come out now. I'm here at your request. We can handle the rest of this shit like men." Like I knew he would, he emerged from the back, and I could see regret on Tiara's face.

"Damn, T, I didn't think you'd fold so quickly. Guess I gotta raise my baby girl on my own after this," Karter said, and before Tiara could react, he shot her in the chest twice.

Pft, pft. The shots from my silencer made his body hit the floor at the same time hers did. I didn't stay long to check pulses. I always made sure to shoot to kill. Leaving out the same way I came, I made sure my head was down so that no cameras caught me.

I ENTERED my place a little while later, and Ming was sitting up on the couch, waiting for me. Walking over to her, I kissed her forehead before heading to the bathroom to change. It didn't take long for her to join me in the bathroom just as I started the shower.

"You wanna tell me what happened?" she asked while hugging me from behind.

"You really wanna know?"

She nodded before responding. "I feel like I need to."

"He killed her; I killed him." I watched her stoic expression in the mirror. Turning, I wrapped my hands around her waist. "How you feel about that?"

"I'm not sure how I feel yet."

"That's understandable. When you're ready, I'll be right here. Just know that I'm going to the furthest extent behind you and Case, putting down anything that poses a threat to us and ours —baby daddies, ex-best friends, uncles, and all. Tell me if that's something you can handle because it's who I am."

"You had me at the furthest extent for me and my son."

Standing on her tiptoes, she pulled my head down to meet her lips. Her lil' mean ass was mine.

3 1

NYEMA

HEARING BOSS YELLING INTO THE PHONE THAT SOMEONE FAILED AT killing Truth, I silently thanked God. While I may not have been his biggest fan these days, the last thing I wanted was him dead. Over the last forty-eight hours, I had stuck close by Boss to monitor what he had going on. During that time, I had a change of heart. I just wanted to recoup the money that Truth had taken out of my accounts and go about my life.

"If you want something done, you gotta do it ya damn self!"

I pretended to busy myself in the kitchen, not wanting to be on the opposite end of his wrath.

"Everything alright?" I asked without turning around to face him.

"Yeah, I gotta go handle something though."

"Wait, come sit down and have something to eat."

From the tone of his voice, I knew wherever he was headed, he had Truth in mind. "I'm not hungry, and I got shit to do!" he snapped, storming off.

I waited until I heard the door close before rushing to my phone. Quickly dialing Truth's number, I hoped that he answered.

"Come on, Truth, pick up this damn phone, man." When the call connected and his voice came through, my mind drew a blank.

"Make it quick, Nyema."

"He... he... hey, Truth."

"**How can I help you, Nyema?**" he asked like I was bothering him. I didn't let it get to me though.

"**I was calling to let you know that you need to watch your back. Your Uncle Boss is after you, and he's the one behind the shooting. I know you may not believe me because we're not on the best of terms, but I'm telling the truth.**"

"**Okay.**"

That was not the response that I expected. "**Okay? That's all you have to say?**"

"**Yes, okay. And thank you for confirming what I already knew.**" He was so nonchalant, as if I hadn't just told him that his uncle was out to kill him.

"**I don't think you understand what I'm saying. Your uncle, as in your father's brother, wants to kill you and your brother.**"

"**I got it. Will that be all?**"

"**Well, seeing as though I provided that information, I would appreciate you replacing the money you took from my account. I mean, it's only fair.**"

"**You're still alive and breathing right now, correct?**"

I didn't understand where he was going with the question, but I responded anyway. "**Yes.**"

"**Then I've been fair enough. Let me go before I change my mind.**"

The nerve of this motherfucka to hang up on me after I just tried to save his life. To hell with the Porter men. At this point, I'd just get my money from Boss and get the hell on. Setting my phone on the table, I went into the bedroom to pack my overnight bag. This shit was for the birds.

While I went through the mountains of clothes I had, the safe that sat in the closet caught my eye. I could feel the palm of my hands start to itch real bad. It was slightly ajar, just waiting for me to open it. I could no longer avoid the voice in my head that told me to check the contents of the safe. Dropping the clothes in my hand to the floor, I inched over to it. My eyes widened in greed seeing the neatly stacked hundred-dollar bills. My pussy creamed at the sight before me. I went to reach for one of the bills and felt something pressed against the back of my head followed by a clicking sound.

"You just had to go and be a sneaky ass ho." Boss' voice was rough, immediately making my pussy juices dry up.

A bitch was caught red handed. Blessed with the gift of gab, I knew I had to talk my way out of this. First, I had to make him believe I wasn't scared. That way, any suspicion of wrongdoing on my part was immediately dismissed.

"Get that damn gun from the back of my head, Boss." I spun around and smacked the gun away. I took a risk on my damn life doing that shit. What I didn't account for was him backhanding me, sending me clear across the room. "Ouch!"

"Are you fucking crazy?!" he berated. He didn't give me a chance to recover before he was on top of me. "I will kill your ass in here, Nyema!" He delivered blow after blow to my body as I curled up in a fetal position to protect my face.

"Boss, baby, please stopppp!" I pleaded, and as if something had clicked in his head, he stopped suddenly. I whimpered and stayed balled up in fear that he'd have more energy in him to continue his assault.

"I knew your sneaky ass was up to something, but I tried to give you the benefit of the doubt. I've been too fucking nice witcho ass, and now, you done brought out another side of me." I remained quiet while he rambled. "Why you tryna steal from me, huh?" he asked, now standing over me.

"I wasn't stealing from you. Why would I steal when I know part of the money is already mine?" In one swift motion, he grabbed my jaw and squeezed tight. "Sssss." The pain that went through my face was excruciating.

"You're only allowed to move around freely because I let you, Nyema. Don't make the mistake of making an enemy out of me. You should already know that I don't care about anyone but Boss. You don't want to be on the losing side of this battle." Letting my jaw go roughly, he left the room.

I heard the door slam and waited fifteen minutes before getting on the good foot. There was no way I was sleeping another night next to that fucking maniac. Returning back to the safe, I swiped my half of the money into my bag, along with my clothes. Call me what you want, but I wasn't a silly bitch. As far as I was concerned, I put my life on the line for this money. I was going to get what was owed to me.

Boss was right about one thing. He royally fucked up when he put his hands on me. For the first time since I'd been dealing with him, I saw the man that was willing to take out his family for a dollar. I didn't bother taking my car when I left. Instead, I ordered an Uber. With the stunt he'd pulled, I could see him tracking my car.

In the Uber, I laid my head against the window, and for the first time in a long time, I felt lost. I could feel the emotion swelling up in the pit of my stomach, creeping up into my throat, ready to burst. Here I was, in the back of a taxi, battered and bruised, both physically and mentally. But neither feeling had anything on the blow to my pride. I prided myself on being **that bitch,** and I should've been exempt to experiences such as this. If karma taught me anything, it was that I wasn't.

"You can let me out right here, sir. I can walk across."

It took me a minute to pull my duffle bag out the backseat, and the asshole driving didn't even attempt to help me. As soon as I was able to, I would be giving his ass a one star. Slamming the door behind me, I paced myself as I walked across the street and up to Tantra. It was still early in the day, so there was no bouncer at the door to deny me access. When I made it inside, it looked like a whole new place. I knew it wouldn't be long before Truth had everything remodeled after Boss paid my cousins to trash it.

"Oh, bitch, you're either bold or real fucking retarded to show your face here." Mina stepped close enough in my face to kiss me in the mouth.

I winced inside, silently hoping I didn't have to fight her. My ribs were already throbbing from the beating Boss put on me. I didn't want to fight, but I would. I may be a lot of things, but a scary bitch I wasn't. "Can you please get Truth for me? It's an emergency."

"Bitch, please. I can't get a motherfuck…" was all I heard before I collapsed to the ground.

"WHAT'S THE DIAGNOSIS, DOC?" I heard Truth ask as I came to.

My eyes fluttered open, and I took in my surroundings. I was in his office with his personal doctor leaning over me. Truth hated hospitals, so he hired a doctor to take care of him whenever he had health issues, which was a rarity. Looking past the doctor, I could see Amiko sitting on his lap in her phone. The doctor smiled at me before standing up straight and addressing Truth.

"She has three broken ribs that are going to take some time to heal. Other than that, she seems fine." She then turned to me to speak. "You have to take it easy. I'm not sure what kind of work you do, but I highly suggest you take some time off for proper healing."

"That shouldn't be a problem, Doctor," Amiko spoke up. "She's unemployed. I'm sure she'll be able to get all the rest she needs."

The doctor smiled again, grabbed her bag, and left. Amiko had a smug look on her face, but what she didn't understand was I had really won. Her man still cared about me, and if him having his personal doctor come look after me didn't show that, I didn't know what other proof she needed. That thought alone put a smile on my face.

"You're sure showing a lot of teeth for a bitch with broken ribs. Truth, you're better than me because I would've let her bleed internally just off GP." I didn't know how I missed Mina standing off in the corner.

"Mina, could you excuse us for a minute?" Truth requested.

She rolled her eyes before moving toward the door.

"Let me go too. I don't know how much longer I can sit here and not go across her shit." Amiko went to stand, only to be pulled back down, making me grit my teeth.

"Look, I only came here to apologize for everything I had a hand in. I know it means nothing to you, but it's the least I could do. Your uncle is the reason for this." I pointed to the bandages that were wrapped around my rib cage.

Truth's facial expression never changed, and I could tell he had no empathy for me. "The last time I was at your house, I heard you threaten to tell Boss' secret. What were you referring to?"

I didn't think twice before I had word vomit. "Boss hired some guy named Karter to murder your parents. He spilled everything to me on a drunk night. The next day, I asked him about it; he acted as if he didn't know what I was talking about." I watched his jaw twitch, and Amiko rubbed his arm in a loving manner. The gesture made me cringe. "He wants complete control of the Porter House. He feels it was stolen from him."

"Nyema, hear me and hear me clear. When you leave this building, don't ever come back. The only reason Doc was called here today is because I have a heart for women. Understand that this was your last pass. If I see you again, your family will be picking out black dresses and suits for your homegoing." I knew he meant every word he spoke. Pulling my shirt down over my bandages, I snatched up my duffle bag, disregarding the pain in my midsection.

"Not sure how much this helps, but the Karter guy was also behind you getting shot." I pointed to Amiko and left out.

I walked a block before using my phone to order another Uber to the airport. It was time for a change of scenery and hopefully a new start, preferably somewhere sunny. Searching for flights to the Bahamas while waiting the five minutes for my Uber to come, I glanced up quickly just as a car pulled in front of me. The window rolled down a little, and I could see Boss' eyes. My first mind was to run, but my feet felt like cement blocks.

"I hope it was all worth it," he said before brandishing a gun and pointing it in my direction. *Pop!* I felt my soul leave my body before I even hit the ground.

32

TRUTH

"Babe," Miko called out to me while still seated on my lap.

I had been staring at my office door that Nyema had walked out of a few minutes ago. When Mina came in and told me that she was passed out inside my club, I was confused. There was no way she thought that I would be inviting when she showed up. Not wanting to attract even more unwanted attention, I had one of the maintenance guys bring her to my office.

Of course both Mina and Miko protested when I called Dr. Onede to come and take a look at her. They both agreed that whatever made her fall out, she deserved for the disloyal shit she had done. Me, on the other hand, I needed to know why she showed up to Tantra out of all places given my ill feelings about her. When she proceeded to confirm my Aunt Pat's suspicions about Boss' connection to my parents' deaths, there was nothing more that needed to be said.

"Babe, come on. Let's go home," Miko spoke again, kissing the side of my head.

It was as if she had completely disregarded that Nyema knew who was behind her shooting. This Karter guy was sent to take me out, and she got caught in the crossfire. Her only concern in the moment was me.

"What kind of man sets his blood up to be killed on some jealousy shit?"

"I don't even have an explanation for it. All I can say is that I'm sorry for what happened to your parents. Karma is going to deal with your uncle."

"Well, call me karma because I'll be the one he has to answer to." I kissed her lips and rubbed her back in a loving manner. "I'm sorry you got caught up in my family drama, and I swear I'm going to make it up to you. Right now, I need you to head to your house. Ralph should be pulling up."

"But I…"

"No buts, Miko," I cut her off. "If what Nyema said was true about him beating her up, then I know he followed her here. He's just waiting for the right time to move."

"I don't want you to do anything that you'll have to live with for the rest of your life. I know you want to avenge your parents, but you don't have to be like him."

"I'm not. He took the coward's way out and hired someone to kill them. I'm gonna look in his eyes like a man before I pull the trigger." My phone dinged with a notification. It was Ralph letting me know he had arrived. I knew she wanted to stay with me, but I also knew she'd be safe with him in my absence. "Come on, your ride is here." Escorting her outside, I made sure she was safely in the car.

After scanning the area once it pulled off, I turned and found myself staring down the barrel of Boss' gun.

"You know, my first mind was to shoot her ass too, but you won't live to mourn her, so what fun would that be? Throw ya phone on the ground and step on it."

I smiled and did as he requested. Even with the gun pointed directly at my head, I had to fuck with him. "Nah, you wasn't gon' do that. I'm starting to think that gangsta shit you talk, you don't really live, Boss. I mean, you set your brother and my mom up to be killed. Then you send the same person to get rid of me. Nahh, you not built for gunplay." *Whap!* The blow from the gun to my head made me stumble a bit.

"Walk yo' ass to the car."

With cameras all around the club, I knew that Mina could see what was going on. Discreetly, I shook my head no. Hopefully, she got the hint that I didn't want her to call anyone for me. I kept moving while he had the gun pressed into my back. I wasn't thinking of a way to make a getaway. I was waiting for the right time to strike.

"You know this is my property. We can do this shit right here and have the footage erased." We hadn't made it to the front of the building yet, and I didn't plan on it.

"You sound like ya father. Can't admit when someone else has the upper hand. That's another reason why I had to get rid of his ass. Him and your mother."

That was all I needed to hear. I needed him to admit it from his mouth.

"Thank you."

"What?"

"For making this easy."

Quickly spinning around, I hit him with a hard elbow to the face that dazed him and upped my .40, sending two clean shots to the side of his head. Watching his body hit the ground, I felt nothing. Stepping over it, I went back into the club, dialing the clean-up crew as if nothing happened. I did what I set out to do, and I knew I'd sleep well at night knowing that I'd avenged my parents' death and kept my loved ones safe.

EPILOGUE (ONE YEAR LATER)

AMIKO

"I now pronounce you husband and wife." When the officiant made the announcement, I couldn't stop smiling.

"I did it, y'all!" Jomy squealed in excitement as Kenneth held her hand in the air.

We had been in Cabo for the last week for a much-needed vacation that doubled as Jomy's surprise wedding.

"Yesss, bitch, you married. Owwww!" Kane twerked in her bridesmaid dress, and the other Elites joined in.

I laughed before being swooped off my feet by the love of my life.

"If you start twerking out here, I'ma have to pop that ass."

Giggling, I pinched his arm for him to put me down. It was good to see my fiancé smiling again. Truth proposed eight months ago, and it felt good to be in love and like with the man of my dreams. It took a little bit to get him back to this point after killing his uncle. To the outside world, Truth was still Truth, but for me, the woman he slept with every night, he was different.

I could tell that him doing the deed affected him more than he cared to admit. There were nights when he would stay up in bed and stare at the ceiling in silence. I never pushed him to talk about it. I let him go through the motions and stood by his side. It was even more crazy finding out that the same Karter Nyema said shot me was Ming's Karter. Chance took care of that though.

"You ain't popping nothing." I wrapped my hands around his neck and swayed from side to side to the music in my head. "You like it out here?"

"Yeah, Cabo's cool. I can really get with the weather out here."

"Well, while I was out yesterday with the girls, I found the perfect place for a vacation home for the Elites." We had been doing so well with the app and the new Elites that I could see us expanding to the tropical paradise.

"You're always thinking about the money, Madam Elite."

"And those two over there." I nodded toward Ming and Case, who were two stepping with Chance. My little sister had come a long way, and I was beyond proud of her. We both found love and had leveled up in the process. Like my boy, Future, said, "Life is good."

MING

Watching Case and Chance as they threw the football around on the beach, tears welled in my eyes. My son had a man in his life who loved him like he was his own and loved me unconditionally. When Chance told me he had to get rid of Karter and Tiara, the only person I felt bad for was their daughter. The little girl would have to grow up with no parents —_all because of their fuck ups. I held onto that for a while until I eventually had to let it go. Everyone had to play the cards they were dealt.

"Cabo looks good on you, Mama," Chance said, kissing my cheek and rubbing my belly. At six months, I was carrying small, and all Chance wanted to do was love on me.

"Thank you, baby. I could live like this forever."

"Nah, thank you for bringing me peace." I kissed his lips and laid back on my lawn chair.

"Forever yours."

"Mine for the taking."

THE END

Did you enjoy the read?
Let us know how much by leaving us a review on Amazon and
Goodreads.

ALSO BY NAI

Seizing A Gangsta's Heart For The Summer

Thug Me The Right Way 2

Thug Me The Right Way 3

A Summer To Remember With My Hitta

Snatched Up By A Hitta

Wet Dreams On Lockdown: The Unit Manager

Santa Sent Me A Real One For Christmas

Bossin' Up On The Plug

Bossin' Up On The Plug 2

In The Trenches With My Hitta

In The Trenches With My Hitta 2

Stealing A Queenpin's Heart

Stealing A Queenpin's Heart 2

A Piece of A Hustler's Heart

A Piece of A Hustler's Heart 2

A Thug's Love Mended My Heart

A Thug's Love Mended My Heart 2

A Summer To Remember With My New York Bae

A Summer Fling In New York

His Hood Love Gave Me Life

His Hood Love Gave Me Life 2

My Thug, My Sanctuary

Thug Kisses For Christmas

For The Love Of My Savage

Charge It To The Game

Charge It To The Game 2

The Swipe 2

By **Toõla**

Melted The Heart Of A Menace

Wet Dreams On Lockdown: Lieutenant Grace

By **P. Wise**

Merry Trapmas

By **Mia Sky**

Thug Me The Right Way

By **DiamondATL & Nai**

Wet Dreams On Lockdown: The Counselor

By **Paris Iman**

Wet Dreams On Lockdown: The Male C.O

By **Tamyra Griffin**

Wet Dreams On Lockdown: The Captain

By **TN Jones**

Wet Dreams On Lockdown: The Warden

By **Shawnice**

Atlantastan

Atlantastan 2

By **Chris Green**

IN The Streetz

IN The Streetz 2

By **Tron Hill**

Coming Soon From
URBAN AINT DEAD

The Hottest Summer Ever 2
THE G-CODE
Tales 4rm Da Dale 2
How To Invest In The Stock Market From Prison
By **Elijah R. Freeman**

Hittaz 5
Coldhearted 3
By **Lou Garden Price, Sr.**

Good Girl Gone Rogue 3
By **Manny Black**

Despite The Odds 2
Hittin' Licks For The Holidays: Chicago
By **Juhnell Morgan**

The Swipe 3
By **Toōla**

Charge It To The Game 3
By **Nai**

This Time Won't You Save Me 3
By **Kyiris Ashley**

Ridin' Forever
By **Telia Teanna**

Atlantastan 3
By **Chris Green**

BOOKS BY

URBAN AINT DEAD'S C.E.O

<u>Elijah R. Freeman</u>

Triggadale 1, 2 & 3

Tales 4rm Da Dale

The Hottest Summer Ever

Murda Was The Case 1, 2 & 3

Hittin' Licks For The Holidays: Atlanta

Wet Dreams On Lockdown: The Nurse

How To Publish A Book From Prison

STAY CONNECTED

Follow
Elijah R. Freeman
On Social Media
FB: Elijah R. Freeman
IG: @the_future_of_urban_fiction